Desert
Light

Desert
Light

Chilton Williamson Jr.

St. Martin's Press
New York

Library of Congress Cataloging in Publication Data

Williamson, Chilton, Jr.
    Desert light.

    I. Title.
PS3573.I45624D4   1987   813'.54   87-4379
ISBN 0-312-00577-6

First Edition

10 9 8 7 6 5 4 3 2 1

For J. O. Tate,
who knows why

Nel mezzo del cammin di nostra vita
mi ritrovai per una selva oscura
che la diritta via era smarrita.

—Dante, *L'inferno*

BOOK

1

1

A PICKUP TRUCK, painted light blue under a spatter of mud and tar, pulled off the highway opposite the Last Chance Saloon & Restaurant and cut its lights; reluctantly, the driver emerged and crossed the road keeping his hands in his jeans pockets and his shoulders bent against the wind. He was a tall man with broad shoulders tapering to a narrow, athletic-looking waist and the long, lean legs of a cowpuncher, wearing a battered hat with a weather-curled brim and flattened crown. For an instant he stood silhouetted against the oblong of yellow light—arms elbow-out from the sides, hands hanging tensely at the hips—before the door closed abruptly upon him and the only source of light was once again the spring moon as it poled fugitively from one ragged silver-edged cloud to the next.

2

SEVERAL OF THE men drinking at the bar raised their glasses to him as he entered, but Richardson stalked past them into the restaurant, choosing a table in a secluded corner of the room where he sat at bay, removing the deerskin gloves but keeping on the denim jacket and hat. Peggy placed a cocktail napkin in front of him, glancing at his face with what he took to be a guarded expression.

"Are you okay tonight?"

"Why wouldn't I be?"

"You don't *look* okay," she explained. "What do you want to drink?"

"Get me a Tanqueray martini up with an olive, very dry."

"Oh, no—not martinis."

"Come out to the ranch with me tonight."

"Don't be funny. Now, what are you going to drink, Chuck?"

"I told you. Or do I have to get it from the bar myself?"

"Suppose I said, 'Take a can of gasoline and throw it in the stove there'—Oh, for God's sake," she exclaimed, "don't answer that. I'll bring you *one* martini then. Is that a deal?"

"You bet."

"Promise?"

"Word of honor," he told her, choosing to ignore the sardonic look she gave him.

4   *Chilton Williamson Jr.*

She brought the martini and afterward, when he had bullied her by threatening to call Bill Gerhardie, two more.

"Liar," she said. "We had a gentleman's agreement. I know—you talked with Hal Pearce today. I think he's nuts to fool with you, if you want my opinion. The only thing worse than having you on the other side in court would be having you on mine."

Halfway through the third drink Richardson became aware of the familiar blood-red moon rising at the back of his mind. He sat holding his head very carefully, as if to maintain equilibrium, remembering a news story about a woman who had burst into flames crossing a city street; according to the writer it was the third or fourth documented case of spontaneous human combustion since the Lisbon Earthquake. Through the octagonal glass sides of the stove he watched the flames swirling upward from the aspen logs, which were feathering into ruins of ash of the most astonishing morphological complexity, recalling Troy and Carthage, Sodom and Tyre, Rome, Kiev, and the holocausts of Dresden and Nagasaki.

Peggy brought the fourth drink without bothering to look at him. He held it to the light, turning it appreciatively in his hand. Richardson considered the martini to be one of civilization's most sybaritic yet most pardonable achievements: a clear vengeful mead bearing catharsis—the twilight of the gods. They had served it in the wrong glass: once he would have cared about that. Across the room Bill Gerhardie sat by the kitchen door writing with a stub of pencil on the back of a meal check and making discreet attempts at catching his eye, which Richardson carefully ignored. Whenever possible he avoided inflicting his rages on friends, whose forbearance in refusing to accept these as proof of his total depravity he found ultimately shaming.

Now and then the pale oval of Peggy's face with its chopped black bangs and bright indignant eyes passed before his own dulled ones. At last he signaled with the empty glass, causing the face rapidly to avert itself and slide quickly out of his field of vision, while Bill Gerhardie jumped from his table and crossed quickly over on silent rubber-soled shoes. His fine, skeptical, Caledonian face was bronzed with sun and carried the sharp scent of good after-shave; trim and fit in a bright silk shirt and creased gabardine slacks, he stood genially rubbing his hands and cracking the knuckles. "Good evening, Mr. Attorney," he said, and grinned like a leprechaun. "May I buy you a drink?"

From beneath the ruined hat Richardson glared at him. "Goddammit, don't call me that."

Gerhardie shrugged deprecatingly. "Sure, Chuck. Whatever you say." His lean face twinkled as, with crossed arms, he rocked delightedly on the rubber soles. "I forget you're just an old sheepherder after all, like the rest of us natives from New York and Aberdeen. Can I buy you a drink anyway?"

"Thanks, Bill, but you might as well save your booze. I'm not going to talk about it."

Gerhardie raised a finger at Peggy, who slunk up to them like a reluctant dog, her fists crammed into the pockets of her apron and her eyes lowered. "Bring Chuck another one of his Molotov cocktails and I'd like a white-wine spritzer."

Richardson swallowed the disconsolate olive and began chewing the toothpick for control. Gerhardie waited until Peggy had brought the drinks and pointedly removed the old glass. Then he said, "Pulasky's saying you've decided to take the case, Chuck."

"That would of course be join, not take, but Pulasky's talking through his ass anyway. I haven't decided a goddamn thing. If he writes in his paper that I have, I'll sue him for a million bucks."

"I apologize for the error in terminology," Gerhardie said, grinning. "I'm not a fancy New York attorney, after all."

"Neither am I, Bill."

Gerhardie shrugged again and permitted his eyes to pass from the holed sweater under the worn jacket to the rain-spotted and discolored hat. "Hell," he said, "I'd take you for a goddamn cowboy any day, at least until you opened your mouth. You've even started eating with your hat on."

Richardson did not say anything, but observed that the fresh drink mysteriously lacked the charm of the four previous ones.

Gerhardie said, "Pulasky wasn't trying to nose into your business, Chuck. He happened to see you at the courthouse on Monday morning with a bunch of papers under your arm and put two and two together."

"If it's anyone's business but ours, we were talking about hunting bears, not a bunch of murdering punks."

"You're figuring on bears this year? What area?"

"North Fork of Scavenger Creek."

"Do you have a bait permit?"

"Tonio does. He's going up tomorrow."

"You're going bear-hunting with *Tonio?*"

"I figure after two days in the mountains with Tonio, Hal Pearce won't want anything more to do with me."

"I can understand that." Bill Gerhardie laughed. "Pulasky and I took him duck-hunting last fall. Tonio wanted to take his boat, but we talked him out of that—we'd seen the boat. We got to the lake around five-thirty and found a dry place near the outlet and told him not to shoot until exactly quarter to seven. I said, 'Now, Tonio, do you have a watch?' 'Oh yes, I have watch!' We went around to the other side of the lake and waited and at six-thirty the shooting started—made as much noise as Gordon at Khartoum. Pulasky says, 'What the hell, a bunch of goddamn Utahans,' but I told him 'No, it's Tonio.' When I yelled at him, he told me I take my hunting too seriously. Then he held up the swan for me to admire."

"He seems serious about bears, though."

"I'm sure. He'll shoot Smokey on opening morning and let you explain it to the game warden because his English isn't good enough."

Two men came through the door into the restaurant, swinging their hands in front of their paunches and grinning self-consciously. They waved amiably at Peggy, then ambled over to Gerhardie and Richardson. Gerhardie said, "Good evening, Bob; good evening, Bruno. Care to join us for a drink?" He and Richardson moved against the wall and both men sat, pinching their pantlegs at the knee.

Bob Pulasky was heavy, gray-headed, and dark-complected, with the shrewd crab-apple eyes and thick-lensed gaze of the country newspaper editor and a disgruntled, suspicious demeanor that suggested he knew more than he was prepared to say. In fact he attended public meetings and events only when strictly necessary, borrowing pens to jot desultory notes on the backs of envelopes and leaving after a quarter of an hour to drink beer in the bars around the square or drop by the jailhouse for a game of checkers with the deputies, these being the two activities that he claimed provided him, as a journalist, with his best material. Every afternoon he and Bruno Bellini, who worked for the Federal Bureau of Land Management, drank a couple of beers together at the Bare Garden before going home for supper; at ten they met again at the Last Chance, where they would sit drinking with Bill Gerhardie until closing time. Rubbing the instep of her right slipper against her left ankle, Peggy wrote down their orders. She kept her body at a careful three-quarter angle to Richardson.

"Ah—Peg? I'll have one more, for a nightcap." Although she gave no sign of having heard him, he felt reassured by the human sound of his own voice, by which he understood that the martinis were maintaining an equilibrium. Martinis could do that too, he reflected. Martinis could do almost anything—not always, however, at the appropriate moment.

"We have a celebrity with us tonight." Bob Pulasky's eyes bugged in mock astonishment behind his glasses. He wiped his mouth with his hand and pulled the cocktail napkin rudely from under Bruno Bellini's liqueur glass. "Can I have your autograph, sir?" Now he was searching his pockets for a pen. Every newspaperman Richardson had ever known carried a pen and notebook, except Bob Pulasky.

"You can all go to hell," Richardson said. "I'm leaving now." He stood but could not get past Bruno Bellini's stomach and the table.

"Now, now," Pulasky said mollifyingly. "There's no reason to be ashamed of distinction. We didn't know you had it in you, Chuck. Always figured you for kind of an ordinary guy, to tell the truth. You're not going to hold that against us, are you? Did you tell Hal Pearce you'll take the job yet?"

Richardson thrust between his teeth one of the small, black cigars he smoked chiefly as a calculated social offense and held a match to it. "I did not, and if you print in the paper that I have, I'll sue your ass, and so probably will he."

"The trouble with these bigshot lawyers," Pulasky observed mildly, "is the sonsofbitches have no consideration. Instead of letting folks catch their breath after a thing like this happens, they just barge ahead into a murder trial right in the middle of mushroom season."

Richardson leaned across the table toward him, breathing smoke from under the hat.

"If the *Fontennelle Fortune* had the guts to take on something more controversial than fishing derbies and Mormon marriages, maybe I wouldn't have to let myself be dragged into some kind of goddamn vigilante action out of an Owen Wister—hell, Louis L'Amour—novel."

Bob Pulasky removed his glasses and rubbed his reddened eyes with thumb and forefinger.

"A small-town paper has to emphasize the positive aspect, Chuck. Our subscribers get all the sicko stuff they can handle just watching the six-o'clock news." Replacing the glasses on his nose, he finished the glass of beer. "Vigilante action?" he repeated. "Since when does the prosecuting attorney's office count for a lynch mob? Although," he added thoughtfully, "maybe you could almost call it that when Hal Pearce agrees to represent the state. I heard him say once that for a defense attorney to turn prosecutor is the same as a Methodist preacher turning pimp. Or something like that." He belched, and contemplated sadly the foam spreading slowly on the inside of the empty glass.

Bill Gerhardie was staring at Richardson like a man catching a glimpse of the other side of the moon. "I don't believe it," he said. "Is this the same guy that comes in here and delivers those fuck-the-world speeches? Last November you didn't believe in voting. You were saying how anybody with the arrogance to run for President ought to be taken out behind the White House and shot at the end of his first term. You were so insistent about it I had to apologize to the women and children in the restaurant and all the bad Mormons in the bar."

Something inside Richardson released very smoothly and quietly, like the trigger-assembly of a well-oiled gun. In the rush of an elation that was equally despair he wished the terrible words he was about to speak to be carved in marble for millions of morons to read and be horrified by. Pulling his hat over his eyes, he leaned forward on his elbows and said, "Fuck the President. Kill them all. Let God sort the bastards out."

The busboys finished racking the chairs on the tables while the waitresses stood around on one foot discussing the mysterious synchronicity of their periods. Gerhardie, Pulasky, and Bellini were exchanging recipes now for blue grouse; they appeared engrossed in their conversation and did not look at Richardson. Peggy came over with her coat on, wiggling her fingers at Gerhardie. "Thanks, Peg," he said. "We'll see you tomorrow night"—and then she was fleeing toward the door. Abruptly, Richardson stood, patting his pockets for the truck keys and treading on Bruno Bellini's foot.

"Good night," Bill Gerhardie called after him. "Don't knock up any more of my help, okay, Chuck?"

3

THE WIND HAD blown the clouds away and subsided, leaving the moon floating free in a silver sky. The cold patted him up and down with tiny frisking hands, and Richardson began to feel entirely better. Across the road he could see Peggy climbing into her little car. The engine turned over with a harsh sound and he stepped onto the pavement in front of the lights; when the fender came to a reluctant halt against his kneecaps he walked around to the driver's side and opened the door. In the green glow of the instrument panel her face had a cold, reptilian look. "Let me go or I'll call the cops."

"Come home with me, Peggy."

"No way."

"I'll behave—I promise."

"Drunks don't keep promises."

"I'm not a drunk."

"You're shitfaced tonight."

"Winston Churchill was seated at dinner with a woman who kept telling him, 'Winnie, you're drunk,' to which he always replied, 'And you, madam, are uglay.' As they left the table she said, 'Winnie, you're *still* drunk'—to which he replied, 'Madam, when I awake in the morning *I* shall be *sobah*, but *you* will *still* be uglay.' "

"You only tell Winston Churchill stories when you're really

smashed." Peggy released the clutch and the car began to roll forward. Setting the toe of his boot on the frame, Richardson hopped precariously beside it on one foot, trying to take over the wheel. "Get off my car before I call the police."

"Please, Peggy. I need you tonight."

"I don't really feel in a mood to be abused, okay?"

"I don't abuse people, only shades—ghosts."

"You drank six martinis this evening," she said accusingly.

"*Five!*" he shouted, indignant.

"Don't yell at me, Chuck. I counted. You paid for five and Bill bought one. Now get off my car. I want to go home and go to bed."

"There's a cop car coming, why don't you signal them?"

"You don't think I won't?"

"I wouldn't underestimate you, but it would be a hell of a lot simpler just to let me in so we can go home."

She sighed. "What about your truck?"

"I can ride into town with you in the morning. Gerhardie won't mind if I leave it parked overnight."

"All right," Peggy said. "God knows you have no business driving. Where is this all going to end?"

The patrol car cruised by slowly, the pale countenances of its occupants turned toward the little car standing slightly askew in the road. Richardson noticed the driver's ethereal face framed by smooth wings of silver-blond hair beneath the brutal-looking cap and waved broadly at it as he ducked inside. "Let's get going," he said. "Damn valkyrie. I'd hate to have to hit a woman, but it'll be a cold day in hell before I let myself be dragged to jail by a hundred-and-ten-pound cunt with a nightstick."

"Male chauvinist pig drunk." Peggy restarted the engine. "Remember, Chuck. You promised."

"Christ, did I? But then drunks don't keep promises, do they."

Subsiding into the seat he became aware of the distant

rumble of the gin, like a storm passing over the horizon: prepared now to make amends for the perversities of the heart. *And that is what the tongue is, a fire. Among the organs of our nature, the tongue has its place as the proper element in which all that is harmful lives. It infects the whole body, and sets fire to this mortal sphere of ours, catching fire itself from hell.* It was amazing, he thought, how you could unlearn adulthood almost at will but never your childhood, which somehow remained, even in early middle age, intact, inviolate, subject to almost total recall, like passages learned by rote for confirmation class or school.

Downtown the traffic light winked a musical yellow; luminous and stark against the night, the frame houses jostled each other with the sharp angles of their simple frontier geometry. Behind the town were the freightyards, the trailer parks, and the motels; beyond them the whale-backed, treeless brown hills, which, like medieval walls, held empires at precarious bay. Although the simple fact of their existence remained a nearly intolerable affront to the moral imagination, it was none of his world anymore; none of his concern. So far as Richardson cared, the Chinese could overrun the Russians, and the Russians enslave the Poles; the Vietnamese butcher the Cambodians and the Cambodians decimate themselves. The Democrats could shoot the Republicans, the Republicans garrot the Democrats; the poor rise up against the rich, and the rich put down the poor. The women could scare the men back to puberty, or the men convert their women once more to chattels; the niggers massacre the crackers, or the crackers the niggers. And fools could write books about these trivia, or discuss them on panel shows or at weekend conferences in expensive resort communities, or on the opinion pages of newspapers, so long as he, Chuck Richardson, didn't have to know about them—didn't have to attend to or even overhear the whining drivel of those "intellectuals" with their egos that were in direct reverse proportion to the value of their ideas and the efficacy of their opinions. Since banishment, rather than death, is man's ultimate dismissal of man, so he had chosen self-banishment; and now, even though after five years it already carried too much of him, he went on loving the country—this barren bony frame that History had not had time to put flesh on yet and to whose nakedness he had responded with instinctive passion, as if it were a woman's. Now he sat watching it stroke past him, silver and wide, under the moon, stretching away in his imagination —section after section, county after county, state after state —in a unified topography of basin and range, prairie and desert; empty, undifferentiated, and splendid. Feeling the pressure of Peggy's tentative hand upon his knee, he gratefully returned it in mute penance for this endemic rage at a world more than half of which was, after all, female.

The moon molded the house and outbuildings to the soft, rounded quality of adobe, beside which the horses stood silver and motionless in the corrals, like trophies. They undressed quickly together in the dark, and Richardson lay on his back beneath a blanket of moonlight feeling his body light, almost weightless on the cool sheet. Outside he heard the slow stamp of hooves, and from the bathroom the gush of water and clank of air: modern plumbing abetting the slow primeval system of female evacuation. He called, "Peg?"

"I'll be there in a *minute*, Chuck."

He lay wanting her, yearning as she approached through the moonshine like a nubile ghost. Instead of pulling the nightdress over her head she sat at the foot of his bed with one knee drawn up to her chin.

"We need to have a talk."

"Not at one o'clock in the morning, for Christ's sake."

"I just want to hear what it is you're going to do about the case."

"The hell with the goddamn case."

"You're almost forty years old," she said. "You're not a

kid anymore, Chuck. You told me yourself you were a good lawyer."

"There are rich lawyers and poor lawyers. There's no such thing as a good one."

"There's no such thing as a good drunk, either."

"Faulkner was a good drunk. Bellini was a good fornicator and my wife would say a good composer, too." The moon seemed to be drawing away his desire like a tide.

She was quiet for a while, staring through the window at the whitewashed night. Finally she said, "There was a girl used to work at the Last Chance. I don't remember what her name was. We called her Carmelita because she drank piña coladas, but she had this kind of colorless blond hair and real white skin. She didn't have a boyfriend and she didn't like the guys she met at the bar. She'd worked in bars ever since she quit high school, she said. One night when she got off work, instead of going home she sat at the bar and had a drink and after a while this ugly little Mexican sat beside her and ordered a beer. For an hour they didn't say a word to each other. Then the Mexican paid for both their drinks and she followed him out. He came back the next night, and the same thing happened. All she said was he had eight kids and something had happened to his wife. After she moved in with him she quit working so she could take care of the kids, and every Sunday they all went to Mass. One night the folks that lived next to them in the trailer park heard these terrible screams—two women screaming at each other. Carmelita was running through the mud between the trailers with just a T-shirt and panties on and this fat Mexican woman with black hair and a long knife behind her yelling, '*Puta! Puta!*'"

Richardson rolled onto his stomach and closed his eyes.

"I think it's sad," Peggy said, "when people can't stop living on the edge."

It was more difficult than he had remembered to counterfeit the easy suspiration of slumber.

"I want to be married," she told him. "I want to have children. I want to start living like a human being for a change."

Richardson said into the pillow, "The only way to quit living on the edge is to fall over it, and personally I'd rather have cancer than kids." Then he lay very still while the dry, reptilian lid closed once again over his heart.

4

UNDULATING WITH A hateful, ironic laughter, the curtains shimmered upward behind the drinkers, a gentle fire-music of beads stirred by conversational zephyrs. Beyond was a perfect spring evening, as expensive as a Tiffany window, in which silver-edged clouds, reproduced with excruciating clarity, floated from one tall glass-and-steel slab onto the next across still intervals of blank sky. Half a block away, on Park Avenue, enameled limousines glided sharklike through the traffic that streamed north and south past a long centerpiece of tulips, waxen-leafed ivy, and lemon-green saplings guyed with wire, stopping with rhythmic precision to let through the taxis cruising east on Forty-ninth Street. He watched as, one after the other, they glided to the curb to discharge lovely women with honey-colored skins wearing bright dresses and escorted by well-groomed men with whom they reappeared almost immediately at the top of the stairs with the avid, expectant expressions of successful people. When the waiter brought the martini Richardson ate a handful of salted peanuts before tasting it. The salt cut exquisitely the oily quality of juniper. "That's it for me," he told the pale concerned faces of the LeRoy Jackson Legal Defense Committee (Morley Thompson, whom *Time* magazine had recently called "America's most important living novelist"; Tony Koestler, the famous criminal lawyer; Christine; and the youngish man with the pink face that always looked as if it had been washed for him that morning and whose name he had difficulty remembering, although his great-grandmother had been a founding Benefactor of the Metropolitan Opera, and who was himself Jackson's editor at Wilder & Lane). "It's your ball of wax, now. I wash my hands of that nigger. I hope they fry him this time"—listening, as if from an immense distance, to the clatter of glasses around the table, the shocked gasps, and Christine, her golden eyes wide and outraged, exclaiming, "Caleb! You of *all* people!"; eating salted nuts and savoring the expensive flavor of Tanqueray, while around them the curtains rippled upward with their silent, scornful mirth.

From the kitchen he heard the blurt of the coffeepot and the hiss of frying bacon—good country bacon, with a hard rind in which a few bristles remained. Her place beside him felt cool to his hand: she must have been out already and fed the horses. On their third morning she had learned to leave bed without wakening him—an act of consideration, he knew, yet one that made him vaguely uncomfortable. A flock of grackles descended upon an electrical wire and balanced precariously there, antic cutout shapes against the static gold of the spring morning. He watched until his stomach could no longer bear their breathtaking backward flirts and quick forward recoveries, then shut his eyes and lay that way for what seemed a long time, hating himself for a fool. He thought, I am like the professional demolitions expert who neglected to take out the last bridge just because it was made of rope. Now he could look over his shoulder and see Hal Pearce following in hot pursuit across it.

Following his resignation from Duncan, Lord and the subsequent move to Jackson he had had himself admitted to the Wyoming bar in order to handle unpretentious local cases should the need arise: a sort of insurance policy to satisfy Christine, who had not believed that one could make her kind of living by combining tar-roofing with the breeding of pedigreed Arabian horses, even with two or three trust funds as a fallback, and who was unpersuaded that the fundamental aim of moving to the country was not to be *in* it merely but *of* it. For this reason, perhaps, she had never formally acknowledged his change of profession: At cocktail and dinner parties—even at ranch barbecues where the guests sat on hay bales to eat and spitted shoats turned slowly behind windbreaks of corrugated iron—she had insisted on referring, smoothly and inevitably, to "my husband, who happens to be an attorney." He had come to resent that more than anything else about Christine, including her taste for blue silk stockings and her fundamental dislike of the male sex, to which he happened to belong. In Fontennelle, to which he had moved again after a year, leaving his wife in Jackson, exactly two people had known—until very recently—that Chuck Richardson had not only acquired a law degree at one point in his well-buried fore-life, but that he had in fact been an extremely successful attorney. These were Peggy and a whore with whom he had spent a drunken, indiscreet, and somewhat boastful night eighteen months ago.

His eyes were screwed shut when his bare feet hit the plank floor, but the morning air had a chill edge and he dressed quickly, snatching up his clothes from the pile in which, in his lust, he had flung them the night before. A century earlier an intrepid stockman named Willard—one of Bridger County's first settlers—had built the house from cottonwood logs hauled from Soda Creek and cut into planks for the square, simple edifice in which he was said to have nocturnally entertained Calamity Jane, and which Richardson had filled with the Chippendale highboys, drop-leaf tables, and lyre-backed chairs that arrived in a North American van three months after the probating of his father's will and for which he could think of no other use—all of them coated with a layer of dust like talcum powder which had blown for two summers now through the myriad spaces between the logs where the chinking was falling out. The house itself had weathered to the color and texture of desert wood, thus acquiring an appearance still more antique than the fine, burdened Eastern furniture better than twice its age. Often it occurred to him that if the West possessed a single defining characteristic it was this aged, almost eternal quality of things dating from the day before yesterday.

His stomach clenched with the puerile fright of that schoolboy he could recall with such mysterious, provoking immediacy; as atonement he shaved in cold water, without soap, the blade scraping and pulling along his cheeks and jaw. Afterward he patted the skin dry with a bandana handkerchief and confronted the dark, brutal, squint-eyed face that stared at him from the glass. The booze didn't show on him yet. Something else did.

There could never be enough of distance between himself and it—that country of iron skies and brazen earth. And yet he, to his shame, had sought it; having caught, from the mellow, modest New Hampshire town of his upbringing, a glimpse of that shining superstructure to which he had attained in ten years through a Harvard LL.D., a Yale B.A., and his Phillips-Exeter credentials, not to mention a handsome wife with plenty of credentials of her own (none of them intellectual), a trust fund, an East Side town house, and a complete set of the *New York Social Register* dating to 1909. Not only sought it but enjoyed it too, he thought; asking nothing better than just more of it—more of that rich cake with its endless layers of money, love, and power.

He recalled that life now, not as he recalled his boyhood, as something of his own, but rather as a thing he had read about in a book—a Russian novel perhaps, the sort of book that left one with a more vivid impression than experience itself. Although there was shame in remembering, as if in remembrance lay the part of his identity he wished most of all to annul, nevertheless pictures of that past would flash unbidden across the back of his mind, forming a rapid-moving sequence he could not immediately shut off.

Then he would see the bright spring sun on the dappled bark and round, dusty-green leaves of the plane trees in the garden behind their house, and feel its warmth on the sleeve of his good Sea Island cotton shirt as he drank scalding Colombian coffee and scanned the ink-smudged, fresh-smelling pages of *The New York Times*. He would hear the sandpaper sound of his fine English oxfords on the pavement squares, feel the morning breeze slap at his face like a referee and the nudge of his expensive attaché case against his knee. He would see the plate-glass window of his English tailor flash back the sun as if in salute, feel the pluck of thumb and forefinger as they seized upon the lapel of good English cloth, followed by the quick, supple tug, like a trout taking a fly, as the tailor drew the last thread through the open buttonhole at the cuff. Then the press and crowding of the steamy, jerking train, and the splendid reemergence into the blue windy canyons of Wall Street filled with florid hurrying men as well-dressed and ruthless as himself, bright flags whipping against a cascade of masonry and glass, the long dynamic cleft absurdly dominated by the sooted spire of Trinity Church, a minute warning pointer against its meager allowance of sky. Finally there was the swift ascent to the offices of Duncan, Lord, occupying a floor and a half of the gigantic building, where he would sit for eight, ten, sometimes twelve or fourteen hours in a padded chair behind a teak desk in his carefully turned-back shirtsleeves, outlining arguments on a long yellow pad with a silver Tiffany pencil or composing letters for the dictaphone; breaking off at noon for squash, a swim, and a shower at the club, followed by London broil and a glass or two of Bass ale at Waverly's. He would hear again, as if his mind were a magnetic tape to which everything in his life had perversely adhered, the crack and ricochet of the ball, smell his own fresh sweat and his partner's sour perspiration, and afterward the clean chemical smell of chlorine on his skin as he dressed his well-kept, powerful body. He would inhale the smoky, cheesy atmosphere of the pub and taste the rich, greasy food and the ale's sharp tang, and hear the loud male uproar of the packed room. And two—sometimes three—nights a week he had escorted Christine to the opera. He would cross the plaza toward the Metropolitan—hurrying as usual to make the curtain—pressing her score of *Norma* under one arm and with Christine herself on the other; savoring the rustle of their evening dress, the play of fountains, and the scent of early spring flowers above the acid odor of city soil: eager with the anticipation of spring and a good wine in the Guild rooms at intermission and even Bellini's music, of which he had heard enough that he no longer responded to it as a dog to a fire siren, though he could not have said truthfully that he actually enjoyed it, the plots, words, and scores of these fantastic dramas having amalgamated themselves into one huge, undifferentiated, unending superdrama that in the end he found suspect because he could not convince himself that life really was like that. Other nights, when Christine was out of town—at Wellfleet or Sag Harbor—he would take a taxi to a little restaurant in Greenwich Village that he enjoyed for its long sweep of polished bar, its mirrors and art-deco architecture, and its aroma of garlic, oil, and shellfish, but particularly for a waitress named Kay with a small waist above a round, mobile bottom, eyes like those of a model in a French daguerreotype, and smooth, luminous skin, who regularly consented to take him home with her if he were willing to sit drinking white wine at the bar until two. Superimposed upon these memories were others of legal conferences in smoke-thickened rooms late at night, meetings of the East Side Democratic Club (of which Christine was a member and to which she had insisted on introducing him), cocktail parties at the New York Yacht Club for the Mayor of New York, and dinner dances at Tavern on the Green for unsavory aspirants to various state and Federal offices—none of which he could look back upon now without a keen feeling of distress amounting to utter loathing. From the sealed window of his forty-ninth-floor office, the sleek, too-confident young man of twenty-eight had gazed upon the rich heart of a vast, careless empire with the blind assurance of the inheritor.

He had returned once two years earlier for his father's funeral in New Hampshire, watching in grim despair as the vast housing tracts, like insect-spawn, spreading to the horizon, lifted toward him under the wing of the plane. They buried his father at four in the afternoon and at seven the next morning he caught a flight home from Boston, the East having, in only a little more than thirty-six hours, left fingerprints on his mind it took him weeks to expunge. He did not own a television set, and perused the newspapers in anger, with trembling hands. Eventually, he admitted to himself that he could not handle the news, to which his brain had the peculiar sensitivity of a drunk to liquor, and quit following national and international events altogether.

On the fatal night he had descended the forty-nine floors to the street, hailed a taxi, and ridden uptown to East Sixty-seventh Street, where, having showered and changed into evening clothes, he had ridden with his lovely wife across town to the Metropolitan to hear *La forza del destino*. During the second intermission the telephone had rung in the Guild room for Mr. Richardson, who thereupon learned that LeRoy Jackson, after hotwiring a car, had driven it at high speed through the plate-glass front of a delicatessen, killing the counterman—a diminutive Jew about fifty-five years of age with an Eastern European name, a bald head, protuberant eyes, and a wide, thick-lipped mouth, whose photograph Richardson cut from the newspaper the following day and carried two thousand miles to Fontennelle, Wyoming, where it rested now in an unopened valuables box in a dresser drawer. Following the call were two hours more of *Forza* and an appropriate gratitude for Giuseppe Verdi, the Metropolitan Opera Guild, and any other circumstance contributing to his absence from home when the furious Governor of the state of New York would be calling his private number at quarter-hour intervals until past midnight: that and, of course, the dreams, still persisting (though at ever-greater intervals now), in which he was fleeing a shadowy, unspecified crime for which, though none accused, he felt himself pursued.

5

PEGGY SAT AT the table drinking coffee and looking through
a pile of veterinary supply catalogues. "You have to hurry,"
she said, "or you'll make me late for work." Besides working
at the Last Chance she had a part-time job as a bookkeeper
for a title-insurance company. "I already ate." She put two
fried eggs, potatoes, and two strips of bacon on a plate for
him and poured coffee. "I fed for you."

"Peg, you're a doll." He pulled out his chair, sat, and began
to eat slowly.

"Are you okay this morning?"

"Not too bad, considering. How about yourself?"

"Just tired," she said. "Tired of bars and assholes with
propositions and confessions to make. Tired of waking up
and not having any clothes or makeup or my toothbrush and
forgetting that you keep the eggs on the outside window
ledge."

"How about of me?"

"You were pretty bad last night, I guess. But you're not
a genuine lunatic, you're a cultured one, like a cheap pearl.
So far I haven't invested that much in you. If I wake up some
morning and feel different, well—good-bye."

"What kind of investment are we talking about?"

"Oh," Peggy said, looking at him over the rim of the cup,

"that would depend on what the market is doing, wouldn't it?"

Women, he thought, are necessary to the order of the universe as a tree is necessary to a lightning storm. The capacity of a certain kind of woman was almost infinite, and Peggy belonged to that kind of woman, in her way. There were few subscribers these days to the notion of original sin—certainly not among these rollicking round-hipped ranch girls, raised to pulchritude under a pagan sun—which might, or might not, be a good thing. And Peggy, though smart—too smart, he had decided, for one of them—was unequipped to recognize his private truth, his blackened pearl, his guilt. For three semesters she had attended a local community college, taking courses in Personal Finance, Accounting I, and Introductory Economics; now, at twenty-seven, she talked of starting an accounting business of her own. Although she had requested his advice about this, he had listened to her only with effort, touched by her innocence rather than by her ambition, which in the past month she had begun to apply with equal energy to his own future. Peggy was appreciative, he could grant her that: most of what she saw in him she admired, and with the rest she was finally lenient. Only she's right, he told himself, I am not a boy anymore. He was no longer satisfied with appreciation and leniency: He had arrived at an age where he wished most of all to be seen whole and plain. He finished the coffee and pushed aside the plate. "Ready when you are, Peg."

She said, with a quizzical look, "You don't look very ready to me."

For the first time, it seemed to him, in a month—since the weather had improved sufficiently for construction work—his hands were not blackened, his nails filled, his clothes filthy with tar. On the drive into town he sat silent, watching the vast, empty country as if in it alone lay salvation: for years he had supposed that it did. It was not, would never be, a comforting landscape; but who the hell, he thought, needs to be comforted? We Americans fly west as geese fly south in winter. Some of us keep running—searching for a suitable vantage point from which to observe the impending disaster. And what, then, to tell Hal Pearce? I guess, he answered himself, you just say Yes or No.

There remained the difficulty that he liked and genuinely admired Pearce, in whom he saw the homely virtues of an earlier time, when a lawyer was a lay philosopher and maybe even a poet; who chose his clients from among those men who loafed on the courthouse steps and through whom he had to pass on his way into court each morning, as well as from among the railroad men, mine operators, and ranch owners who had the money to pay his fees. They had met in Jackson before he and Christine had become finally estranged and he had moved to Fontennelle and bought a forty-acre ranch with the modest equity he was able to scrape together: Albeit reluctantly, Richardson had been impressed by a quality of empathy that remained nevertheless too personal to be vulnerable to inflation, either by politics or vulgar idealism. They had hunted duck and elk together, and Christine, taking what he had considered to be slightly fatuous pity on an aging bachelor, had invited Pearce to dinner. Now, imagining her in Jackson pursuing her slightly mad scheme for annulment and plotting a dramatic return to the East, he was grateful that she was ignorant of his dilemma, any suspicion of which—he had no doubt of it—would encourage her to extend for a year anyway an uncomfortable hitch to a husband liable to be coerced into partnership with an attorney whose reputation had long ago crossed the Hudson as triumphantly as Caesar the Rubicon. And yet he knew, with painful, shrinking, and innermost certainty, that what finally compelled was not admiration for Hal Pearce but outrage at what he recognized increasingly as a personal threat of the kind he had—naïvely, it now appeared—imagined he had succeeded in outrunning.

Peggy drove slowly past the square with its moving electric

sign that read this morning CONGRATULATIONS JIMMY POWELL—EAGLE SCOUT: Whatever the failures of provincial America, he thought, it had at least the virtue of coherency —identity. Bob Pulasky stood on the sidewalk letting himself into the offices of the *Fontennelle Fortune*. He turned to wave, his eyeglasses flashing like small near-sighted suns, but Richardson did not return his greeting. "Drop me at the courthouse, will you?" he said.

"What about your truck?" she asked, surprised.

"I'll walk down and get it when I'm through."

She looked at him then. "Through with *what?*"

"Just some business."

"I see," she said. "Why couldn't you have told me that last night, Chuck?"

"Because it isn't your business, it's mine."

He raised his eyes toward the figure of Justice, that gilded whore, holding her scales above her head and treading the black points of the fir trees like a medieval witch on iron spikes. At the foot of the marble steps he got out, unfolding his body sharply like a clasp-knife. Overhead the flag snapped smartly in the breeze.

"Chuck?" she said, softly.

She was leaning across the seat now, smiling at him.

"What is it?"

"I'm real proud of you."

They always were, weren't they?

He closed the door and went up the steps and into the building without looking back, his bootheels clattering in the dim rotunda with a sound like the shades of deputized lawmen clapping for a thing they would have called Justice.

6

Slumped in the chair that seemed barely large enough to contain him, his bootheels resting on the edge of the desk, Hal Pearce raised his eyes from the book lying open on his lap and regarded the square of lemon-colored sun across the neatly piled papers and ring binders, the touch-tone telephone with its array of buttons, the walnut pipe-rack with its row of charred, dirty pipes, and the hand-shaped, time-rubbed, fragrant-smelling Zuni jar presented to him thirty years before by an Indian drifter out of New Mexico he had got acquitted of a murder charge and which he had used since that time to keep tobacco in. He rejoiced in contemplation of the day's work as it rested before him, awaiting merely his breath and touch to quicken and move it once more upon the world. The desk would have to do, he thought. The corners were chipped and rounded with wear, the wide surface of golden oak scarred by generations of boots, the drawers stiff and swollen; still, it possessed the appropriate weight, solidity, and character. He had had it carried up from the basement by the sweating building superintendent and his cursing assistant and installed in the special prosecutor's office because he could not, certainly *would* not, work at the cramped contraptions of tin and plasticized wood they equipped offices with nowadays. From his private law offices in Jackson, nearly two hundred miles distant, he had brought two armchairs, a sofa, a small glass-fronted bookcase and a second, old-fashioned rotating one he kept within arm's reach, and a wide Navajo rug, flung down in disharmonious protest against the blank green institutional walls of what ordinarily was the meeting room of the Bridger County Board of Commissioners. He drank from the mug of now lukewarm coffee Mary-Elena had brought him and applied himself once more to his book. He read:

> *Faust.* Where are you damn'd?
> *Meph.* In hell.
> *Faust.* How comes it, then, that thou art out of
>   hell?
> *Meph.* Why, this is hell, nor am I out of it.
>   Think'st thou that I, who saw the face of
>   God,
>   And tasted the eternal joys of heaven
>   Am not tormented with ten thousand hells,
>   In being depriv'd of everlasting bliss?
>   Oh, Faustus, leave these frivolous demands,
>   Which strike a terror to my fainting soul!

Hal Pearce stirred his large, not fat body satisfiedly in the chair, rubbing the corner of the page between his broad fingertips. The poetry and drama of Marlowe he considered superb: at times he suspected them of rising to greater heights than Shakespeare's. Before his love of law, he assured himself, came his love of rhetoric—twin from the same muse—inherited no doubt from his Mississippi ancestors: He believed that no lawyer could be worthy of his profession and at the same time ignorant of the literary and moral canon that had arisen as a shoot from the identical root. He loved it all, especially the works of pre-Christian antiquity, the Enlightenment, and the Romantic era; he loved the language of the Bible too, while disdaining mildly its message, having a marked preference for the Old Testament for its frankness and rough bucolicity. He read Homer, Aeschylus, and Sophocles; Herodotus and Vergil; Ben Jonson, Marlowe, and Shakespeare; Swift and Montaigne; Gibbon, Voltaire, and Rousseau; Byron, Shelley, and Tennyson; Taine, Bancroft, and Macaulay; Emerson and, of course, Thoreau. He loved not only the ideas of these men but—and perhaps even more—their words and the music these words created; loved the drama, history, and motion they evoked. He loved the the thick, fingersome richness of old editions ordered from New York and London, and the crisp, lithe suppleness of modern paperbacks. He loved the smell of paper, ink, and glue, and the way tobacco smoke crept into the pages and imprinted itself there with the words. Most of all, he loved the fact that he—despite undergraduate and law degrees acquired from the University of Wyoming—had discovered, for and by and of himself, the incredible richness of books.

He was at his desk each morning by eight, though Mary-Elena, who generally arrived at the same hour and sometimes earlier, never allowed him to be disturbed before a quarter to nine. For forty-five minutes her presence beyond the closed door was pure Negative, a silent invisibility blotting out all intrusion, while he sat behind the big desk, not moving except to turn the page or raise the mug of coffee to his lips; sometimes just sitting, watching as the sun crept upon the piles of documents it seemed almost to levitate as he marshalled the thoughts and emotions and roles for the combats that—he finally believed—were unjust and unsought impositions levied upon helpless clients whose innocence should have obviated the necessity of argument in a court of law. He believed it—yet had caught himself worrying, the past couple of years, that the habitual courtroom display of weary resignation to a changeless round of wholly unnecessary pleading was hardening now into an actual weariness that was slowly grinding down the fierce energy that had relentlessly directed his mind to such effective result. Although he went on winning cases, like an aging slalom racer he had begun to experience intimations of a stiffening somewhere —of something that might lock in time, without warning, snatching away his balance even as it treacherously increased his momentum.

An edgy May wind gusted through the lowered transom from the wine-blue sky in which small round clouds like gun-patches floated. Through the tall embrasured window he saw the budded trees feathery among winter-rusted pines, and beyond the trees the dollhouse shapes of grimy bungalows crowded upon their dingy out-buildings—garages, toolsheds, doghouses—on paltry iron-fenced plots. For a moment he sat thinking of his ranch on the Hoback River, of his fields and horses and the apiary he had started the year before last and to which he devoted much of what little spare time he had, aware of a depression rising like a small cloud at the back of his head. If, he assured himself, to do what I am doing—have to do—and indeed have done, it were necessary for me to do it, to live in this place—well then, I would do it. But thank God it is not. Any one of these houses could have been his father's in Buffalo—also a coal town— in which his childhood had been spent. Staring at the wide picture windows behind which the curtains seemed permanently drawn—had he ever, he wondered, had a view of them open?—he felt that he was nevertheless of these people, had come from them at least: agonized with them in their pathetic, overmatched encounters with powers their lives had not prepared them to confront on equal terms. As long as, he thought—watching an oddly familiar small boy of about eight pedaling furiously around a corner of one of the bungalows on a fire-engine-red tricycle—he continued to be gifted by this special empathy, his duty would continue to be clear, his future couched in that special assurance enjoyed chiefly by artists, saints, and other similarly self-sufficient people. Crinkling his eyes into a squint he continued to stare at the image of the plain and appallingly vulnerable community from which he had come and whose sworn and habitual defender he was and—for better than thirty years now—had been.

The sun flashed benignly behind a pair of the little white clouds arranged like spectacles as the wind gave the transom a final brisk rattle, causing Hal Pearce to close the volume on his thumb and return it regretfully to its place on the swivel bookcase. Then, swinging his boots decisively off the desktop, he drew himself up to his full height—six foot four in heels—and pawed at the scudding papers as he took the breeze gratefully on both cheeks. He exclaimed, "Ahhhhhhhhh!"—stretching his arms upward from the shoulders and shaking himself down like a big dog. Closing his collar, he pushed the knot of his necktie into place, buttoned his vest, and brushed his trousers at the knees. He felt good because he was going bear-hunting on the weekend, and he hadn't had many opportunities recently to hunt anything that didn't go about on two legs rather than four.

His pocket-watch said eight-forty-three. Forbearing to press the electric button on the desk he sat again instead, clasping his hands behind his large silver-haired head, rocking gently in the old swivel chair and confidently anticipating the punctual appearance of Mary-Elena.

She slipped through the door at precisely a quarter to nine, holding a clipboard in one hand and an electric coffeepot in the other. At their first meeting he had been instantly struck by the tall, slender figure, which he took for that of a retired ballerina until he became aware of a slight rigidity of carriage uncharacteristic of a dancer. She had been thirty-two then; now, at thirty-six, she was, if anything, more handsome still. Her auburn hair was drawn back and fastened with a coral clasp at the nape, emphasizing the classic, marbled quality of the head, with its nose and chin only slightly in excess of the ideal, and the large, black, disturbing eyes that appeared intermittently to be striving to soften the severe expression which threatened to unsex her. This morning she had on a white sweater with long sleeves fitting tightly at the wrists and set off at the throat—to which her long, febrile hands rose constantly—by a string of matching coral beads like blood-drops. After refilling his cup, Mary-Elena set the pot carefully on the blotter and stood with the clipboard pressed to her chest like a singer awaiting instructions from the pit.

"It's been a *terrible* day already," she said, "and it's hardly begun yet."

His hands still clasped behind his head, he smiled upward at her. "You could have fooled me," he said. "It's been quiet as a church in here."

Mary-Elena accepted the compliment with a slight elevation of her chin, while one hand went on twisting the coral necklace.

"Who wants what this morning?" Pearce demanded, tasting the coffee.

Mary-Elena gave an elaborate sigh and communed with the clipboard.

"Sam Caldwell from the Department of Criminal Investigation called at eight-oh-three about the lab tests and wants you to call him back—said it's extremely urgent. About eight-ten Ted Williams from the State Highway Patrol called to discuss his subpoena to the preliminary hearing. He said to tell you he's on duty the rest of the morning and he'll try to get back to you after three. At eight-fifteen you got a call from Bob Brown of the *Bear Valley Ranger-Bulletin*—"

"That son-of-bitch," Pearce remarked over the edge of the cup.

"—wanting you to comment on a column by Herb Crawford in the *Casper Star-Tribune* saying you've compromised your integrity as a defense attorney—"

"That's enough," he interrupted, frowning and holding up a large hand. "Jesus Christ, Mary-Elena, you know better than to bother me with crap like that." Although they had never discussed the subject directly, he understood that Mary-

Elena was tacitly in agreement with Crawford's point of view. Mary-Elena, though not a sensuous woman, was nevertheless a passionate one: believer, fighter, advocate. Born of Greek parents in Rock Springs, she had gone east to study voice at the New England Conservatory of Music, returning after five years of unsuccessful striving at becoming an opera singer to Wyoming, where, accepting a job as a women's-issue lobbyist in Cheyenne, she poured into the cause of feminism the emotionalism she had been thwarted from conveying in the roles of Verdi's, Donizetti's, and Bellini's for the most part profoundly anti-feminist, if strong-minded, heroines. He had become acquainted with her after taking the case of a woman executive who had suffered a nervous collapse upon being dismissed from an engineering position with a nationwide construction company, and had hired her five months later in a capacity that had come to include everything save actually rising in court to confront a jury. Mary-Elena lived in a small rented house in Jackson that he felt guilty visiting, although he paid her a very good salary over which he held no discretionary right of disposal. In her late twenties she had married a good-looking restaurateur twenty years her senior who owned a string of nightclubs around the state and who, if he had been asked about it, would have defined a woman's issue as something prescribed for in Leviticus. The marriage lasted thirteen months, after which she lived again out of apartments, driving twenty-five thousand miles a year around the state and chain-smoking cigarettes at three or four late-night meetings every week. She had given up the cigarettes finally, replacing them with endless cups of black coffee and boxes of rich candy that had no effect whatever upon her figure, to which she had had tailored an impeccable, seemingly inexhaustible wardrobe. "Now," he said, "who else wants a piece of my hide today?"

"Bob Brown said he'll call back," Mary-Elena told him.

He glared at her, angry now. It was a question he had

decided for himself two months before, and which he felt no obligation to take up again. Making decisions was after all chiefly a matter of proficiency, and he had made a lot of them in his time. At fifty-eight years of age, a wealthy and successful man with plenty of experience, he had grown dismissive—not even impatient—of criticism. If that was a fault, he assured himself, most certainly I have earned the right to it. Because when the need to listen is really there, I know it; can feel it.

"A Mr. Tom Axehelm from KTVR in Cheyenne called at eight-forty-five to ask if you can go on 'Cheyenne This Morning' with the Governor next Tuesday at ten. I told him you had a court date tentatively scheduled in Omaha for that date. Was that right?"

"Absolutely. Anything else?"

He noticed the bruised places on her wrists the coral beads had made. In a brittle voice she said, "Christine Richardson wants you to return her call as soon as possible."

Hal Pearce removed his hands from behind his head and began drumming his fingers on his knees in rippling, musical motion. He sighed, and regarded Mary-Elena archly over the tops of his Ben Franklins. "Did she say what it was about?"

Mary-Elena shrugged her slim shoulders. "Did you actually imagine she'd tell *me?*" she demanded with a short laugh, looking past him through the window, where scattered flakes of snow were falling through the dimmed light of a high plains spring. Mary-Elena he knew distrusted Richardson but positively loathed his wife.

"What time did you say she called?"

"About a quarter till."

"Did you get the impression it might be about her husband?"

"I got the usual impression," Mary-Elena replied frigidly.

"If he doesn't make up his mind in forty-eight hours, I'm going to ask Keith Wilson in Sheridan." Hal Pearce thrust two fingers of his right hand into his vest, then removed them and selected a smelly pipe with a well-chewed bit from the rack. "I suppose I'd better call her, huh?"

Mary-Elena did not say anything.

"If you'll get her on the line for me in fifteen minutes," he said, grinning at her, "I'll sign those goddamn letters you were bothering me about yesterday afternoon."

He read over the letters rapidly, with satisfaction at her professionalism and his own fluent style, and signed them with the enormous Mont Blanc fountain pen he had paid a hundred dollars for and used especially for the purpose, admiring the calligraphic design that was more like a monogram than a signature on the expensive cream-colored paper. He became so engrossed in signing letters that he was not at once aware of the flashing red light beside his elbow. He lifted the receiver and heard Mary-Elena say angrily, "Mrs. Richardson on the line to speak with you."

Her voice vanished with a click and was replaced by an interval of absolute silence, shattered suddenly in its turn by a clashing sound like that of Ajax falling upon his sword and which he recognized instantly for the braceleted armature of Tiffany & Company. "Hi there!" Christine cried. "Am I speaking with Mr. Hal Pearce, the Great American Defense Attorney?"

He heard quite definitely the equine snort of smoke against the mouthpiece. "What can I do for you, Princess?" He had been calling her Princess for nearly five years now, having discovered somewhat to his surprise that she seemed to enjoy it.

"Has my darling hubby been in to see you yet?" she asked. Her speech was American, despite intimations of the Mayflower Society and the Quai d'Orsay; her voice shimmered with Tiffany's truest luster. It was, he thought, an upper-class tomboy's voice, a startling and thoroughly original combination of male joviality and female aplomb. He imagined the bracelets pumping like piston rings on the gesticulating, tawny arms, the golden tiger's-eyes blazing.

"I haven't heard a word in a couple of days, Princess. If you're talking with him in the next day or so, better tell him time's running out. I'm not calling him about it again."

"I'm not supposed to *know*, Hal—remember?"

"Have you two spoken recently?"

"I tried to reach him the other night," Christine said, "but the little slut that answered the phone didn't give him the message—apparently. I just get so *fed up* sometimes, Hal."

He said, "What made you think he'd been in to see me?"

"Oh, I don't know, MESP I guess. What I call Mated Extrasensory Perception." She gave one of her little snorts of laughter—perversely attractive, as he remembered—and blew smoke at the mouthpiece again. "He wants us all to think he's just some old sheepherder, but he's still Mr. Bigshot pretending to be the Virginian resurrected in 1984."

Some part of him appreciated Christine Richardson, in small doses at least. "Listen, Princess," he told her. "We have a date to go hunting together this weekend and I promise I'll do my best with him—not for you or even for him, but because he could make a damn valuable assistant if only he could pull himself together and fly straight for a while. But if he wants to make the boat, he'd better get his ass up the gangplank in one big hurry."

"Okay," she said. "Please, do. And thanks for calling back. Take care. *Ciao!*" And hung up.

He sat for a while, starting again to fill the pipe he had taken up three-quarters of an hour ago, kneading the tobacco between thumb and forefinger and sprinkling it liberally across his lap. What was it, he thought, that was so attractive finally about that bitch? Maybe one day he would ask her husband.

Again the light flashed; the intercom this time. He raised the receiver and, speaking through clenched teeth around the pipestem, said, "Yes, Mary-Elena?"

"Mr. Richardson is here to see you," she told him in a poisonous controlled voice. "Can you see him now or should I have him wait?"

He paused, trying to decide which of the two of them annoyed him more. "Ahhh!" he said. Then: "Mary-Elena, ask Mr. Richardson if he wouldn't mind waiting a *couple of minutes.*"

He replaced the receiver in the cradle, then, sitting back in the chair, knocked out the pipe and started leisurely to refill it while his eyes pursued an oddly familiar-looking little boy pedaling furiously around a corner on a tricycle painted a poignant fire-engine red.

7

CLOPPING DOWN THE echoing linoleum corridor Richardson thought, I sound exactly like the *Grand Canyon Suite*. A single door in the line of oaken ones paned with pebbled antique glass had been replaced by a slab of raw steel, blank save for a peep-hole set in its harsh gray face. The county, he guessed, was taking no chances with the drug crowd. He punched the bell hard and waited for Mary-Elena's eye to appear in the lens, standing close against it to prevent her from getting a clear view. Abruptly the hole glared at him, an eye within an eye; there was a pause followed by the grating noise of unfiled metal as the door swung inward. "Hello," Mary-Elena said over her shoulder, already on her way back to her desk.

"Howdy," Richardson said, to irritate her. He removed his hat and tossed it at the wooden coatrack. "I want to have a talk with Hal if he's got a minute."

Not looking at him, she said, "He's on the phone right now."

"He going to be on long?"

"He'll be on as long as he needs to be," she explained coldly. "If you'll have a seat, I'll let him know you're here as soon as he gets off the line."

He sat, crossing his legs, and watched while Mary-Elena replaced the headphones over her ears and began to write very rapidly on a steno pad. Her profile he thought was fine, her thighs within the tight black skirt finer still, the fact of her dislike for him seeming only to increase her attractiveness. Drawing a package from his shirt pocket he lit one of the little cigars. The match-head made a tearing noise along the sole of his boot and Mary-Elena looked up quickly from her work; he wondered how she had heard it through the earphones. He tilted his head and blew a gusher of blue smoke at the ceiling.

"Would you mind not, this morning?" she said. "I seem to be coming down with a cold."

Richardson shrugged and, stubbing the cigar in the spittoon between two fresh butts, glanced impatiently at the red button that continued to flicker unevenly beside Mary-Elena's elbow. At a right angle to her desk a word-processor rested on a smooth maple-wood counter flush against the dead-looking wall painted an institutional green and on which faded squares and oblongs showed where picture frames had recently been taken down; overhead the single good fluorescent tube flared steadily fainter. It was assuredly not Hal Pearce's style, but despite Mary-Elena's elegance he could not help thinking that this dreary suite suited her Calvinist soul. Already after two weeks the place smelled of Justice, pervaded by a chemical odor like that in a doctor's office: redolent of despair, corruption, and death.

The red light died suddenly and Richardson saw Mary-Elena's eye dart at it. For amusement he counted the seconds before she lifted the receiver. He had reached a hundred and sixty-eight before she said curtly, "He's off the phone now. He'll be with you in a couple of minutes," she added, after hanging up.

Mary-Elena and Hal Pearce worked together, he reflected, like a Puritan conscience in a cavalier breast: He had never been able to understand why the lawyer wanted her around. It had occurred to him that they might be romantically conjoined after hours but he had immediately dismissed the idea. Though stolidly masculine, Hal Pearce was as conventional a bachelor as he was a floridly theatrical and idiosyncratic attorney.

"He can see you now," Mary-Elena announced. Checking her wristwatch ostentatiously, she added, "He has another appointment in forty-five minutes."

Hal Pearce's face had that English clarity that was almost translucence, like afternoon rain on the Serpentine or the music of Purcell or Sullivan. It was a face completely lacking in the smooth conventional looks of the standard twentieth-century-hybrid American masculinity, a face that would go forever unfulfilled by its natural complement of powdered wigs and linen cravats—as also, apparently, by the attention of beautiful women raised to accept their standards of male physicality from Southern California and West Palm Beach. And yet, indisputably, it was a handsome face—strong and indomitable despite the lines and pouches of late middle age and a faint, almost indistinguishable, slackness at the corners of the mouth that hinted at a so-far-controlled tendency toward self-indulgence. The silvery hair fell just above the ears in backswept wings and the china-blue eyes were clear and alert, their pink rims suggestive less of weariness than of a sad disillusionment in which, however, you found yourself not entirely prepared to believe. The large body—not fat at all, just tall, wide-built, still powerful—was dressed in a patternless pearl-gray vested suit tailored in the Western style, white shirt, and black silk necktie; on the desktop before it an enormous silver Stetson rested on its crown beside a pair of black Western boots polished to a high gloss and with the half-soles worn nearly through. Hal Pearce, Richardson thought, resembled more than anything one of those remarkable characters from the antebellum South who had combined the identities of planter, scholar, lawyer, entrepreneur, and statesman, and to which he himself had added the paradigmatic role of Western lawman. He filled—dominated—the room, as he filled and dominated every room—including a court of law—in the way sea-sound fills a beach or the glare of the sun a desert. Watching him, Richardson understood, with a twinge of envy, that the key to this man's enormous presence in the world was his fundamental and unshakable acceptance of it. "Well, my friend," Pearce said, wreathed in blue tobacco smoke and not lifting his chin from his steepled fingers, "have you an answer for me this morning?"

Richardson dropped into the facing chair and swung his boots onto the desk until the toes were nearly touching the lawyer's. He drew out another of the offensive cigars and lit it. "Mary-Elena wouldn't let me smoke outside," he said.

"Mary-Elena suspects you of having an impure attitude," Pearce told him. "She doesn't regard you as a committed person."

"Committed to what, for Christ's sake?"

Hal Pearce shrugged. "Just committed period, I guess. You do look like hell, you know—that hair, those pants."

Richardson considered the faded jeans—untarred it was true, but stiffened with horse sweat, frayed at the cuffs, and pulling their seams along the legs—the sweater unraveling at the elbows; the scarred, cracked sharkskin boots with the half-soles peeling back from the toes. His hair, he realized, was falling forward into his eyes, which would be bloodshot; his head throbbed like a failing engine. Oh well, he thought: Never apologize, never explain.

"Never mind about all that," Pearce said. "What about it, Chuck? There's a bunch of work to be done right away and I've got several out-of-state cases to deal with besides. You're going to have to shit or get off the pot, now. Did they ever tell you at that candy-ass law school back East they call Harvard what the worst fault in an attorney is?"

"Idealism. And they didn't have to."

"Wrong. 'There is grief in indecision,' as Cicero tells us. And after indecision, cynicism."

Richardson masticated the cigar. The tobacco was stale, almost tasteless, and biting to the tongue, but it made a good cover. "Listen," he began. "You would have to understand something first. If I do this thing it won't be for Our American Way of Life or the Basic Principles of a Free Society or the American Bar Association or the Rotarian Club. It will be my personal, gold-plated, limited-issue, this-offer-good-for-thirty-days-only commemoration of every man who ever had the simple bravery to take the law into his own hands in the days before there was any such curse as law—"

"Stop right there, now." Hal Pearce was holding up a hand as wide as a traffic cop's, palm out. "That'll be enough of that," he said. "A prosecutor can't afford to listen to any more of that sort of thing." He lifted his boots off the desk and, leaning back in his chair with his hands behind his head, squinted at Richardson. "I don't give a damn what you call it," he said, "so long as you don't repeat it to me. But I *will* tell you that you, an Easterner—not a Southerner or a Westerner—not forty years old yet, have not earned the right to defend lynch law. You know, my friend, you'd be a decent human being if only you'd just quit talking so goddamn much. The important thing is that you and I are in fundamental agreement about the significance of this case—are we not?"

Richardson took a long pull on the cigar, and gagged. When he had recovered himself he replied sullenly, "Yeah, I guess."

"Then it's settled." Abruptly Pearce reached for the intercom. "Don't go away yet," he said. "I want you to do me a simple favor. It won't take more than an hour or so of your valuable time and I believe I can promise you that you won't find it wasted."

"Okay." It occurred to Richardson to resent the faintly ironic stress on the word *valuable*, but he decided to let it go. "What is it?"

"There's somebody I think you might be interested in meeting. I'm going to have Mary-Elena find out if it can be arranged this morning." As he spoke he held the receiver away from his ear, permitting Richardson to hear Mary-Elena's sharp, impatient voice saying, "Yes? Yes? Hal? What is it?"

"About our friend's request for a meeting with the prosecutor's office—would you call Wainwright right away and see if he can arrange to meet us at the jail in half an hour?"

Hal Pearce sat for a minute in silence, pressing his fingers to his chin. "This should be *very* interesting," he remarked at last. "For you and for me, both."

8

TOGETHER THEY WENT along the corridor and, without waiting for the cramped elevator, down the stairs, across the rotunda, and around the weathered pile of the courthouse to the new jail building which was modern, efficient, and equivocal, with as little of tragedy about it, he thought, as a daycare center. Entering by a side door, they found themselves in a linoleumed passageway, incandescent with sealed light, in which their boots made no sound at all. In a square yellow-painted cubicle at the end of the corridor two deputies in brown uniforms sat playing checkers at a card table, which, together with a soft-drink machine, portable television set, and several folding chairs, were its only furnishings. Both deputies wore blond sideburns and both of them were soft-looking and fat, though one was fatter than the other. They had the television switched to a morning news-and-talk show from New York but with the audio button off, so that the only noises in the room were the creaking of chairs, the whisper of the game pieces across the board, and the low threshing sound of circulated air. The deputies looked up from their game as the two men entered the room and one of them said, "Good morning, Mr. Pearce." Their plump faces showed a liverish yellow in the even fluorescent lighting.

"Bill Wainwright not here yet?" Hal Pearce asked.

"Not yet, Mr. Pearce."

"Boys," he told them, "I'd like for you to meet Mr. Chuck Richardson of Fontennelle. I've asked Mr. Richardson—who's an attorney and, I'm here to tell you, one hell of a good one—to join me as assistant prosecutor, and he's been generous enough to at least consider the offer. How's our friends doing this morning?"

The officers glanced at one another as if their wits in combination could provide perhaps an answer to his question. At last the fatter one said, "Munger's just finished eatin breakfast and the other one's at the infirmary havin that broke wrist looked at. They still got the girl down at Bear Valley Hospital."

Hal Pearce sat down heavily in one of the light folding chairs, setting his hat carefully on his knee. He glanced warily at the television screen, where a man who appeared to be either a terrorist or a mobster, a black hood over his head, sat in a chair for an interview. There was an empty fourth chair but Richardson, wearing his hat, remained standing stiffly by the door. Jails made him nervous, in the way that hospitals made other people.

"Do you want me to turn off the TV, sir?" the fatter deputy, whose nameplate said Smith, asked.

"No," Pearce told him, setting his hat on the television. "I'll just sit here and watch Mungerism destroy the world via satellite communications until Mungerism's defense counsel arrives."

"Hell, Mr. Pearce," the other deputy said. "You meet ever' kind of puke in this work, but I never seen anything like this one. I didn't know they made 'em like that anymore."

Hal Pearce glanced at him then, his blue eyes clairvoyant and stern. "They make them like frogs in a dark and dismal swamp, my friend," he said. "Civilization is just a floating bridge across billions of Mungers, and always has been."

"You know," the deputy said respectfully and in a surprised tone of voice, "I never thought about it that way, but I guess you're right, sir." Hitching his chair toward the set, he turned up the volume and regarded the screen with fresh interest.

A man came into the room holding a Stetson hat in his large red hands. He had on tan trousers cut long over the heels of his tall yellow boots and a green polyester jacket with imitation brass buttons, beneath which a patterned Western-style shirt lay open at the neck, its cuffs protruding nearly to his sunburned knuckles. His thick orange hair was plastered close above his freckled red face, from which faded yet alert blue eyes protruded. Something in his carriage, as well as a slight self-consciousness of demeanor, made Richardson think of a countrified, second-string version of Hal Pearce himself. He did not believe that the absurd cuffs, which caused him to resemble a hayseed in a George Ade fable, were entirely ingenuous.

"Morning, Bill." Pearce's voice was cordial as he rose from in front of the television to extend his hand. "I hope I'm not putting you to any inconvenience, calling on such short notice."

"No, sir, not at all." Bill Wainwright shifted the hat from his right to left hand for the greeting, and back again. His manner was like that of a bulldog confronting another, larger. bulldog in its own back yard: tentatively friendly but on guard, prepared to spring first if need be.

"This is Chuck Richardson, Bill," Pearce said. "As you've probably heard, I've asked him to work with me as assistant prosecutor. I don't suppose you have any objection to his accompanying us, do you?"

Except for their color, the blue eyes were exactly those of a bulldog—quite a smart bulldog—as they aggressively held his own for a long moment. Of course he doesn't want me to, he thought. Of course he doesn't want any of us to. Probably he has no better idea than we do what this lunatic wants to tell us—insists on telling us. And the poor son-ofabitch can't do a thing about it.

"Well," Bill Wainwright said doubtfully. "Heck," he agreed.

"I guess I don't have an objection. But, as I'm sure you folks will appreciate, on behalf of my client I intend to monitor this interview real carefully."

"Certainly, Bill," Pearce assured him politely. "We're all three professional attorneys. We don't begrudge you the obligation to set whatever limits you see fit to fix."

Deputy Smith unlocked the heavy door, and they followed him through it and along a close corridor smelling of lye and laundered clothes. Descending a short flight of stairs, they continued through a second corridor with slotted windows just under the ceiling and giving at ground level onto an asphalt-covered parking lot. Here the passageway widened abruptly and they reached the first line of cells, each a neat rectangle evenly lit with that same sealed-in light and containing a bed and a washstand. Deputy Smith halted in front of one of them. "Okay, Munger," he said. "You got company."

In the center of the floor he saw a torn magazine and a pair of slippers; other magazines lay scattered across the bed, which was neatly made and empty. Staring, he saw for a moment nothing more. Then a movement just beneath the ceiling caught his eye: a leg being pulled up from the stretched-out position in which the figure had been reclining in the window-slot. Drawing itself together suddenly like a shadow, the figure dropped with feline lightness to the floor, from where it watched them in a crouching position. It had on a gray pajama-like suit and white socks that emphasized the waxen, almost colorless flesh; the head was close-shaved and squared at the jaws and temples, giving it a flimsy, ill-made look, like a fruitbox on which the mouth was a thin purple stain filled with wide-spaced rodent teeth. The close-set eyes were like holes bored in a mask held precariously in place before Nothing.

"Good morning, Willie," Wainwright said. "This is Mr. Pearce and Mr. Richardson from the prosecutor's office—the folks you were wanting to talk to."

The figure approached in a slightly stooped position and gripped the bars with its waxen hands. Deputy Smith removed a key ring from his belt with a rattling sound. "Get away from the door, Munger," he said, "and I'll let these gentlemen in to visit with you."

The eyes, Richardson thought, were like something glimpsed back of the stars, at the bottom of the universe, on a bad night. Staring at them, he remembered with a feeling almost of reassurance LeRoy Jackson's sloed ones in the black, mobile, expressive face, at once insolent and pleading, torturing and tortured, feckless and intense—human. With a prickle of horror he observed a small cross on a chain hanging against the triangle of gray skin revealed by the open pajama neck.

"What for?" the mouth demanded. "What I got to say to them I can say just as good this way."

"Now, Willie," Wainwright said hastily, "you remember you wanted to talk to these gentlemen, and we agreed—"

But the prisoner was not looking at him now. " 'Works for the prosecutor's office,' " he mocked. "Well, kiss my ass. I tell you what—if I was on the outside I'd take his fuckin head off for him."

Richardson discovered that Willie Munger was not looking at Hal Pearce at all. The eyes—colder, flatter, more deadly than a snake's—were set like the twin barrels of a shotgun upon his own.

"I'm warnin you, Munger," Deputy Smith said. "Show respect. The next time you see Mr. Pearce and Mr. Richardson here may be in court." Holding the key between thumb and forefinger, he turned away to the three men. "You want to visit with him today, or wait until he's ready to behave himself, sir?" he asked Wainwright.

Richardson was vaguely aware of Hal Pearce's silent bulk at his elbow, and of the defense attorney's excited protests to which his client remained oblivious. Like a cobra's, the eyes seemed to hold him, making him incapable of motion or even of breath.

"Hey, dude." The flat, dead voice spoke again. "Do yourself a favor and get lost, willya? You ain't ever goin to find where I live."

And then—like the cobra—the creature spat, the gob of phlegm hocked neatly onto the linoleum floor at his feet, as Richardson, in recoil, flung his hands up to his face and Deputy Smith's bellowing filled the corridor, summoning the running feet that drowned attorney Wainwright's plaintive exclamations, together with the prisoner's uninterrupted stream of flat, monotonal cursing.

When they returned to the television room the second deputy was sitting over the unfinished checkers game watching a terrorist gang hurling grenades into the streets of what was apparently a Middle Eastern city. Richardson and Pearce shook hands in turn with the mortified defense attorney, for whom Richardson could not help feeling pity, and the two men together walked silently down the linoleum tunnel into the bright windy morning full of gusting light and the scouring white clouds.

"How about it?" Hal Pearce asked at the bottom of the courthouse steps. "You still up for hunting bear this weekend?"

"*Jesus Christ Almighty!*" Richardson removed his hat and wiped the band with his bandana.

"I'm up for hunting something," he said.

9

"Look at that asshole," Hal Pearce suggested. "Where do you suppose he's headed now?"

Richardson said, "He thinks he's going to where he set the bait. According to what he told me several days ago, it's in exactly the opposite direction."

They stood watching the diminishing figure struggle away from them across the talus slope that made one wall of the long valley. From time to time it paused, teetering and holding its rifle above its head for balance, then went on, moving cautiously but with unswerving surety of direction.

"What would you make of that if you were a bear?" Pearce asked.

"I guess I'd figure my long-lost Uncle Albert had escaped from the circus finally and found his way home."

"Doesn't he carry a compass with him?"

"He does, but it might as well be a pedometer."

Hal Pearce laughed suddenly. "Do you take Tonio hunting with you very often?"

"I'm empathetic somehow. Always have been. And he's a great cook."

"You think he'll find his way home for supper?"

"If he smells the right campfire, maybe."

Pearce swiveled on his heels to scan the green walls of the

surrounding mountains. "It doesn't appear that he's got much of a choice," he said.

Far below them, the torrenting spring-filled creek tore at the red clay banks, swirling down amid clumps of orange willow; above them, silver mountain peaks tilted fractured snowfields against a cloudless sky. The day before, Richardson had coached the pickup, grinding and fishtailing in the unquickened mud, as high as the first snowbanks, where they had made camp in a small, damp park marked with snow-drops and the tentative hoofprints of deer, and Tonio had prepared a supper of elk steaks, fried potatoes, rolls, and coffee, to which they had added whiskey and two bottles of wine.

Tonio worked as a short-order cook at a Fontennelle lunch counter where his talents—which extended to elk heart stew, beef Wellington, lasagna, and exquisite Italian cakes—were insufficiently exercised. His wide features were more Slavic than Italian, his skin very fair save for a spot of intense color on each cheek so exact they looked painted by an Austrian toymaker, his round, nearly lidless eyes a rich chestnut brown matching his curly abundant hair. A childhood accident had damaged his vocal cords, leaving him with a high-pitched voice that contrasted absurdly with the powerful physique distinctively and habitually attired in a loose blouselike shirt, heavy peasant shoes laced halfway, and a ubiquitous plaid cap worn backward on the round skull. For two years Richardson and Tonio had been companions—fishing on wind-swept, snow-chilled mountain lakes in August; hunting antelope across golden, sage-spiced plains in September; drinking apple schnapps as they trudged on snowshoes across the lavender-and-pink shadows of January after cottontails to shoot, or whiskey in Tonio's trailer, which was so crowded with guns and fishing tackle, snowmachine parts and the tore-down truck engines, chainsaws, and cuckoo-clocks Tonio rebuilt in winter, that by spring his movements were confined to a path running from the front door to the bedroom and from the bedroom to the toilet.

With that peculiar sense of jealous and exclusive possession experienced by every sympathetic white man beginning with the first fur-trappers and Indian-fighters—as well as, he presumed, the Indians themselves—Richardson regarded the mountains as being by right of unique appreciation his unrecognized personal demesne. In wet, blustery spring, following the receding snow line upward along treacherous trails, he hunted them for bear; returning in fall for deer, elk, and more bear, he slipped out with his kill from beneath the descending portcullis of winter. In summer he explored the endless succession of valley and range—still an almost trackless wilderness of timber and talus, willow and high meadow—on horseback or on foot, alone or in company with the Fontennelle County Search and Rescue, locating and retrieving impacted four-wheel-drives, strayed climbers, or the wreckage—mechanical and human—of lost airplanes. Standing now with Hal Pearce on the hogback above Scavenger Creek he surveyed through the field-glasses the eastern slope of Deadman's Ridge, where, in August, Search and Rescue made camp for three workless, womanless, restraintless days of poker, whiskey, guns, and more whiskey.

"He said he wanted to have a look at that crossing where he found tracks last night," Hal Pearce said. "He thought it would take him only ten minutes or so to do that."

Richardson did not reply; instead he began humming "The Bear Went Over the Mountain" under his breath. When he had hummed it four times over he kicked a rotten pine log with his boot, breaking it in two and disturbing an angry colony of ants. Now the figure was out of sight, vanished into a stand of the tall black timber. "Come on, Hal," he said after a moment. "If we don't go after him he'll end up in Jackson sometime around Labor Day. We can bring the guns, and if we don't see any bears we'll shoot Tonio instead. Dressed out you couldn't tell the difference anyway."

They doused the fire and filled the pockets of their vests with shells. Richardson took a compass reading on the spot where Tonio had disappeared and they set out, moving across the ridge at an ascendent angle. For a quarter-mile they slogged through the damp, gripping clay that showed crimson beneath the blue boluses of sagebrush before they reached the talus, a slide of iron-colored shards like smashed pottery, over which they went spread-armed, banking and trimming like clumsy hawks against the sky. An equilibrium of speed and balance, Richardson discovered, produced an irresistible momentum and he found himself bounding across the scrabbled gray brow like a mountain goat, intoxicated by motion and the thin fine air. The assurance of well-being he had experienced the previous evening expanded to elation as he flew over the broken, bitter rock beneath a high and perfect sky, his body poised as a dancer's. Glancing back once he saw Pearce's bearish shape following deliberately, not faltering or winded, just steadfast and unhurried. It occurred to him that Hal Pearce was at his best in the mountains, and unexpectedly he felt himself overwhelmed by a feeling almost of love for this man who was old enough to be his father and yet was approaching the age of sixty without issue. He raced on, feeling his heart begin to pound and his lungs tighten, until a stone turned abruptly under his boot and he lost it all— lurching through space with jagged points flying at him like spears and just time enough to thrust the rifle above his head so that when he landed it was in the absurd position of a cast-iron figure on a battle monument.

He sat panting, holding the gun across his knee and waiting for Pearce to catch up. He had hunted last with the lawyer four years earlier, for elk, going much of the time on horseback, and while he had been impressed then by the older man's stamina, he was surprised now to find it apparently undiminished: although Hal Pearce's physical movements were as slow as his mental ones were lightning-quick, he possessed the rugged unstoppable motion of a machine. Richardson watched him driving forward: a big man in a fringed deerskin jacket, weather-stained hat, and heavy boots, carrying a pair of binoculars around his neck and a .7mm rifle on his shoulder. Despite something of the far, ineffable look of the scholar-bachelor in his china-blue eyes, he appeared most naturally himself equipped with gun and hunting knife and in the rough clothes of the outdoorsman, which served to convey the atavistic core of his personality as riding habits and yachting clothes might the effete reality of the hard, city-bred attorney. Together they rested on the shattered face of the mountain under a stunted pinyon pine, sharing water from Richardson's canteen as, carefully, they glassed the flank of the opposite ridge.

"The dumb sonofabitch," Richardson said. "I apologize, Hal. I should have left him in town this weekend."

"That's all right now," Pearce told him. "I don't have to shoot a bear." He stood suddenly and stared around the palisaded horizon, shading his eyes with his hand under the hat's wide brim. "What goddamn gorgeous country it is," he said, removing the hat and holding it against his belly as if he were delivering a speech, while the wind whipped his long silver hair and teared his eyes. " 'The fatal gift of beauty,' " he quoted. "There are things, my friend, that were made too perfect for their own good, like a beautiful woman, or these Rocky Mountains, or maybe just the ordinary human life we used to enjoy in this simple, dispersive, symbiotic civilization called the American West. And after four thousand years of codifications and treatises, statutes and constitutions, all we can say for the Law is that it can perhaps be the agent by which some fragile thing of value may have a chance to prevail, or at least hold out for another day, another week, even—who knows?—another century."

Richardson felt his neck prickle, as if a person unseen were holding a gunsight on the back of his skull. He said: "It's not a question of laws and constitutions. It's a question of putting enough distance between you and Them that the sonsof-bitches can't find you."

"Maybe so," Hal Pearce agreed, squinting. "But in that case, friend Chuck, you haven't run far enough."

Abruptly, Richardson began striding away from him across the talus. "Come on, Hal," he called over his shoulder. "I'd like to at least get a shot at something today."

Beside an outcropping of rock at the edge of a line of timber the waffled prints of running shoes were superimposed upon a burnt-out match lying on the soft red clay. Tonio had stopped to light a cigarette before entering the forest.

"Why the hell didn't he wear boots this morning?" Pearce demanded irritably, scraping over the prints with the side of his shoe.

"He thought he could climb a tree easier if a bear chased him. I asked him—that's what he told me."

In the cold emerald-green glitter of the woods they tracked him easily across the corn-snow to the crest of a ridge where the fir-trees stopped and the south slope fell steeply away in a tilted sagebrush meadow plumed with unleafed aspen. In the valley below a line of beaver ponds lay strung like fallen stars along the silver thread of a creek. Scowling, Hal Pearce surveyed the country through the glasses. "I don't see a thing," he said shortly. "Well, Caleb—where do we go from here?"

"If I know Tonio," Richardson told him, "he wasn't able to resist checking out those beaver ponds. Of course, if he'd taken a shot at anything we'd have heard it, but I'll bet dollars to doughnuts we find his tracks there anyway."

The heavy guns pounding their backs, their ankles turning painfully on hummocks of brush and matted grass, they reached the valley floor sweated through by the ripening spring sun. At the second pond Richardson discovered Tonio's prints among the fresh spoor of elk. "That no-good, would-be, poaching bastard."

"Screw Tonio," Hal Pearce told him. "Suppose we take a little rest?"

Sitting on a gnawed aspen log with its still-green top lying in the water, they drank from the canteen and shared the elk sandwiches Richardson took from his pack. When they had finished they removed their hats and lay back against the hill, feeling the warm sun beating against their skins through the wind-chill. They would hear the wind starting out of the domed silence of the cirque, rising above the soft, pervasive sound of rushing water, constant and omnipresent, as if the world itself were flowing rapidly to its end; building like a hurricane in the great bowl to hurtle suddenly upon them with the irresistible force of a freight train until, as suddenly, it would be gone and they would unscrew their eyes and stare once more at the palisade of granite and snow standing like a fortress against the sky from which tall white clouds moved heavily on flat, gray bases. Watching them, Richardson felt as exquisitely and fragilely situated as an egg in an eggcup.

"You know," Hal Pearce remarked, closing his eyes again and folding his hands on his chest, "I never did learn the full story of that case of yours, back East."

"I don't recall telling you *any* of it. Anything you heard you must have got from Christine."

"It wasn't Christine," Pearce assured him quickly. "I apologize for mentioning it anyhow."

Five shots close-spaced as machine-gun bullets cracked suddenly, creating a long, unbroken uproar in the cirque's blue shadow. When finally it ceased the rock walls seemed to hang tentatively in place like shattered safety glass.

"Utahns—goddamn Ubangis," Pearce muttered.

"It's Tonio," Richardson told him.

"You think he's got onto a bear?"

"Hell, no."

"Whoever it is, he's a good mile away," Pearce said. "Maybe two."

"Sure. But he isn't going over that cliff; he's got to come

back through the bowl. Retracing his steps to camp is going to seem like making a detour over to Salt Lake to Tonio, but he won't have a choice. All we have to do now is sit here and wait for him like a couple of ant-lions after an ant."

"Suits me," Pearce agreed. "Do you happen to have another of those elk sandwiches? We'll maybe grant old Mr. Bear a stay of execution. You know, Chuck, the older I get the more I prefer just to let live things live."

They finished the water and the sandwiches and afterward sat without speaking while Hal Pearce squinted gratefully into the sun and Richardson dug small holes in the dirt with the heel of his boot. At last he asked, "Would that be some kind of problem for you?"

"Would what be a problem?"

"That business in New York."

"Oh, no. I'm not worried about it. It happened a while back, for one thing. For another, it was an Eastern story, and folks out here don't pay much attention to Eastern horse-shit anyway." He stopped then. "I guess that wasn't the most gracious way I could have put it, was it?"

"It don't hurt my feelings any," Richardson said sourly. "I'm not an Easterner."

"But you grew up in the East. You lived half your life there."

"Sure. I can't change any of that. But it was all going sour by the time I hit thirty. For some reason it took five more years and the death of an innocent man before I did anything about it."

For a while they were silent again, staring at the mountains. Then Pearce said, "I suppose that must have been kind of humiliating, huh?"

"You bet your ass it was humiliating. That nigger took me right to the cleaners. It was humiliating and it was personal and I took it that way. I'd been walking around for months talking like a combination of Ivan Ilych and Clarence Darrow and then carried the whole load of bullshit to the

Governor. It didn't make any difference to me that he was full of shit himself, and as a matter of fact it didn't make any difference to him, either. The phone call I got afterward damn near took out my hearing."

Hal Pearce chortled. "I've taken some of those myself," he said. "The best way is to let them run out of gas and then when they stop for breath invite them to fuck themselves. Works every time—almost."

But Richardson wasn't listening to him. He sat, instead, with his knees drawn up, peeling the bark from a branch of willow. He said, "To be honest with you, I got over that part of it pretty quick. I was just another guy that told his old lady 'Okay, dear,' one too many times. Christ, it wasn't even my kind of law to begin with. The first time I was introduced to him was at a party in Greenwich Village *after* —do you believe it?—I'd got him released on bond on the rape charge. The publisher was going ahead with the publication of his novel and the folks at the Endowment for the Humanities and the Defense Committee wanted to hold a big shebang for him. He had on a wet suit—"

"A *what?*"

"Wet suit—what you wear skin-diving. It had kind of a soft, velvety look; like a seal. For all I know they're wearing them to state dinners at the White House now. Edmund Burke said you can't indict a people. He was wrong. What you can't do is *save* a people."

Hal Pearce chewed thoughtfully on a piece of willow bark Richardson had involuntarily flung at him. "Go on," he said.

"There's only one thing more. I decided, All right—fuck the humiliation. If you can forget it isn't humiliation anymore. But for years afterward I had dreams—still have them. This was a guy who had raped a woman, and at the suggestion of a bunch of politicians who had given him money and praise and contracts and parties and were embarrassed for doing it now, I let myself be henpecked into pulling his chestnuts out of the fire so he could hotwire a car and kill an innocent man with a wife and kid at home. I saw a doctor about it and he said it was perfectly normal—the Vietnam vets are still going through it. In the dreams, I had killed a man without remembering details like who or how or why—just that I was guilty and they were going to find out about it and about *me*. And yet the terrible part was that I was like a ghost that nobody could see or recognize until this Thing I had done was discovered—when what I really wanted was to be hauled outside the city limits and driven away with stones."

" 'But how in *nature* was I wrong?' " Hal Pearce murmured.

"Something like that. Anyway, I won't be one of your cause or activist lawyers, because salvation, if it exists at all, is a personal thing. A century ago people came out here because they wanted to grow up with the country. Now they just want to escape going down with it. I want to be one of the best horse-breeders in the state and one of the best elk-hunters in the county, and that's *it*. If I've learned one thing in thirty-nine years it's that life is a one-on-one proposition, and I refuse to let go of that. And if after listening to this you decide you don't care to have me within a hundred miles of you when you prosecute this case, then there'll be no hard feelings whatsoever."

For a while they sat, hugging their knees and staring at the iron-blue cirque. From behind a cloud a spear lanced forward suddenly, a silver shaft tipped with a hurtling silver point. It flew overhead and onward and they sat silent while its rumble slowly filled the bowl like water rushing into a sink, and then as slowly drained from it.

"You know," Hal Pearce said, "I don't agree with all of what you've been saying, but I do with some of it. Maybe as much as half." He reached for his gun. "Do you suppose we'd better walk on a little farther and see if we can find out what's become of our friend Tonio?"

10

THEY WERE MOVING up a talus-strewn wash banked by blue-bells, moss flox, and mountain larkspur down which a gutter of foaming water tumbled when Pearce laid a hand upon Richardson's arm. "There's our goat," he said. "Looks as if he might have started to get worried." Several hundred yards above them a figure pranced, and signaled frantically with its cap.

Richardson removed his own hat and waved it, whereupon the figure commenced a hopping downhill shuffle in the direction of a crescent-shaped stand of timber that made a barrier between them, wide at the center, tapering at the ends. As they approached it they saw an apron of new grass fronting a ridge of damp blue snow sooted with pine needles. Tonio was halfway to the trees now, still waving his hat and shouting; they could hear the voice, but not yet the words. "He seems to be pointing into the woods," Pearce said. "Maybe the guy *is* onto a bear."

"I doubt it," Richardson replied shortly. He understood he should have thought twice before allowing himself to be drawn into argument, and felt the day was now spoiled for him.

They were nearly to the timber when Pearce dropped abruptly to his knee on the soft ground. "A big one," he exclaimed in a harsh whisper, pointing to the clawed print in which water was seeping. "Fresh, too. He's in those trees all right. Must have come here to drink and Tonio surprised him."

They checked the magazines of the guns and slipped on the safeties. Tonio had halted his descent above the timber. He had apparently stopped shouting but continued to gesticulate fiercely. Hal Pearce said, "You go in from the left and I'll cover the right. Can you make Tonio understand he's supposed to come down the center?"

It was chilly in the trees, which were thicker than he had expected and very dark: at first he could discern a hem of light at the periphery, but as he moved deeper into the timber it disappeared. The snow too was deeper, heavier than he had imagined, and once he stumbled and nearly fell over a submerged log. He picked himself up, cursing silently, and, rechecking the safety, moved ahead among the spiked dead branches that scraped at his face and clothing even as he avoided snapping them. He guessed he was now very close to the heart of the little forest, and stopped once to listen for sounds of another presence. He walked further and emerged suddenly into a choked clearing in which a ruined cabin stood. Its roof had been crushed by the weight of accumulated winters, while three of its walls, though sprung outward, remained standing; the front wall lay partly buried beneath a flood of tin cans, bottles, and other trash that spilled in a cornucopia of rubbish from the black interior. Holding the rifle tightly beneath his arm, Richardson began a cautious perambulation of the building. He had passed across the flattened wall and was picking his way over the refuse, when Tonio emerged with what was for him incredible speed and stealth from the trees beyond and, with his fist, beat a reverberating tattoo against the frail wooden backside of the cabin.

Richardson was remotely aware of a fusillade of shots above the furious black wind, bad-smelling and hot, that sent him sprawling on his back amid the bottles and cans, passing over him with the force of a charging behemoth. He lay for a moment waiting for his head to clear, then rolled onto his belly to retrieve his hat and gun. He saw Tonio, his eyes and open mouth forming a triangle of vacant and utter astonishment, staring at Hal Pearce, who was kicking tentatively at a black shape stretched in the underbrush. The thick fur appeared unruffled, but beneath the carcass a deep pool of blood was forming. "Well, I'll be goddamned," Richardson said. The stench of bear was already causing his eyes to smart.

"You know," Hal Pearce told them, "I feel pretty dumb sometimes, thinking how I had to go to law school and afterward spend fifteen years in so-called practice just to learn to do in a court of law what my father taught me to do in the mountains between my twelfth and sixteenth years: to learn that justice is only one of those basic things, like killing or simple human decency."

They skinned out the bear, and Richardson cut the best meat for steaks, wrapping it into the pelt and leaving the rest beside the torn remains of the antelope carcass Tonio had placed in the ruined hunting cabin. He worked quickly, hardly speaking, and when he was finished spread a cover of branches over the corpse, whose human similitude was more than he could stand.

BOOK

2

1

ALTHOUGH HE HAD not been present to witness the scene, he could imagine it clearly enough: the salmon-colored pile of the old courthouse sharply angled by the clear May sun as three white-and-black patrol cars, traveling fast, came around the square and drew up in front of the building. With the clarity of actual memory he saw a cop emerge from each of the cars to snatch open the curbside door and hurry his handcuffed prisoner unceremoniously across the sidewalk and up the steps past the office workers who had left their desks to stare at the two men and the girl jerked upward in sullen defiance. He saw the expressions of elaborate self-awareness on the officers' faces, like those of amateur thespians taking a bow at final curtain, and the private cars cruising past, slowing to look but not stopping, while the reporter for the *Fontennelle Fortune* stood around in the basement trying to borrow a dime to make up the thirty-five cents for the soft-drink machine. It was not, he knew, that the town had failed to be shocked by the events or that already it was losing interest in them, because nobody under the age of ten had been unaware that morning of the arrival of the short motorcade from Green River. It was simply that it had not yet had the opportunity to devise a public face appropriate to the outrage, or even to consider, in the shock of its embarrassment, the possibility of doing without one. Each morning, wearing a moderately respectable corduroy jacket, clean shirt with necktie, and washed jeans, he drove past the blank, relucent, curtained windows toward the courthouse, unpleasantly conscious of an apparent inversion of light, like that in a room in which the lights have been switched around, giving familiar things the displaced, faintly sinister quality of objects in a dream. For nearly a week, hurt and increasingly angry, he had detected signals of veiled hostility from everyone he encountered before he recognized that he was himself the source of that hostility, which was only the outward expression of a disillusionment such as, he believed, ought not to be suffered twice in a single lifetime. A crime, or crimes, had been committed worthy of a society of mad dogs—in the face of which Fontennelle knew merely the shrinking embarrassment of Rotary and the Lions' Club.

Newspapers around the state, and some in adjacent ones, followed the case assiduously, while the *Fortune* had contented itself with a single story printed the day after the arraignment and concentrating on the honor cast reflexively on the city by the choice of one of its citizens as assistant special prosecutor. The morning the story appeared Richardson had phoned Bob Pulasky's office but—fortunately—found him out; he did not call again. After he had finished scanning the newspapers, Mary-Elena would bring him the transcripts, evidentiary accounts, and police photographs, to which he would devote the rest of the morning; then, if Hal Pearce were in town, they would lunch together in the small but relatively elegant dining room of the Hotel Fontennelle. In the afternoon he would meet with potential witnesses, law enforcement officers, representatives from the Department of Criminal Investigation in Cheyenne, psychiatrists, ballistics experts, and investigators from the Federal Bureau of Investigation and the Federal Narcotics Agency. Around six-thirty they would break for dinner with Mary-Elena, usually at the Last Chance Saloon, where they were often joined by

Tom Greenspan—the youngish, delicately built man with a bald head, swarthy complexion, and furtive, ratlike eyes who worked as Pearce's special investigator—and afterward return to the office to work until ten or ten-thirty. He was putting in what amounted to fourteen-hour days, seven days a week, rising at five to feed and returning home at eleven to feed again and water before collapsing into bed for six hours of numbed sleep; drinking too much coffee; his reserves of clean laundry steadily diminishing and the pile of soiled clothes as steadily accumulating in the dry sink beside the stove; his roofing business neglected at the apex of the season; his eyes bloodshot from too little sleep and the reading of too much fine print; and his brain exhausted by reams of detailed horror. Perhaps, he thought, it is because I am almost forty that I am experiencing so viscerally this descent, ledge by ledge, into the maelstrom of terror and filth. Arriving home close to midnight one evening he put his hand on the telephone, finger extended to dial Pearce's room at the Best Western motel to say this was it, he had had enough, he was through. As spring slipped into summer the light came early now, yellow and warm, the sky a shiny blue by eight and the prairie emerald-green beneath a wash of blue sagebrush. He wanted to feel eight hundred pounds of muscular horseflesh through his gloved hands on the end of the longe-line, to smell the hot odor of tar and feel its sticky warmth on his face and arms; he wanted to eat big meals with plenty of wine at evening and afterward lie with Peggy, feeling the velvet sky draw the day's heat from his skin like a poultice. And all the time he knew that it was no good—that he was in too deep now, not so much for Hal Pearce's sake but for his own, because the case had ceased to belong to Hal Pearce somehow.

It had been at first an astonishment, ultimately an affront, that the special prosecutor showed so little of passionate commitment to the case. Calmly smoking his pipe, he would write notes and summations for himself on legal pads with the Mont Blanc, give impromptu interviews to the press, and talk amiably with the hard-faced men from the DCI with no stronger emotion evident upon his face than that slightly weary, scarcely engaged expression that in unguarded moments occasionally left his mouth and eyebrows but never the eyes themselves. Much of the time he was out of town —flying to Cheyenne for a television appearance, to Omaha for an out-of-court settlement, to Chicago to deliver a bar association lecture—leaving Richardson, Greenspan, and Mary-Elena to hammer together a scaffolding for the preliminary hearing. In emotionally elevated moments Richardson was nearly as infuriated by Pearce's phlegmatic demeanor as by the town's cold impassivity—even if there were moments still when he envied them. The worst part of self-regeneration, he discovered, was the self-consciousness that came with it, as when at dinner the first night Bill Gerhardie, maintaining an equivocal expression, had contributed four bottles of red wine before tactfully withdrawing, while Bob Pulasky and Bruno Bellini, arriving later in the evening, had contented themselves with smirks and a round of complimentary liqueurs. During that meal too Mary-Elena had grown increasingly cordial to the point where, upon leaving the restaurant, she had given him a cold, henlike peck on the forehead and said, "Welcome aboard"—causing him, a man of thirty-nine years, to squirm like a high-school graduate primly congratulated by a maidenly teacher who had made no secret of her previous reservations concerning him.

Sometime between noon and one o'clock he would hear the tramp of deliberate feet outside the door of his cubicle, followed by the rap of knuckles and Hal Pearce's voice: "Ready to go for some grub now?" Together they would leave the courthouse to walk the three blocks to the Hotel Fontennelle, blinking the dust from their eyes and tucking the ends of their streaming neckties into their shirts. Or they would meet at the hotel, Richardson hurrying into the dark, cramped, dingy lobby to find the older man seated in an overstuffed armchair reeking of stale tobacco, with a fresh folded copy of the *Star-Tribune* or the *Denver Post* on his lap and a handful of cigars in the breast pocket of the pale-gray suit, writing in a pocket notebook with the Mont Blanc or, if there were people in the lobby, just watching, listening. Then they would walk from the thick brown atmosphere of the lobby into the restaurant, where silver daylight slanted down through tall windows across the white linen tablecloths set with heavy old-fashioned service and fresh-cut flowers in silver vases—a place where the town's daily business was accomplished by the bankers, lawyers, real-estate and insurance men, and small-company presidents who lunched there. Often they brought a guest—a DCI man or someone from the district attorney's office—and the talk, after beginning with business, would grow desultory, social, while Richardson watched Pearce's large hands toying with napkin and place-setting, the leonine head nodding beneficently toward the Lions, Rotarians, and Chamber of Commerce men in polyester suits and bolo ties, eating steak and fries and liver-and-onions and drinking cup after cup of hot black coffee: thinking how perfectly suited this Galahad actually was to the provincial milieu into which he had been born and in which he had chosen to live, not just in order to defend it but because he loved it. Even if only for that, he was willing to grant Hal Pearce some measure of greatness.

Entering the Fontennelle Café one gusty, blue-and-yellow noon, they seated themselves at a corner table by a window. In the square the new-leafed trees made a foam of pale green above streets blowy with dust through which the staggered rows of grimed windows flashed dully. The sunlight made a warm napkin across his knees and, resting his chin in his hand above the menu, Richardson gazed contentedly at the long whale-backed shape of Shoshone Ridge, whose riveted flanks seeped into brilliant green like an unfinished chalk sketch. Without looking at the waitress, he said, "I'll have the special today, please."

"I don't remember seeing that one before," Pearce remarked when the girl had gone.

"Who?" Richardson asked. He had been watching a semi-trailer carrying sheep pull down Main Street. Shearing season had arrived without his noticing, and he had been thinking how, if he were not exhausted after work, he would like to drink whiskey and beers at the Ewe-Turn with the Aussie and New Zealand sheepherders who, exquisite in their Carnaby Street clothes, commandeered the bars for two weeks every spring.

"They've hired a new girl," Pearce explained," but you were too busy daydreaming to notice. Knowing you, you won't miss her a second time."

Richardson tasted his coffee. "They're making new ones every day."

"That's right," Pearce agreed. "They probably made this particular one in time for your twenty-first birthday. That's why I thought—"

"Lay off my personal life, Hal. Whatever you've been generous enough to leave me of it, that is."

Hal Pearce spread the silverware on the tablecloth and smiled. "I suppose that *was* adding insult to injury. Nevertheless, I'm not going to apologize. As Carlyle said, work is the only solution. 'Suffer, suffer into truth.' God knows you're old enough."

Soft clouds raced on flat silver bottoms across an enamel sky. "Oh, cut it out," Richardson told him. "You're starting to sound like my wife, or ex-wife, or not-wife, or whatever the hell she is—or thinks she is."

"Actually," Pearce corrected him gently, "that was Aeschylus."

The waitress returned carrying a loaded tray and served them while Richardson continued to stare glumly at the square. When he took up his fork he caught the other watching him with an amused, faintly ironic smile. Wooden-faced, he began to eat. The girl was a tall redhead with white skin, long, shapely limbs, and a front as buoyant and shapely as a swan's.

They applied themselves in silence to the stew, thick slabs of fresh-baked bread and butter, and scalding coffee, and sat back to allow the redhead to remove the plates. When Pearce proffered a cigar Richardson accepted it, and they smoked quietly while the girl brought the check and refilled their cups. The café was nearly empty. Across the mountain-face a herd of antelope browsed, glimmering and eliding like motes of light among the cloud shadows. A white-and-black cruiser turned the corner sharply and went on up the street, the thick barrel of its racked shotgun standing at brutal attention beside the driver. "Well," Hal Pearce demanded, "what is it we've decided to go for, Chuck? Or *have* we decided?"

"My vote is we go all the way with this one, Hal." The cruiser stopped in front of the city hall and the patrolman, a heavyset man in khaki, climbed out and entered the building, his holster slapping against his wide hips. Several times during the past week Pearce had broached the question, without displaying much eagerness to resolve it.

"You know," Pearce said, "I did everything but take an oath when I passed the bar exam that I would never willingly seek a man's life, let alone the lives of two men and a woman—a girl of twenty-one. And at fifty-eight years of age, after thirty-three years at law, I can still assure myself that I have been faithful to that determination. I'm going to have one hell of a time with this, Chuck. Particularly with Wainwright expecting—hoping—that we'll demand the death penalty so he can make whoopy-do against it. That's the only reason, after all, he agreed to touch the case. He has his heart set on being the Clarence Darrow of Wyoming, you know."

He sat with one hand thrust into the pocket of his trousers, rapping a tattoo on the table with the other; feeling an icy wind emanating from huge, steadily beating wings held fast in some fold of the desert as the wide chrome mouth of the van rolled silently to a stop beside the two women. He saw it going very fast across the night and a Laocoön figure emerge from it, struggling against a black sky stained by the ruddy glow of the trona mines and pulsing to the blast from the great dark wings.

"Fuck all of them," he said at last. "They deserve to die for what they did. I'd like to drop the pills myself: One—two—three."

"It must be comforting to have such an uncomplicated view of life," Pearce remarked dryly. "I've never been able to achieve it, myself."

"Life *isn't* complicated, it's perfectly simple, like every other harsh and hopeless thing. 'Justice flows from the barrel of a gun,' as Chairman Mao liked to say. And I don't see why the girl makes any difference. One life isn't more valuable or pathetic than another, just because it happens to be female. Goddammit, Hal—they've Californicated all the rest of the country. There has to be some point or some place to say, 'This far and no farther,' and make it stick."

Hal Pearce placed his carefully refolded napkin on the table, shoved back his chair, and sighed. "All of which, however," he said, "has no bearing on the fundamental question of the morality of capital punishment. It's two o'clock already. Shall we be getting back to work now?"

The little round clouds had spread and flattened and the wind had turned cold, bearing scattered flakes of snow like winter seeds. Richardson strode rapidly up the hill holding his hands in his pockets and keeping a little ahead of the older man. Above the trees he could see the blind, brazen Whore maintaining her slow, indefatigable tramp in place.

It's the girl he thought suddenly—the girl who was responsible for his perturbation, verging now on panic. The police glossies showed a ghost, a ghoul—a mere negative of a human being with gaunt cheeks, vacant eyes, and hair as stiff and straight as cave ice. More than anything he had seen or read—more than Willie Munger himself—she appalled him, he discovered. He feared that, confronting her in court, he would be undone by the horror: he feared that he would disgrace himself. Words would fail him. He might even flee.

2

W HEN SHE WAS seven her parents had taken her to the Salt Lake City Zoo, where she had felt so sorry for the animals as they stalked back and forth in their cages or sat quite still in corners that she had burst into tears and had to be fed ice cream before she would stop. Now she herself was in a cage, and she couldn't be bothered even to look out the window.

It was like convalescing from a nearly mortal illness you could remember only disconnectedly, in fits and spasms. The people who cared for and visited her were like doctors and nurses in a hospital, people who were there solely for her well-being. Three times a day they brought her food—it was quite good food—and every other day clean clothes, neatly ironed and fresh-smelling, like bread from the oven. Each morning they gave her a towel and washcloth, and she would wash herself thoroughly at the little basin in the corner. Her body was like a bulb that had been set aside for a long time in a dark place and which, returned at last to the light, had already begun to plumpen. Twice a week they allowed her to shower with the other women, of whom there were two; both heavy-set, dark-complected women in their thirties who looked unkempt even without their clothes and stared at Jenny with unwavering insolence while they bathed. Each day the attorney appointed to her by the court arrived to sit on the neatly made-up bed and ask questions. He was a limp, owl-faced young man with glasses and no necktie who wore brown suits and cowboy boots, appeared nervous, unhappy, and chain-smoked cigarettes. He carried a plastic portfolio under his arm and wrote down everything she told him in longhand on pads of yellow paper. Jenny explained to him that she did not want to see Munger and Weber ever again and asked him please to call her folks in Mosiah, Utah, and tell them not to come visit her.

Because she did not understand whatever it was that was happening inside her she paid attention to her body instead. As often as they allowed her to she washed her hair and rubbed herself with the cold creams the owl-faced attorney brought her, extending her long white legs and arms and caressing her skin with her fingertips. After several weeks of the good meals she learned were catered by a local motel she worried that she was growing fat and began to exercise herself, at first for an hour a day, then, because there was little else to do, two, and finally three. They would not permit her to lie around undressed, but at night, in the quiet dark, she would unbutton the gray pajamas and explore her body with her hands. It had a clean, delicate, sweet odor, as if anointed, and appeared to be concealing some intimate secret. She would have slept a great deal during the day if they had let her.

After several weeks the owl-faced young man's questions became irksome to her. In the hospital, too, the white-coated doctors had asked her this and that, but their queries had been almost solicitous and of a strictly personal nature: even the tests they had given her had been no more than a minor nuisance. It was different with her attorney, who sat for what seemed hours writing out her reluctant, often disjointed answers to disagreeable questions that forced her into cruel, relentless confrontation with events that, having survived them, she, with the callous forgetfulness of the very young, had already forgotten. He asked her about her relations, first with Seth Weber and afterward with Willie Munger; whether she had had a previous familiarity with drugs and if Munger had used them to—as he put it—"take advantage of" her. He asked her if she had herself accepted money for cocaine, marijuana, and heroin, and inquired into the details of Munger's dealing. He even asked—with a confused, embarrassed indirection that amused her—if she had been a virgin when she met Weber, and clumsily demanded an intimate account of her sexual encounters with both men. Lastly, he made her relate the events of the night itself, beginning with Munger's plan to disable the Collins women's car and ending with her arrest the following morning. He had, it seemed to her, a more thorough recollection of the facts than she herself did, prompting her every other sentence and propping up her reluctant account with constructions she could only regard as lies. Her statements became increasingly perfunctory after that, until at last the attorney, throwing up his hands above the yellow pad, exclaimed irritably, "Look here, Ms. Petersen, do you want my help or not? God knows you need it." She had explained that her only worry was meeting Munger and Weber in court, but he said Stop worrying about Munger and Weber and worry about Mr. Pearce instead. After he had mentioned Pearce repeated times she found herself developing a curiosity about the prosecutor, and wished to be allowed to meet him. From the owl-faced attorney's description of him she imagined somebody out of an old movie.

This unremitting concentration upon Munger and Weber and what she thought of simply as The Night should have had the effect of projecting them upon her sleep, but it did not happen. Instead, she would lie peacefully on her back, drifting across shifting planes of consciousness, between the immediate present and the distant past, as if she were stitching a mental quilt and her mind, having rejected a prematurely sewn-in square, had cut it away and was now restitching the two large pieces directly together. One moment she would be staring up through the dark at the faint glow from the barred window, feeling rather than hearing the nocturnal hum of the sealed building, as if it were a spaceship or submarine, while the next instant she would be watching herself in tableau, a noontime study in gold and bronze: her own tawny female form silhouetted against the gelding's sorrel flank at the center of an oval of yellow dust enclosed by a fence of fresh-peeled posts. Beyond the corral she could see the hayricks, green-gold and fragrant, the bales fitted carefully to each other like the stones of a well-made house, under a sky that was a fierce yellow-white except where it made a seal of blue against the red canyon wall. From the creek she would hear a birdcall—a stream of liquid sound on a single breathtaking note—and for another moment or two she would hold it all motionless, poised, perfect about her; before she —the girl in the picture—would deliberately spoil it. Holding the bridle on her shoulder and swinging the nosebag in her hand, she would run abruptly from the corral toward a grove of cottonwoods, which began, abruptly, to seethe, as if in response to this fresh burst of her wild, uncontainable restlessness.

With increasing urgency, the owl-faced attorney mentioned a thing he called the Preliminary Hearing in a voice that suggested the Day of Judgment. He would repeat his questions over and over, revising her answers painstakingly and making her restate them exactly. After several days of cross-examination she was so nervous that her responses could be unscrambled only after three or four attempts, and her appetite fell off. Then one night she dreamt, for the first time, that she was again in the black van being driven at terrific speed away from the Preliminary Hearing. Again she felt Munger's body heavy upon hers, his rough beard and fetid breath against her face, and woke with a little shriek to fumble her way in the dark to the washbasin, where she rubbed herself down with soap and water. The next morning she was at first vague and finally snappish with the attorney when he attempted to rehearse her: he became angry, accused her of having what he called "no understanding of our adversary system of justice," and went away early. Jenny was relieved to see him go and spent the afternoon drawing with colored pencils on the pad of artist's paper they had given her in the hospital and which they continued to allow her to use in prison.

He returned the next day, his round face pale and moist-looking, his eyes red and irritable behind the owlish glasses that magnified them to a comical degree, making her want to burst out laughing when she looked at him, and gave her another lecture. Either, he said, she would cooperate with his efforts to save her from a lifetime in prison, or he would ask Judge Thurlow of the district court to find another defender for her. He was emphatic about it, tapping the end of a ballpoint pen on the legal pad while she sat with her hands in her lap, clenching and unclenching her fists and observing his incipient paunch, receding hairline, and the spot of egg yolk on the front of his Western-style dress shirt. After he was through, she said in an offhand voice, "I want to talk to Mr. Pearce."

The ballpoint pen skipped nimbly out of his stained fingers and rolled beneath the bed. "You want *what?*" the owl-faced attorney said.

"I want to talk to Mr. Pearce. They have to let me do that if I want to, don't they?" She thought his eyes were more like a fish's than an owl's now behind the ridiculous lenses.

"You have the right if you want to," he said, "but I can't advise it. As your attorney I am completely opposed—"

"Will you call him for me today?" she asked.

"Today?" he repeated in a bewildered voice. "Why, I don't even know if he—I would have to have time to prepare—"

"No," she told him simply. "I want to talk to him alone."

She observed that the pad had started to quiver on his knee and that the pale hand, streaked thinly with black hairs, trembled as it groped along the floor for the pen. He stood abruptly, cramming papers into his plastic portfolio, which was splitting at the ends. "You'll be alone all right," he said over his shoulder. "You'll be more alone than you ever dreamed it was possible to be if you don't smarten up in a big hurry."

The next morning he did not appear, and for the space of a day and a half she fretted. Perhaps he would refuse to call Mr. Pearce, or perhaps Mr. Pearce did not want to talk with her. She imagined that he must be a very busy man. She attempted to draw but was unable to concentrate; when dinner came she picked at the fried chicken and ate only the too-sweet cake, lying afterward on top of the blanket, hearing the stir of people in the corridor, knowing that visiting hours had started. You were allowed to see your lawyer in the cell but family and friends had to use the visiting room. Suddenly she heard a sound on the other side of the door and swung her legs off the bed, expecting the owlish attorney. Instead the matron had brought a man she had never seen—a man older than she, yet not old, certainly much younger than she had imagined Mr. Pearce to be. He had a tanned, battered, handsome face with a brutally muscled jaw and a wide mouth whose full, sensuous lower lip contrasted sharply with the thin, ascetic upper one; eyes the color of two gas jets slightly squint beneath a dark jutting brow; and black hair that glinted blue, like gunmetal, falling in sleek wings from an off-center part. It was a face she might have been frightened by were it not for the inverted, self-directed quality of the anger she read so plainly there.

Sitting very still on the bed, Jenny stared at this man, clasping her legs in her long arms and resting her chin on her knee, waiting for the thing she already knew was going to happen. It had been a long time since anything had been required of her, but now, without warning, she found herself overwhelmed by a presentiment that suddenly something was.

3

RICHARDSON SAID, "I'M Chuck Richardson, from the special prosecutor's office. I understand you want to speak with Mr. Pearce. He's out of town for the week, but you can talk to me if you want."

Instead of the long-nailed, stiff-haired harpie, anonymous in black Levi's and shapeless black sweatshirt, of the police photographs, he saw a girl in crisp gray pajamas looking as healthy and wholesome as a schoolgirl home after two weeks at a Swiss spa. He guessed that, standing, she would be tall and that the brown hair, pinned now against her ears in lapped, lustrous wings and fastened at the nape by a simple tortoise-shell clasp, would fall nearly to her waist. Her features were so pale and even that, despite the soft flush of cheek and the light freckles over the bridge of the nose, she seemed almost plain for such a pretty girl. Then he saw that it was not a question of pretty or plain, just a strong, well-formed healthiness only slightly rubbed around the eyes, which were a cool gray and had a demure, almost grave expression. With a loathing amounting to fear he noted her long-waisted tomboy's figure, which appeared to have only recently acquired its female contours, and the dimpled girlish elbows below the rolled pajama sleeves. Her flesh was plump and rosy, like that of a freshly fed ghoul he thought. He noticed too the long hands, well-proportioned to the arms, and their clean, manicured nails, which he tried vainly to imagine pressed against a trigger-guard or gripping the handle of a shovel, tossing down the rattling gravel. At his back the cell door clicked softly shut and he whirled in involuntary panic, as if they had locked him into a lioness's den. Somewhere in the pockets of the shabby corduroy coat there were matches and the little black cigars; he found them at last, fallen behind the lining and through the torn pocket, and fingered one out. "Mind if I smoke?" he asked; and she answered him: "Please go ahead." It was a country voice, having about it the quality of well-water, supple and soft as the muscles of her white throat.

They had forgot to leave him a chair and he would not sit beside her on the bed. He walked with what he hoped was a casual stride to the window and stood smoking, gazing out at the muddy undercarriages of parked vehicles; thinking how living halfway below ground level like this would be like having one foot in the grave. After a while he said, inanely, "So, you're Jenny Petersen?"

Keeping her eyes demurely averted and holding her hands loosely clasped in her lap, she sat without answering him.

"From Mosiah, Utah—is that right, Jenny?"

Her eyes lifted toward him then, brushing his face like a bird's wing. "I tried to make them quit," she said, "but they wouldn't. I told him, over and over, but he never believed me."

Drawing on the cigar, Richardson contemplated the asphalt cracks in which new grass was springing, unsure whether he was repelled or impressed by her control. "All right," he said after a moment. "But why don't we take it from the beginning?"—thinking: If she's just going to deny everything, why am I wasting my time?

Like an obedient, highly aware child, she began right away talking, drawing her knees up to her chin and clasping her legs in her arms. Once she had started he found he could not look at her, the facts seeming to acquire from the spoken narration an unbearable reality mere news accounts, transcripts, even the photographs, had not been able to convey. He stood smoking by the window, watching the slow twilight deepen almost imperceptibly—it was the start of the second week in June now—and hearing the soft, terrifying voice describe how Willie Munger and Seth Weber had discussed "getting" Jamie Collins, who had been Munger's Fontennelle drop until Munger decided that he was holding out on them, undercutting their stuff by peddling another dealer's at lower prices from which he extracted a higher commission. Finally, they agreed to send him a warning through his sister, who lived with the mother on what remained of the Collins ranch after the rest had been sold to the subdividers and who had a job as a practical nurse at the county hospital in Fontennelle. The plan, Jenny said, was invented by Munger, who gave Weber the job of disabling Mary Collins's truck before she began the hundred-mile trip to Rock Springs for her weekly training at the larger hospital. Munger's idea was that Weber "do something" to the truck so that it would run ten or twenty miles before breaking down in the desert. Mary Collins worked a night shift, eleven until seven, which gave them their opportunity. They would follow the truck until it quit, and offer Mary a ride. After giving her what Munger promised would be "a good scare," they would leave her along the highway with "a message for Jamie."

At first, she said, everything had worked fine. Shortly before seven on the evening of April fourteenth, a Saturday, Weber slipped into the Collins garage and did something—she didn't understand what—to Mary's vehicle, doubling back afterward to where she and Munger sat waiting in the van he had parked on a street corner so that they would have a clear view of Mary Collins coming along the one-way street. A little after nine the truck—a green Ford with a white cap over the bed—braked for the Stop sign and made a left turn, heading up the access road toward the highway south. Weber thought he had made out a passenger riding in the front seat, but Munger said No, he'd had a good look into the cab and there wasn't anyone in there but Mary Collins.

They tailed the truck at a discreet distance for eighteen-and-a-quarter miles by the odometer before the brake lights flashed ahead of them and Munger slowed from fifty-five to thirty miles an hour. When they got to the Ford it was sitting on the shoulder of the road with the hood up and a hand-kerchief tied to the radio antenna, limp in the windless dark. The door on the driver's side was open and a woman sat behind the wheel with her knees out and her feet on the running board. Beside her was another woman who looked just like her, only older.

Jenny said Weber had said something in a sharp whisper then, but Munger had told him to shut up. He told her to slide open the panel door and ask the women did they need help and would they like a ride someplace. She thought the Collinses seemed very nervous at first, but when they saw her in the door they looked relieved and climbed out of the truck. Munger whispered to Weber, who went and looked under the hood of the pickup, shook his head, and told Mary Collins they'd have to get a wrecker from town. She knew from the sound the panel door made when he shut it that it was locked this time.

For a while the women didn't seem to notice that they hadn't turned in the direction of town, or maybe they were just hoping too hard. Munger explained to them how they belonged to a secret society called the Immoral Minority that had more than a thousand members. She thought he must have made up the Immoral Minority on the spur of the moment; he was always making up things like that, she said. Mary Collins said that was very interesting and she was on her way to work in Rock Springs, where her mother was going to spend a week with relatives. Munger asked them if they would like to be members of the Immoral Minority too, and they said No, they didn't think so—they happened to be Catholic. Munger said in that case he was sorry but they would have to Do Something about them, because the Immoral Minority was a secret society and he couldn't risk anyone telling people about it. At first she said the women only laughed in a nervous kind of way but finally they started to scream and throw themselves against the sides of the van. Munger pulled over then and climbed in back with her and Weber, and the men tied them with nylon cord that wouldn't stay tight. The Collinses flopped around like fish on a beach until Munger and Weber wrestled them out of the van into a gulley, where Munger handed her his .22-caliber revolver and told her to shoot them both in the head. She was screaming, she said, hanging onto his arm and telling him to stop and make Weber stop, and the women were screaming back, shouting Please, please, tell him no, don't let them hurt us. She told how she had fired the six rounds into the air and thrown the gun as far as she could into the prairie, but after he and Weber got the women tied properly Munger searched around with a flashlight until he found and reloaded it, while Weber took a roll of toilet paper from the van and went behind a juniper tree.

When they were gone she had knelt beside the women, trying to get the cord loose and calm them, telling them it was all right, that the men were only trying to scare them for a joke. She still almost believed it herself, she said, until she discovered Munger watching them from a distance, smacking the butt of the pistol into his palm and grinning. When the old lady discovered that her hands were free she quit thrashing about in the dirt and rose on her knees with her arms extended, as if she were trying to embrace her. With one hand she grasped a charm bracelet, holding it forward as if urging her to accept it; until, at the moment at which, finally understanding, she reached for it, Munger jumped as if he had seen a ghost and shot Mrs. Collins twice through the chest. Then, seizing her under the armpits and wresting her away from the dead woman, he had shouted, "Goddammit, Weber! Take care of the other!"; and it had been from a prone position that she had watched him hand the gun to Weber, who shot Mary Collins three times in the head. Finally, they had dug two graves in the clay and gravel, and Munger made her lie in one of them for a while as punishment for trying to betray the Immoral Minority. He even had Weber throw a couple of shovelfuls of gravel over her before telling her to get her ass up out of there.

They went back to the van, where the men finished a six-pack of beer and smoked a couple of joints each before burying the bodies. She didn't remember the trip to Rock Springs—she thought she must have been hysterical most of the time—but did recall that Weber was scared and wanted to drive straight home. Munger told him, What the fuck (she faltered then, looking up at him like a school child caught writing a bad word on a lavatory wall), they hadn't left any witnesses, had they? They spent the night in a Rock Springs trailer court with one of his contacts, and were arrested just after noon at a Burger King where they had stopped for a late breakfast. She would never forget, she said, the look on Munger's face when one of the deputies told them how Mary Collins, her soft palate blown out, a fragment of slug in her neck, and a bullet graze behind her left ear, had dug herself out of her shallow grave and crawled nearly a mile to the trail leading back to the highway, where she had been discovered at dawn by a sheepherder to whom she managed to give a description of the murderers less than an hour before she died.

4

HE HAD TURNED involuntarily toward her from the window
and now, as she finished speaking, he stood facing her, watching her lips fall silent like those of a woman suddenly de-
ceased. Gently, he asked: "Jenny, when Willie Munger and
Seth Weber told you to invite those women into the van,
you knew what you were doing—being asked to do. Didn't
you?"

She gave him a quick, anguished look from the corners of
her eyes but said nothing.

"When Munger jumped in back of that truck and told
Weber to help him tie them up, did you try in any way to
prevent them from doing so?"

"I was crying," she said, "shouting at them to stop. I tried
to take the cord away from them but I couldn't. They aren't
big guys but they're both real strong."

"But you and the Collins women made three. Couldn't
three women, two of them young and strong and the third
only fifty-nine, have fought off two men—both of them
under the influence of drugs and alchohol—long enough at
least to—"

"Munger had the gun," she reminded him, "and Weber
carried a knife."

"And when Munger handed you the revolver it didn't
occur to you to use it to protect two innocent people in some

way other than just firing into the air, as if you were dealing not with two deadly human beings but a herd of wild horses? Can you honestly tell me, Jenny, that such a thing never occurred to you as you stood there with a gun in your hand watching those women brutalized?"

She leaned forward, clasping her hands between her knees, and began to sway slowly from side to side on the edge of the bed.

"I was *afraid*," she said. "I was afraid I might have to shoot them—Munger and Weber—and I didn't know if I could do that. But the big thing was—I didn't really believe *they* could either." She closed her eyes as her voice dropped almost to a whisper. "Even after they did *It* I don't think I actually believed it. It wasn't until Willie made me lie in that hole that I . . . *knew*."

For the first time her composure broke; her shoulders shook and the nails of one hand made long purple furrows in the palm of the other. Fascinated, he stared at her.

"You *knew?*"

She looked squarely at him, then almost boldly.

"He pushed me," she said, "and I grabbed him by the hair and started kicking him. His hair was thick and matted and I kept pulling it with my fists and suddenly it was *all for real*. It was the realest thing I ever felt in my whole life."

He stood, not feeling his tired legs, profoundly moved in spite of himself. *No* he thought *you must never be weak—a fool!—that way again. Never. Never.* "What was it you wanted to talk to me about?" he said.

She looked at him, in astonishment this time. "I told you."

"No," he replied, "you didn't tell me. That wasn't it, Jenny. I haven't heard a thing from you this evening I didn't know already, from whatever source. Even the newspapers. Maybe," he said, lifting his eyebrows at her in an ironic gesture he was instantly ashamed of, "because there *isn't* anything else?"

"I told you everything," she said simply.

Richardson pinched out the end of his cigar and, after a moment's hesitation, pocketed it. He took his hat from the floor where he had placed it.

"I'm sorry," he said. "Tell your attorney we might be willing to plea-bargain for information, but not for sympathy. When he's ready to talk business, have him give us a call."

He didn't have to look back at the healthy young woman in washed gray pajamas sitting on a bunk bed with her knees clasped in her arms, staring at the floor.

5

WHEN HE EMERGED from the jailhouse flocks of starlings were brushing the final light from the sky with a dry winnowing sound, and he stood for a while on the sidewalk, smelling the cold, pine-scented air and hearing the faint blare of music from the propped-open doors of the bars around the square. "My God," Richardson said aloud. He could not ever remember needing a drink so badly in his life.

Richardson drank downtown when it was his deliberate intention to get drunk and when he did not want to have to worry about whom he inflicted it on. Fontennelle, a city of only five thousand inhabitants, contained a dozen saloons—more than enough, he had discovered, to suit every alchoholic mood. For conviviality, there was the Bare Garden, offering go-go girls nightly and frequented chiefly by oil-riggers, construction workers, whores, and dope pushers. For bellicosity, there was the Number One Pit, where men from the coal mine upbraided the company and the government, chased their raw whiskey with beer, and occasionally picked a well-chosen—often brutal and uncontrollable—fight. For melancholy or moroseness, there was the Ewe-Turn, patronized mostly by outlanders—ranchers, sheepherders, forest rangers, and surveyors—who, preferring a woman, had nevertheless grown too shy and too introverted to approach one until the whiskey that conveyed the glory also retracted the power. Tonight Richardson selected the Ewe, where he found a place among five or six leather-faced men sitting with their hats pulled over their eyes and their elbows crooked around their drinks, staring silently at the backbar while the jaded barmaid leaned against the register trimming her fingernails. After a drink or two he would understand what the matter was; after three or four it would be less hopeless than he had feared; after five or six he would either know what he was going to do about it, or else he just wouldn't give a damn.

He sat drinking in severe abstraction, feeling the words she had spoken working their way into his flesh like thorns: *The realest thing I ever felt in my whole life.* He imagined the long white hands entangled in the filthy matted pelt, shaved since by the jailhouse barber to a stubbled shadow over a scalp well-scrubbed with PhisoHex. He saw her in the clean gray pajamas, holding her knees under her chin—girlish and terrible, radiant with that unnerving calm that seemed imbued with a gently blinding significance—and again he exhorted himself *No. Not ever again. You're a man now—no longer a callow, pussy-whipped kid with fancy clothes and a fancy degree.* He forced himself to imagine the Collinses, hurling themselves like panicked birds in a cage against the panels of the van; kneeling in the damp clay with their hands tied at the small of their backs as they stared into the needle's eye: the aperture of Munger's small-calibered instrument, which in another millisecond would widen for them to contain all of space and time. He reassured himself *Of course she's guilty. Evil points only to evil, by which evil is proved.* Recalling the zombie of the police glossies, the transformation seemed to him in retrospect more horrible still: the rosy, blood-sated flesh, gorged and tranquil in reptilian suspension. Like a film director viewing the daily rushes, he saw the scenes she had described with such chilling calm, played over again and again—the tumult in the van, the struggle in the sagebrush and clay, followed by pistol shots and the sound of bodies dropping like Muslims on their faces in the dirt.

Suddenly his mind was screaming, Stop! Cut! Hold! Hold it right there! Back it up! Go back!, and it was as if someone were trying to oblige but fumblingly, infuriatingly, the frames jostling one another out of place and focus while he fought desperately to recall which of them contained the discrepancy, the jarring detail, the startling but unobvious inclusion or elimination, the what's-wrong-with-this-picture surprise. And then he had it—the episode of the bracelet. The girl had told how Mrs. Collins, on her knees, had tried to give her a charm bracelet; she had not made it clear why. But of one thing he was certain: she had not mentioned it before. It was not included in any of the transcripts.

He drank one more martini and left abruptly, leaving a ten-dollar bill for the barmaid. He found the truck key without having to grope, but had difficulty fitting it to the lock. With forced lucidity he reminded himself to have it recut at the hardware store in the morning and started the engine, letting it idle as he deciphered the luminous dial of his wristwatch. Cautiously he pulled away from the curb, circled the square, and drove slowly out of town under the glare of the arc lights. Ahead he made out the electric sign of the Last Chance Saloon where it occurred to him to stop for a nightcap; an idea he was contemplating attentively when he became aware of other lights, flashing blue-and-red in the rearview mirror. Obediently he drew onto the shoulder of the highway and stopped, awaiting them with the sober confidence of a Mormon bishop.

At sight of the capped blonde head he was stunned to momentary paralysis. Recovering his aplomb, he rolled the window down and passed his operator's license to her. "Would you get out of your vehicle please, sir," she said, firmly ignoring the offering.

He put one leg out and stood tentatively, keeping a hand on the doorframe as he tried to grin at her.

"Have you been drinking, sir?"

"Have I been drinking?" He paused respectfully, as if to

give the question the attention it deserved. "Why no," he said finally. "Unless you'd call a glass of wine at dinner—" He paused again, screwing up his eyes comically at her as if to suggest that naturally she must recognize that a glass of wine could hardly be classified as—

"Recite the alphabet from A to Z," the girl ordered. "Not slowly—say it as quick as you can."

He complied, the letters rolling off his tongue with little or no differentiation that he could tell between them. He gave her a broad, congratulatory smile, generously inclusive of both of them.

"Touch your left forefinger to your nose, holding the right hand out, and repeat in reverse. Walk seven steps toe-to-heel and back. Stand straight and put your head back until I tell you to relax."

Richardson executed these manuevers with dignity and exactitude and was turning to climb back in the truck when something cold and thin closed about his wrists with a nasty click. "Get in the car," the girl said. Her partner, whom he had not noticed before, stood beside the cruiser, holding the door for him with the expression of a doorman in a chic apartment building observing the expulsion of a noisy drunk.

He stumbled on the frame and discovered that his hands were extraneous now to his equilibrium. Other hands shoved at his back and then he was inside, staring at the racked shotgun standing with the thick brutality of a bazooka beyond the wire partition. The cruiser made a swift U-turn in the road and headed into town on wide silent tires. He must have dozed for a couple of minutes then, because the next thing he knew they were stopped outside the jail.

They pulled him from the car, the male cop handling him this time, as if he were a trained bear, while the girl went ahead of them through the door, her bottom firm and insolent in the uniform trousers. They had him sit in a chair and told him to breathe into the machine while the girl wrote rapidly in a small black book.

"Why howdy there, Mr. Richardson," a voice said. Looking up, he saw the fat deputy standing in the door with a puzzled expression on his face. "What in hell's going on here?" he asked the city cops.

"This man is point-oh-three over the limit," the girl said severely. "We picked him up driving north on 385 with his headlights off."

"Just take it easy, folks," the fat deputy said.

Richardson watched them whispering together. Then the male cop came back and roughly unsnapped the handcuffs. "Okay, that's it," he barked. "Deputy Smith here's going to drive you home."

Richardson rubbed vigorously at his chafed wrists. "I'm drunker'n a waltzing piss-ant," he told the city cop. "You read what the machine said. Go ahead and lock me up."

"It's okay, Mr. Richardson," the fat deputy explained. "You'll be all right in the morning." He grasped him by the elbow then, and began to lead him from the room.

"Thanks for the date," Richardson told the girl as the deputy led him past her. "We'll have to try it again some time when I'm feeling in better shape."

He stood obediently by the sheriff's car, waiting for Smith to open the rear door, but the deputy invited him to sit with him up front instead. On the way out of town they stopped at an all-night café, where Deputy Smith bought two cups of strong black coffee. In the moonlight the prairie lay like a black silk dress dropped in folds. Deputy Smith drove at a steady seventy miles an hour, flicking his spotlight over the deer that browsed above the cutbanks along the right-of-way. "Game and Fish have duck fits when they catch us doing that shit," he remarked in a satisfied voice.

Through the window he could see the blue glare of the television Peggy had brought out with her from town. Deputy Smith swung the car around magnificently in the drive and stopped it in front of the gate. "Need a hand inside?" he offered, with wide generosity.

Richardson shook his head and shut the door without saying good night. He watched the lights go up the dirt road to the highway, where they turned east and started moving very fast toward town: from time to time a finger of white stroked out as Deputy Smith spotlighted a deer. He went on through the gate and up the walk to the porch, where he halted, looking for his keys; a town girl, Peggy kept the doors locked after dark. His first thought was that he had left them in the truck, before it occurred to him that the cops would have retained them after having the vehicle impounded. He rapped loudly at the door, which opened after a delay to reveal Peggy, barefoot in a yellow nightgown.

"For God's sake," she said. "Hal Pearce has been calling all night, he says, from Denver. I just got off work. He wants to hear about your conversation with that girl." She hadn't seen the deputy's car, and in the half-dark, he supposed, he didn't look too awful. "He left a number and said if you got home before eleven-fifteen to call him back."

"What time is it now?"

"Eleven-thirty." Her voice sounded suddenly suspicious as she leaned to favor him with a sharper scrutiny. "Are you okay? Where have you been all evening? I fed before I went to work."

He pushed past her through the door without replying and went on to the bathroom, where he began slowly to undress, bracing himself with one hand against the wall. He opened the faucet and ran hot water into the tub, waiting naked on the folded-down toilet while the room filled quickly with steam until the electric bulb in the ceiling burned like a tiny sun through the fog. He began to breathe with an exaggeratedly deep and rhythmic action, feeling the moisture scald his lungs as it lay in hot concentrated droplets on his flesh, leaching his body of the poison. He heard the doorknob being wrenched and Peggy shouting through the mists, "Do you want me to reheat your supper now, or what?"

"That would be great, Peg. Thanks."

He shut off the faucet and walked, dripping, to the bedroom to dress in faded army fatigues. Sockless, he padded on to the kitchen, where Peggy had set a place at the table, and sat with his chin in his hands while she filled his plate for him. She had moved out from town the week before to help, she said, with the livestock and prepare, before going to work herself, a hot meal for him on his return from the courthouse; for the past seven days the dogged conscientiousness of women in trivial or mundane matters, which had always puzzled and frequently irritated him, had seemed—in service to profound female desire—nothing less than terrifying, however welcome the convenience.

When the phone rang she set aside the half-filled plate to answer it. He watched her face darken as she listened, the corners of her mouth pulling tight.

"It's for you," she said, averting her eyes as she passed him the receiver.

"Hi, tiger!" The ebullient voice soared above the distant clash of gold, the smokey triumphant snort. "I've been reading all about you in the papers!"

He knew then—without astonishment or shock, just a dull and hopeless despair at his own fatal gullibility, which he had been assuring himself for four years had been bled finally from his system, while all the time it had been circulating in his blood, dormant but potent, like malaria. Drawing a long breath, he said, "The one thing I can't figure is why, if you thought I was too dumb as a man to see what was happening, it didn't occur to you I'd be too dumb as a lawyer to be of use to Hal Pearce, or to you, or, for that matter, to myself. I thought four years ago I'd proved *that* to you, anyway, but obviously I was wrong. Or perhaps we both needed another lesson. So thank you, Christine. I'll try not to forget this one for another eight. Good night."

He ate supper alone and afterward rinsed the dishes and dried them before joining Peggy in bed. She was lying on her side, stiff as a dried codfish and as silent, though he knew by her breathing she was awake. He was thirty-nine years old and there were plenty of truths he did not understand about women—except for such fundamental ones as the importance of never turning your back on them; those which, all his life, it had been his misfortune to have mislaid just when he had need of them most.

6

"Even the assholes on the Ethical Standards Committee can't think of everything," Richardson told him. "Sometimes an attorney has to rely on just his own sense of common decency."

They sat facing one another across the big desk, its scarred top a welter this morning of newspapers, unopened mail, and the stubs of airline tickets in their paper wallets. On the floor three battered leather attaché cases rested with their tops propped open against the wall, spilling more papers across the Indian rug. Hal Pearce leaned back in the swivel chair with his coat off, his boots on the desk, and his pipe in his mouth, looking florid but tired despite his relaxed demeanor; Richardson kept both feet planted on the floor while he gripped the arms of the chair, his upper body bent tensely, as if prepared to spring forward at any moment.

"Now, now," Pearce told him, holding up a hand. "Just hold your horses there, Chuck. What's this all about? You didn't spend the night on the town, did you? You look god-awful."

"My wife," Richardson said. "This was all Christine's idea, wasn't it? You hired me as a favor to her."

"Now hold your horses," Pearce repeated mildly. Deliberately, he knocked the dottle from the pipe and stuffed fresh tobacco into the bowl with a large finger. "I can't afford favors like that to anyone, Chuck. I invited you to join me in this business because despite your mouth and your martinis and your girls, you're a smart guy and a hell of a good lawyer—when you want to be."

"Thank you. I appreciate the flattery. But I imagine the description applies to a number of other people you might have asked who didn't have a gorgeous Minerva weaving webs behind their backs."

The special prosecutor scowled at him suddenly through the sweet blue smoke. "Don't go too far, friend Chuck."

Richardson stretched out his legs until the toes struck against the apron of the desk with a sharp sound. "I wasn't suggesting anything like that," he said. "You did it for me—I know that. Was it out of pity?"

"Not pity, no. Maybe concern, partly."

"Then you should have saved it."

"It isn't a pleasant thing to see a man rot, Chuck."

"Then why scoop me out of my shell if I'm such a terrible spectacle? Not to mention whether I rot or don't rot is my business—not yours, not Christine's, anymore."

"I wasn't thinking in terms of business. Not entirely anyway."

"*Jesus Christ!*" Richardson leaned forward and brought his fist down hard on the desk. "Why the hell does everybody think they've got to save me?"

"I'm afraid I can't answer that." Hal Pearce struck a match and applied it to the bowl. The head pulsed like a tiny red heart, and expired.

"Well, I can," Richardson told him. "In my wife's case, at least. In her view the only thing worse than a poor husband is a poor ex-husband. Christine knows even she can't squeeze blood out of a stone."

Pearce raised his hand again. "Let's not get into personalities," he said. "I'm genuinely fond of your wife, and she is, after all, still your wife. Also, we've got plenty of work to do and next to no time at all to do it in. Tell me about the girl, will you?"

Richardson slumped in the chair and contemplated his steepled fingers. He did not answer immediately.

"Mary-Elena said you were with her almost two hours."

"That's right. I was."

"Well?" Hal Pearce appeared to heave slightly with impatience, like a bear turning over in winter. "Were you able to get anything out of her?"

"Something of interest, maybe, but not necessarily of meaning—and absolutely of no use."

"Can you elaborate on that?"

Richardson removed his chin from his fingers and sat upright in the chair. "There's something not right about that girl, Hal."

"Of course she isn't right. She's not in there for flat feet, you know."

"That isn't what I mean."

Pearce was watching him carefully now. "Then what do you mean?" he asked.

"I can't say exactly."

The pipe had gone out, but Pearce continued to suck contemplatively at the bit and stare at the separating layers of blue above his head. "She didn't have anything to give you, at all?"

"Not really."

"Then what was the point? Do you think what's-his-name wants to plea-bargain?"

"Wise? He wasn't there."

"You must be joking."

"Apparently it was at her request."

Pearce relit the pipe and puffed crossly on it. "I see what you mean about there being *something* wrong," he said dryly. "But why the hell did it take two hours?"

"She talked. I listened."

"About *what*, for Christ's sake?"

"How it happened."

"And in two and a half hours you learned nothing more than you knew already?"

Richardson shrugged and stared at his fingers again.

"The hell with her then," Pearce said finally. "We don't need her cooperation to nail her ass. That stud farm of hers has already talked enough to put them and her both away for a thousand years. According to Munger's testimony, she was acting like a little harpie that night, right in the middle of it all—spitting, kicking, begging to be allowed to pull the trigger herself. Her fingerprints are all over that gun."

Richardson got up suddenly and jerked away the chair. "I'm going out for a while," he said. "If anyone's looking for me tell them I'll be back in a couple of hours."

"Go right ahead," Pearce said, grinning. "That nice fresh wind should be just the thing for a hangover."

He went out, slamming the door behind him and jostling Mary-Elena, who stood bent over the file cabinet. She turned and glared at him.

"Nobody expects you to *be* a gentleman," she said, "but can't you at least try *acting* like one?"

The crash of the outer door was music to his ears, and he paused for a moment in the corridor to appreciate it. For reasons he was unable for the moment to identify, he was very disappointed in Hal Pearce.

7

HE COULD NOT have said for what purpose he had driven the thirty-five miles from town, let alone how he had known from the moment he had walked out of the courthouse that he was going to do it. He had taken the pickup—redeemed that morning from the impoundment lot at a cost of twenty-five dollars—instead of the unmarked sedan the county had placed at his disposal, thinking that even now, in June, the prairie would be treacherous, the creeks swollen and the washes muddy. It was a country in which spring was not a season but an act of imaginative will, as if the land finally achieved completion by mind itself, upon which its harsh, elemental beauty was largely dependent; a country meant for people of strong faith or—like himself—of no faith at all. He had set out like any tourist, traveling toward his destination merely because for some reason it had become an imperative for him to be able to say: These eyes have seen.

And it was good to be out of the office, he thought, away from the phones and the clatter of office machines, the drone of laconic lawmen and Mary-Elena's spring-loaded freneticism. He rolled the window down and let the cold wind scour the cab while he admired the stainless blue of the sky in which a few clouds floated, the sage spreading like blue coral across the shimmering green plain, relieved only by the eruptive Indian reds and yellows of the sculpted buttes.

He overshot the trail the first time and, swinging around on the highway, retraced his route at a slower speed, measuring the miles in careful tenths on the odometer. At last he came to it: a rutted trail scratched in the face of the prairie and linked tenuously to the blacktop by a battered cattleguard overgrown by milkwort and false rye and to which a sun-bleached cow's skull was lashed by a length of rusty wire. The soil was white and hard as old bones but after the first hundred yards he drove in low gear, and when he reached the first of the wooden stakes from which bits of orange ribbon still flittered he got out and went the rest of the way on foot.

A cold wind whinnyed in the hills and hollows and feathered the stiff ends of the sagebrush, but the sun was hot on his back as he picked his way over the sour chert; walking with his eyes on the ground, every tumulus, depression, and runnel of which owed its familiarity to that mosaic of black-and-white prints which, taken together, revealed in minute geomorphic detail a landscape as alien as the moon's.

He had visited the site once before, with Hal Pearce and several men from the DCI. There had been, as he remembered, little to see, just the tire marks and the footprints—mostly obliterated by wind and the light spring rains—the scuffed, trampled places in the rabbitbrush, the piles of shoveled clay and gravel. Only the twin depressions, less graves than subsided barrows, had impressed him; while now, standing again above the weather-beaten cavities from which the sheriff's department had removed the preserving canvases for the photographers, he felt that he was on the verge of some private, yet tremendous, thing.

It had been the shallower of the two, he recalled, in which first she, and afterward Mary Collins, had lain. He dropped on one knee beside it, feeling the earth like a cool compress through the denim—hearing the stroke of the night wind, seeing the white fingers winding themselves into the matted hair. Carefully he ran a hand over the rough dirt, smoothing it back and forth; he took a little in his palm and held it out as if weighing it, the clay, faintly moist, crumbling in the ridges of horny skin. Then he stood and, after rubbing his hands absentmindedly on his clean pants, began walking rapidly back to the truck. Around him the prairie teemed with renewed life: he heard everywhere the peremptory cries of sun-warmed gophers and in the middle distance saw the bright hound-colored shapes of antelope grazing across valleys of new grass under the sickled shadows of circling hawks. As if from nowhere a small white cloud like a sponge appeared, sprinkling him with a few drops of rain as he hurried on.

Abruptly he stopped, his body arrested in a rigid scissored position from which he recovered clumsily after a moment before wheeling about and returning at a dog-trot to the site, where he stood once again above the barrow, clenching and unclenching his hands in indecision. At last, moving slowly and with great deliberation, he began pacing off the area, square foot by square foot, holding his squinting eyes painfully to the ground and pushing aside clumps of rabbitbrush with his boot as he went, searching for the gleam of spiderweb metal. For nearly two hours he walked out the unmarked plot with the painstaking thoroughness of a Civil War buff scanning a battlefield with a Geiger counter, while the sun dropped toward the west and the hollows between the hills pooled with shadow. At last, straightening partway, he stood looking toward the setting sun, his hands hanging limply above his knees and his shoulders rounded with discouragement.

Of course, there was nothing, had been nothing—not with the body, not with the desert, that bitter, silent witness always accepting of death but eagerly condemning lies. What, after all, he thought, did I expect? As what, he consoled himself on the drive to town, would actually finding it have proved? No more than that the thief, having mislaid her theft, had after four weeks in prison imagined a way to turn her loss into gain. *Goddammit, Richardson!* he warned himself, slamming his fist against the wheel. *When will you learn? When the hell are you ever going to goddamn learn?*

104   *Chilton Williamson Jr.*

8

EVERY AFTERNOON NOW the lozenge of light swung closer, until, stretched on her back upon the bed, she felt it pass finally across herself from head to foot, as if her body were a sundial. For weeks she had lived outside time—pleasantly sealed like a fly in amber and not caring for movement because the energy for it did not exist yet. Since her first impatience with the owlish attorney, however, there had been a difference: she was no longer content to drowse and wash herself and eat, like a yellow cat. It was as if she were coming alive again by stages, and her mind, its bodily shell restored, had begun once more to assert itself.

One evening, having asked for and received a pad of lined letter-paper, she stretched on her belly across the bed and wrote in block letters across the top of the page CHAPTER ONE: the beginning of her autobiography. She had read Patty Hearst's story several years before and now it occurred to her that her own might be no less a subject for a book. But after making several false starts and staring at the crossed-out pages for the rest of the evening she decided that an autobiography was not a sensible project. As she grew stronger her mind worked more cannily, sharpening her instinct for self-preservation: it seemed to her that whatever she wrote might be used against her, the way Owlface had misused—though to different ends—what she had candidly and truthfully revealed to him.

Of nearly equal importance to her decision was the discovery, arrived at after hours of painfully frustrating labor, that she could not write. The images were present but she could not translate them into thoughts with a beginning, a middle, and an end. Perhaps, she thought, she should tell her story in pictures then: she had been a professional artist for a year, drawing funny portraits for a dollar apiece, from which Paoli Brothers had deducted fifty cents. She had observed, at any rate, that words apparently had little impression on Mr. Richardson. Although she had met him only the one time, she had come to feel that Mr. Richardson was the one she had to explain to—the person she would have to *make* understand, whether he wanted to or not. She was still talking to Owlface every day, but only in the most perfunctory and inattentive way.

Using the cheap white drawing-paper and pencils she had brought with her from the hospital, she began working—fitfully at first, then with greater, more sustained concentration. They would interrupt her to shower or for meals or exercise, and immediately afterward she would resume drawing, propped on pillows against the wall with her knees drawn up for an easel. She found that after two years she was out of practice, but also that her proficiency returned with gratifying speed.

The first scenes she tried were circus ones, because she remembered the circus as being, for some reason she could not have expressed in words, the best part of her life: a brief twelve months of living inexplicably interjected between seventeen years of denial and two of outrage. The best and most ambitious drawing showed herself standing in the sawdust ring under the big tent making a pony leap through a flaming hoop. In fact, her work with the horses had been limited to exercising them twice a day and shoveling out the trailers when they were on the road, but working them in the ring under bright lights and in front of all the people was how she liked to think about it. For the faded blue jeans, baggy workshirt, and sloppy pigtail she had worn around the pens she substituted a white satin suit with silver buttons and a wide blue sash, flowing hair, and a whip trimmed with ribbons. Next she drew the pony, fat and shiny, with a luxuriant mane and tail. After that she had to stop to consider how to finish the picture. After thinking about it for most of the afternoon she finally decided to put in Nick Mahu, the clown, wearing his ape suit. Nick had been an unprepossessing man in his late forties, with scraggly gray hair around a bald spot and reddish, malevolent eyes. When drunk he had often exhibited a violent temper, and had once made a bid—barely distinguishable from attempted rape—at seducing her. Although she had never considered him much as a man, a clown, or an ape, instinct told her that art was the drama of opposites, so she went ahead and put him in—a hairy, dumb-looking gorilla prancing about on its hind legs as if it were a legitimate part of the act, when what it actually had in mind when it was drunk (as it usually was at the end of the show) was breaking everything up and stealing the applause for itself. When she had finished the central composition she began sketching in a background of faces, like melons ranged in tiers around the ring, all of them with their mouths open in expressions that might equally have represented killing laughter or outraged horror. When she was done with the drawing she shuffled it into the pile of unused paper where it would not be noticed, satisfied that she had managed to express something of significance.

In the course of the long, haggling sessions with Owlface she had acquired, out of sheer necessity, the facility of discussing the two years spent with Munger and Weber without actually recognizing them or legitimizing them as part of her present reality. Even as—prompted and badgered by the infuriating man—she recapitulated the facts in minute detail and afterward listened in disgust as he rewove them into the official version—a horrible travesty he assured her "would fly" and that she began to imagine in the shape of a bird, half-buzzard and half-raven—she was aware of granting them a merely tentative validity. Her life had become a process of maintaining two opposing states of consciousness. It was exhausting, but she accepted it as a medieval prince might have accepted the absurdity of having to solve a riddle set him by a harsh, implacable Lady to whom his life was forfeit if he failed. Her life, she recognized with the clarity of perception returning strength had brought her, depended now upon the ability to manipulate nonentities.

She concluded that Owlface was what in school they had called a space cadet. At the sight of him arriving each morning with his bursting portfolio under his arm, his round shoulders and absurdly magnified eyes, she wanted to giggle, but by the time he finished with her and was preparing to leave she felt sober and even a little scared. Her own lawyer was a jerk and Mr. Richardson didn't seem to understand. She thought of asking to see Mr. Pearce again, but she didn't dare go over Owlface's head a second time. He had asked a lot of smug questions about Mr. Richardson's visit in a tone of voice that said, I warned you not to play with fire, but you wouldn't listen to me. Now you've made things worse, but don't worry. If you promise to follow my advice exactly I'll see that you get out of this mess all right. She was, she recognized with a feeling of genuine astonishment, becoming very shrewd.

One morning she noticed at once that Owlface was in an ugly mood. He began by criticizing the carelessness and imprecision of her answers and went on to scold her for inaccuracy in recalling her cues, which he attributed to her failure to pay sufficient attention to his prompting the day before. Stuffing papers violently into the portfolio, he shouted that, in the event of an adverse decision on the part of the jury, he would not in all fairness to himself accept the blame.

After he had gone Jenny resettled herself on the bed and wrote a short note to Mr. Richardson asking if he would visit her again. It was very important that he come soon, she said. Then, after folding the sheet and tucking it inside the envelope, she lay on her back with her arms behind her head and stared at the ceiling, thinking of him.

She was in bad trouble, needed his help, and had asked for it now, and yet she felt it was a strange kind of plea she was making—a cry for help in which the promise of it seemed to echo, as if two people were shouting to each other across a canyon, question and reply confused by distance and the gusting winds. Remembering the battered, corruscated face, the agony behind the angry gas-blue eyes, she thought again, Maybe it's me—maybe I'm the one that has to do It. Only she didn't have the slightest idea what "It" might be.

9

ENTERING THE SHADOWY old building out of the sun-blue morning, Richardson felt like a man who discovers that he has inherited a fortune the day after deciding to take holy orders. He was rousing the ghosts again from their corners, and this time, unmistakably, they were mocking him. Hurrying across the rotunda he bounded up the stairs to the second floor, clenching the letter in his fist. He had known the instant he saw it lying on the kitchen table among the bills, the seed and equipment and outfitters' catalogues, that the writing on it was hers—the fatly formed, cute, entirely characterless script of the young half-educated American female. She had addressed it simply to Mr. C. Richardson, Fontennelle, Wyoming, and they had delivered it to his RFD box instead of to the office.

"The next time you ring that way you can come in through the mail slot with the rest of the bad-news telegrams," Mary-Elena told him. "Is it honestly too much to ask that you remember to carry your office key?"

Richardson jerked his thumb at the closed door. "Is *he* in there?"

"You ought to know his schedule by now. He never sees anyone before nine."

"It's twelve to right now."

"I'm sorry," Mary-Elena said, compressing her lips. "When

you get to be where Hal is you can arrange your schedule to suit yourself."

He went on through to his own office, where he sat drinking coffee and paging unconsciously through the morning papers. At one minute after nine she put her head into the cubicle. "He'll see you now."

"Good morning, Chuck," Hal Pearce said as he entered. "You're Johnny-on-the-spot this morning, aren't you?"

"Look at this."

Richardson thrust the letter across the desk and watched as the big hands slowly turned over the envelope before removing and spreading the paper. He saw a flicker of annoyance pass across the china-blue eyes. Then Pearce refolded the letter and held it out in a dismissive gesture. "Well?" he demanded in an irritated voice.

"She wants to talk to me again."

"I know. I just read her letter."

"Maybe we should both go this time."

The blue eyes widened behind the filament of smoke, which rose as straight and calm as woodsmoke on a still October day. "For what reason?"

"I think you should hear her for yourself."

"Why?" Pearce asked. "Do you have any reason to believe she means to add anything to what she told you a week ago?"

"It isn't a matter so much of what she *says*."

Pearce tamped the pipe bowl with a deliberate finger. "I'm beginning to understand," he said. "She's offered you a tin cup, or rather what you think is a tin cup. Will it hold water?"

"I don't know. Maybe you will."

Pearce nodded sympathetically. "Let's call it a hunch, then. An intuition."

"Whatever, Hal. You know—you've had them. You're famous for making them stick in a court of law, too."

"Yes," the other agreed. He had been striking matches as they talked, as if the succession of minor ignitions appeased him for something. At last he emptied the pipe and refilled it from the Zuni jar, in whose even glaze a tracery of fractures spread like the capillaries in a dissolute's cheek. "But hunches shouldn't come out of thin air, they should come with a nail to hang them on, like that tin cup. Where's your nail?"

Richardson remained silent for a moment, weighing his reply. Inexplicably, her letter had wiped away the disappointment of not finding the bracelet, which nevertheless remained a story too unsubstantiable for introduction into this evidentiary crisis. "Talk to her yourself and maybe you can show it to me."

But Hal Pearce was smiling again, weary but still patient. "Imagination, friend Chuck, is like ambition: a good servant but a bad master. I hope I'm not offending you when I suggest that yours may have—temporarily—run away with you."

"That could be, of course. My feeling is that imagination works best off the leash, like a good dog. It's got to stray a little if it's going to flush the bird."

The tolerant smile widened to a grin. "Does that apply to bears, too?" Hal Pearce asked. "Or were we just working with the wrong kind of dog?"

But Richardson was refusing to be put off now. "What I'm saying to you, I guess," he said quietly, "is maybe I believe in her."

"I guessed that." Hal Pearce shifted his weight more comfortably in the chair. "At least that's out in the open now, though I have to tell you I don't myself find much to believe in." And when Richardson remained stone-faced: "Listen. Shall we review—briefly—the facts?" His voice was still patient but a note of quiet irony had come into it. "Jenny Petersen is—or was—a runaway from what was—apparently —a normal, decent home. For the past two years she had lived what I am old-fashioned enough to describe as a depraved life, first as a whore to the most degraded kind of criminal, then as the communal property of two of them. She permitted herself to be drawn—evidently without either resistance or compunction—into their criminal activities, ending finally with a pair of brutal murders, the execution of which she clearly did little, if anything, to thwart—which she in fact, on the testimony of two witnesses, participated in with a peculiarly bloodthirsty glee and afterward—and this statement does not admit of contradiction—made no attempt to report to the police, although she was not without opportunity to do so. After three weeks of psychiatric observation and more than a month in prison she invites us to listen to her story at first hand—a story differing not one jot or tittle from the one she told the J.P. at her arraignment.

"And now I'm going to tell you something, Richardson. In thirty-plus years at law I have discovered that justice, like life, is essentially a simple thing. I'm not talking about a procedure now, or a profession, or that elaborate political bullshit in which law courts all too frequently become enmeshed. I'm talking about what has come to be buried under layers of institutional and bureaucratic procedure and technique but can never be suppressed entirely because the pattern exists in the very genes of man himself: an eternal triangle, if you will, expressed in three simple but venerable words— *crime, vindication, punishment.* And it is because I believe that they are not just the basis of law but the whole of it that I am the kind of attorney I am: a country defense lawyer who abominates Causes with a capital *C* and whose job differs from that of the prosecutor chiefly because it consists of taking the monkey off the back of the innocent rather than placing it squarely on the shoulders of the guilty.

"So you see, I am not entirely unsuited to the prosecutorial role. It is just that, for the first time in my career, the question of who deserves to hang appears to me of greater moral compulsion than the question—ignored by most prosecuting attorneys—of who does not."

So that was that, he told himself. That was how it always ended for these flamboyant idealists: when their idealism aged to a degree of brittleness, it cracked in two, like those concrete-hulled transports the navy built in absurd numbers during the Second World War and which went down like rocks, carrying everything with them. It was a personal tragedy as well as an intellectual one, even if at the moment of catastrophe those people unfortunate enough to be caught in the maelstrom were too busy clinging to bits of debris to register the appropriate pity. And what of it? Richardson thought fiercely. Let the dead bury the dead.

In a voice as even as he could make it he said, "I understand. Then you won't see her?"

"Among other things, I have to be in Billings most of the week. Finally, of course, my seeing her depends upon the ultimate disposition of the three cases, whether they are to be tried jointly or separately. For the time being, however, the answer is no. You, I take it, intend to talk with her again?"

He drew a long breath. "With your permission, yes."

Hal Pearce regarded him at length with his head cocked sideways and one eye almost shut. "You know, Chuck, I'm beginning to think you have no instinct at all for women."

"Oh, for Christ's sake, Hal. Is chivalry completely dead?"

He left the room quickly, before he could get really mad, stalking by Mary-Elena who gave him a flashing look from her black eyes as he passed her desk on the way to the little office, where he shut the door and sat for a while, staring at the sour green wall and smoking one of the black cigars. He was thinking that he understood at last what the trouble with Mary-Elena was. She wanted him.

10

HE FELT HIMSELF as chagrined by her radiance as he was unprepared for it, standing bashful as a schoolboy with his hat in his hand, watching her through the bars while the matron unfastened the door. She had been drawing: an assortment of colored pencils was scattered on the bunk behind her and she was holding a pad of artist's paper in her hand. He tried to ignore the long legs and torso, the shiny hair tucked demurely behind the little ears, the grave, plain-pretty face. She was not chubby yet but she had gained enough, while her composure had become so settled that a slight anxiety at seeing him seemed to spread visibly outward from her center like ripples across a quiet pond. The matron brought him a chair and left them.

"If you're going to stand," Richardson told her, "I will too. This way I feel like a turkey-necked legionnaire in a wheelchair."

She gave an anxious laugh that did not show in her gray eyes and sat obediently on the bed again, staring at her clasped hands. Reaching abruptly for the half-finished drawing, she laid it face-down at the foot of the blanket.

"I'd forgotten that you draw," he said.

"It isn't drawing really, just messing around. I used to do a lot when I worked for the circus. I never had any lessons though."

"It must be tough having to figure it out for yourself."

"Oh, no," she told him simply. "It just comes." Then she looked him straight in the eye. "I want you to be my lawyer."

My God, he thought, I couldn't have done it better than that myself: I couldn't have done as well. He said, "I already represent a client in this business, Jenny. My client is the state, which regards you as its legal enemy. You know that."

"I know it," the girl told him. "So what?"

He had to turn away to the window then, to regain not just composure but, he felt, breath itself. He stood watching a small boy on a red tricycle pedaling at breakneck speed along the sidewalk with the reckless, innocent abandon of fools and children; groping not for words but for the inspiration that would suggest them. Finally he said, "I want you to tell me more about the bracelet, remembering that you are talking not to your attorney but to a member of the prosecutorial staff. Do you understand what I am saying to you?"

"The bracelet?" Her voice was surprised and almost sullen, as if she thought he was trying to elude her.

"The bracelet Mrs. Collins tried to give you just before Munger shot her."

"Oh, that. I told you about that last week."

"I remember you did. What I don't understand is why you never told anyone else."

She gripped the edge of the bed with white knuckles. "Because I forgot about it. Because I was scared at the time and when I remembered it it wasn't important anyway."

This time he pulled the chair forward and sat in it, looking as deeply as he could into her cool gray eyes. "What happened to that bracelet, Jenny?"

"I don't know," she told him. "I can't remember whether I took it from her or not. That's what she wanted me to do. Maybe I took it and lost it—afterward, when they made me—" She stopped and stared again at her hands, where the nails were imprinting tiny white moons in the rosy flesh of the palm.

"All right," Richardson said. "Tell me again, now. From the beginning."

"The *beginning?*" For the first time, her voice rose almost to a wail.

"Not everything," he reassured her. "Just the part about her offering you the bracelet."

So again he stood with his back to her, his hands gripping the bars of the window while, speaking in the neutral, inflectionless voice he recognized by now as the one she used when talking about The Night, she recounted how during the struggle the women had kept glancing at her—the girl tight-lipped and silently proud, the mother bawling and rolling her eyes—as if they expected that somehow she would provide help, or perhaps (it occurred to him as he listened) simply pity; how, after the men had wandered into the prairie, she had worked as fast as she could at the knots, only to discover as she finished Munger grinning at her, anticipating the moment when he would spring forward to avert their escape; how Mrs. Collins had used her final moment of near-freedom to thrust the bit of chain—thankfully, was how Jenny had interpreted it—at her equally helpless liberator, who remembered only the plunging body of Munger followed immediately by the inconsequential snapping sound of the .22 pistol.

"Can I stop now?"

"Yes," he said, remembering Hal Pearce's cup and the nail to hang it on. This wasn't it, wasn't enough. He wanted it to be, but wanting didn't have a thing to do with it.

When finally he did face her she was still braced on the edge of the bed with her head lowered, staring at her hands, which she held pressed between her knees. When Richardson saw that her shoulders were trembling he hurled himself at her, like a coyote after a lamb.

"Both Willie Munger and Seth Weber," he said brutally,

"have testified that that is not the way it happened. They have claimed repeatedly that from the moment Munger gave the order to tie those women you were in it up to the eyeballs. They have accused you of spitting, scratching, and kicking the victims. According to Munger you even wanted to be the one to pull the trigger."

She shrugged in a matter-of-fact way, suggesting that she could be neither responsible for nor concerned by other people's lies, and for an instant he was with her again, rooting for her: not just sympathetic but admiring.

"That woman's skin was found under your fingernails," he added viciously, squinting to observe her reaction.

"She wouldn't hold still," the girl explained. "I guess I must have scratched her trying to get the cord off. I tried to tell her, but she just kept on screaming."

For what seemed a very long time they were silent. Richardson tried to imagine that he was alone in the cell, but while the girl made no sound—seeming not even to breathe—her presence behind him was overwhelming. Finally, he said, "Maybe you know, or maybe you don't know. It isn't a simple thing for a lawyer to have himself dismissed at will from a case. I can't just walk out the front door and come in again by the back one. I would have to talk to Judge Thurlow, who is the district judge, and persuade him to release me from a legal, professional, and moral obligation. I haven't had any dealings with Thurlow, but most judges, if they would allow it at all, would make an attorney jump through hoops before turning him loose in the middle of a case. As for my representing you afterward, that's probably one of the craziest ideas I've ever heard, though I suppose maybe legal in a technical sense. I'd have to read up on that one. It sure as hell would look terrible to a jury, though."

"We can work it out," she remarked, almost offhandedly.

She was leaning against the wall with her knees up, and he noted with astonishment that she had been drawing: holding her head a little to one side and sucking at her lower lip, and he understood then that she had not really been listening to anything he had said for the past seven or eight minutes. He wanted to slap her, but she looked up just then and gave him a sweet smile. "It's done," she said.

"It's *what?*"

He stared at her helplessly as, holding the pencil between her teeth, she held out the pad to him, still wearing her sweetly ingenuous smile.

"It's only a sketch, I had to hurry to finish it while you were still talking. Aren't you even going to look?"

He didn't have the slightest idea what she was talking about but he took the pad from her and stood staring at what looked to him like a pineapple resting on a topknot of leaves until he realized he was holding it upside down. He corrected for that, and looked again.

It was a sketch of a face instantly familiar to him—a dark, battered-looking face but without mark or outward blemish, as if the damage had been accomplished from within: hollow-eyed, with a thin mouth and wide, muscled jaw. She had laid on shading for effect, with the result that the complexion, beneath the waxen gloss of the hair, had a sooty look, while the deep-set eyes—outraged, implacable, and lost—glared from their black sockets. It was a harsh, self-abused face, at once unrelenting and appealing, tormenting and tormented, and which he recognized the next instant as his own.

11

"Well, Princess," Hal Pearce's voice said; she thought it sounded tired over the phone. "We lost him today. He broke clean off, but he's still out there with the hook in his mouth."

"*What?*" Setting down the Campari-and-soda, she stubbed her cigarette violently in the Waterford dish. "Wait a second, will you, Hal, while I turn down the stereo?

"The Beach Boys are *great* when you can't listen to Mozart any longer," she explained when she was on the line again. "Now, what are you trying to tell me about my darling husband?"

"He quit this morning. Not the case, just the prosecution. Apparently he's going to try to represent the girl against me."

"You're *kidding!*" Dropping cross-legged on the carpet with the telephone between her knees, she lit a fresh cigarette and reached behind herself for the drink.

"Unfortunately, I'm not."

Christine flung a strand of streaked-blond hair over her shoulder with a golden clatter. "I don't be*lieve* it! He must have gone com*pletely* bananas this time!"

"All he told me was that he believes in her."

His voice seemed to her to be touched by irony. "Oh, for God's sake. We're talking about a man who's going to be forty years old in December, Hal."

"Not forty, Princess. Maybe twenty—or ninety."

"God," she said again, almost bitterly. "He really is impossible, isn't he."

"I have to agree. But why couldn't you have warned me earlier?"

"Now, Hal, you know that's not fair. We both knew it was a gamble." Tipping the glass, she caught the lemon peel on the tip of her tongue, drawing it playfully between her teeth.

"No," Pearce told her, "the law itself is a gamble. This was shooting myself in the foot—a deliberate, premeditated act of self-mutilation."

"Well," Christine said with a tragic sigh, "at least we tried, didn't we?" The small crystal-and-silver traveling clock on the walnut table said five minutes to seven. "Christ, I'm supposed to meet someone at the Matterhorn in fifteen minutes and I'm not even dressed yet. Listen, Hal, let me know what happens, will you? Last time I called, one of his little tootsies answered the phone and then he almost bit my head off. Thanks again for calling—okay? I'm sorry—and *ciao*."

Instead of dressing at once she continued to sit for a while on the floor surrounded by strewn record sleeves, running her fingertip around the rim of the Campari glass and staring at the Tetons turning purple with evening. *Grands Tétons* in French meant Big Tits, a fact she often mentioned at Jackson cocktail and supper parties for the mild discomfiture it produced. Of course she was not surprised by Hal Pearce's news: nothing her husband had done in the past four years had astonished her. Under the circumstances it couldn't be lust, and she wasn't interested enough to sort out which among all the possible crazy reasons was the right one: he was, after all, such a terrible innocent. Naturally, Hal is mad about it, she told herself. Now he has to go out with the egg still fresh on his face and find himself a new assistant prosecutor. It was typical of him, though, that he hadn't mentioned what must be the terrible embarrassment.

She thought, If I don't do it now, when will I ever do it?

After sixteen years, how did you go about getting a Greenwich, Connecticut, marriage annulled? That left divorce, which she had been considering for eighteen months now without coming to a decision—partly because it was messy and partly because divorce proceedings, unlike necessarily those of annulment, tended to acquire a momentum of their own. For a year and a half now he had vegetated on the ranch he had bought with the money his father had left him, busy with nothing apparently but his horses and his girls, while she remained in Jackson in the condominium inherited from her own father, drinking Camparis-and-soda, listening to Wagner and Mozart, having infatuations, and waiting for him to cry uncle. She hadn't expected it to take him so long to demand that they settle one way or the other: it hadn't occurred to her that he would be able to endure even a year in that attenuated state, which had actually suited her extremely well. Although she was drinking more than she was used to and smoking altogether too many cigarettes, the perennial problem of the male animal was well in hand. She found plenty of attention in Jackson, while a mere two hundred miles down the road was the reasonable excuse she had not seen in over six months now for declining compromising (even faintly disgusting) situations. For her—who had spent her entire adult life in a titillating aura of hysteric suspension—limbo was not a problem.

Now the clock said seven-twelve and she thought, Robert will be more than happy to wait a half hour for me in the bar! She herself would not tolerate being made to wait, but there was gratification in rushing in to find a man, husky-voiced from cigarettes and with his necktie pulled away from his wilting collar, tapping his fingers on the wood and looking red-eyed and slightly stupid from alcohol. She mixed a fresh drink and carried it into the bedroom where, stripping off her jeans and shirt, she began to do her face, which was handsome rather than pretty and possessed a natural severity that tended to obviate makeup. She was thirty-seven and looked it, she thought; the only woman her age she knew who freely admitted to being over thirty-five. She had other defects—things a lot worse than being thirty-seven—she would admit to also, though never apologize for; among them the admiration of money and social position, willfulness, a congenital incapacity for love, and—still at thirty-seven—a commensurate incapacity for deciding what it was she wanted to do with herself.

When she had finished she stood for a moment regarding herself critically in the mirror. At least, she thought, I am not vain: if they don't like what they see they can buy dinner for somebody else. Flinging the shirt and jeans across the shower rod, she marched into the bedroom. Another defect she would admit to was untidiness, even slovenliness. Yes, she told herself, you might as well face it, kiddo—you're filthy. Closets stood open upon racks of crowded clothes, drawers hung halfway out of the Regency bureau, while the bed and chairs were buried under piles of lingerie and record sleeves. Without pause for reflection, she snatched a shirtwaist of turquoise silk and threw it across the bed. From the bureau she selected a pair of nylon stockings and, from its precious Florentine box, the necklace of delicate sterling silver links her mother had bought in Mayfair to wear to the coronation of Elizabeth II. It was slightly tarnished and as she fastened it around her neck she reminded herself that she must tell Carmen to polish the silver on Friday. (She had tentatively planned to drive to Fontennelle that morning but felt she could trust Carmen in her absence.) Divorce, she thought, as she drew the smooth silk over her head and buttoned it in back, was a terribly final thing. When you had gone straight through the list of available possibilities the one thing left to do was start over again from the top.

When she came out of the bedroom the clock read a quarter-to-eight and the peeled log walls and polished wood floors of the front rooms glowed pink in the blood-red light of the sun. The condominium was part of a resort development built on property that had formerly belonged to an ex-governor of the state. Her father, who had used it two weekends each year for skiing and in the fall for a "hunting" weekend in which to play cards and drink Wild Turkey, had filled it with a lot of hideous log furniture in the Three Bears style and some Indian rugs and hangings. Through the plate glass window she could see the elaborately dressed wedding party that, earlier in the evening, had crossed the street from the Unitarian Church—a small structure of rusticated logs surmounted by a rude cross that looked like two sticks fastened together, and which had been included as an afterthought by the developer, presumably to create a sense of community —to enter Le Chanticleer, a French restaurant designed to resemble a Swiss chalet. Watching the guests climb into their expensive polished cars, she wondered what the ex-governor would think now of his ex-cattle ranch, and was stricken suddenly by the nameless, terrifying, irresistible grief that blew upon her once again as if out of a black void. At such moments as this it seemed to her that nothing in life—her life, anybody's life, life itself—could compensate for the knowledge that it had given her twelve generations of ancestors and money as her sole dowry and distinction, and that however hard and devotedly she might try, her overshadowing accomplishment—that of being born—lay behind her. This was both her greatest, most radical defect, and the one to which, in all her thirty-seven years, she had never confessed.

The sun descended upon the horn of the Grand Teton, where it seemed to rest for a moment like a shining eye at the apex of a gigantic pyramid; as, glancing at her wristwatch, she thought suddenly of poor Robert, slumped over the bar with his Gibsons and his cigarettes, tapping the wood with a patient, drunken, metronomic finger.

BOOK

3

1

"I HEARD YOU got some purty horses here," Mr. Peepers said. "I come clear over from Idaho to have a look at that stud of yours."

The two of them stood resting their elbows on the rail watching the horses run smoothly around the corrals—tails flowing, heels smoothly clicking, dark legs blurring like spokes—while Jenny came across the yard from the tack-room, carrying the saddle and blanket and holding the bridle over her shoulder. She had put her hair into a braid and wore blue jeans that nipped her figure in the flattering places and a hot-pink shirt with yoked shoulders and pearl buttons down the front. Mr. Peepers was not looking at the horses now. He was a tall, lean, jug-eared man with long teeth stained brown by tobacco and a moled hatchet face that might or might not have been a sign of Indian blood and that bobbled forward on his skinny neck like a paper lantern on the end of a pole.

Richardson said, "He's three years old, Mr. Peepers, three-quarters broke, and pretty comfortable under the saddle un-less you happen to be in it. He didn't grow last winter like I hoped he would, and I'm a mite heavy for him yet. He's got no trouble carrying a trim little thing like Jenny here, and there's no mare's going to object to carrying him for five minutes, either."

"Not *that* little," Jenny corrected modestly. Abruptly the colt lipped her arm, and she whirled and slapped the velvet muzzle, which resounded loudly under her hand like a ripe melon as the horse flung up its head.

Mr. Peepers gave a loud, ostentatious laugh, exposing his pinkish gums and crinkling his yellow eyes. "That's good," he said approvingly. "She don't cut him no slack. How much you taking for a trick?" he asked, placing a pinch of tobacco under his lip and turning again to Richardson.

"Seven-fifty."

She fixed the bosel and browband, spread the blanket, and placed the saddle on it while the colt Sennacherib nodded placidly, its eyes patient and unperturbed. Reaching under the belly, she drew the cinch smartly through the girth ring as the hooves lashed suddenly sideways, and then they were flying together around the corral, the girl grasping the mane in her fists and hanging there, making the colt take her full weight. It stood finally, and again she pulled upward on the cinch, nimbly dodging the quick hooves. She was panting now. The soft blue air carried gently to his nostrils the scent of female flesh, edged sharply by sweat.

Mr. Peepers's jaw dropped slightly and his brown, pupil-less eyes looked moist. "Looks like you got yourself a cowgirl," he observed in a husky voice.

Jenny fastened a length of bailing string to the cinch and let it dangle innocently beside the left flank; then, quietly, she reached under the belly for the girth ring, drawing the string lightly through as the colt laid back its ears. Speaking in her quiet, gentling voice, one hand pressing the withers reassuringly, she pulled lightly on the string, drawing cinch and girth into place about the barrel until the cinch came neatly through the ring and with a sudden, astonishingly muscular jerk, she tied it off in a neat windsor as the colt soared angrily on pivoting hooves. Mr. Peepers guffawed and applauded, with a sound like dry bones rattling. "Well,

I'll be dipped in shit," he exclaimed. "That little gal of yours is a natural."

Then she was mounted, her right boot securely in the stirrup against black outraged motion, the horse dancing sideways, fighting for its head.

Mr. Peepers asked, "She ain't your daughter, is she?"

"No, she isn't."

"She workin for you?"

"That's right."

"Local gal, I expect."

"Utah."

"Is that a fact now." Mr. Peepers chose a straw from the ground and began carefully to pick his teeth with it while Richardson continued to watch girl and horse stamped in raging symbiotic motion against the cloud-barred gold of the western sky. "Kind of a long way from home, ain't she?"

"I guess."

Mr. Peepers spat out the straw and drew a package of cigarettes from his shirt pocket. "Care for a cigarette?"

"No thanks."

Mr. Peepers tapped one out and placed it between his yellowed teeth. He ignited a paper match on his thumbnail and sheltered it in the cup of his hand.

"Look at that action," Richardson told him. "You never saw a smoother gait than that animal's got. It's in the genes."

"Sure is a purty horse," Mr. Peepers agreed disinterestedly, as the hot-pink shirt whirled on around the corral, a dollop of ice cream on a rich black cake. "Didn't you have a gal out here workin was involved in them highway murders last spring?"

"Only seven hundred fifty bucks," Richardson reminded him. "Some of the best Arab blood in this part of the country."

"Seems to me like somebody tole me—" Mr. Peepers began.

Squinting at the antic centaur shape battling itself to stasis upon the red medallion of the sun, Richardson felt doubt pierce his heart like a shard. He said: "Look here, Mr. Peepers. You didn't come here to talk about any stud fee. Maybe you won't mind telling me what you did come for."

The cigarette dropped from Mr. Peepers's mouth and hastily he began scraping dirt over it with the side of his boot. "Why, sure enough," he mumbled. "You bet! Like I said— I been hearing plenty about them horses of yours, and—"

Richardson clapped the man's narrow head between his hands and wrenched it around until the yellow eyes held directly on the circling horse and rider. She had Sennacherib in control now, cantering him easily about the corral: each time they swung past he could hear her sharp breathing above the animal's stentorian heave. He panned Mr. Peepers's head as if it were a movie camera, keeping it focused upon the graceful double figure.

"Take a good look at her, Mr. Peepers," he said. "Tell me when you've looked enough. And then get your ass off my property and don't ever bring it back."

She drew up in front of them with a gay little salute and began the dismount. Before her left foot was free of the stirrup the horse was on its way up again. She got her leg over fast, catching the right stirrup with the toe of her boot, and rode it up, down, and up again, her body pressed along the plunging withers as, letting out the reins and then drawing them in hard, she brought the animal almost to its knees. Then she was upright in the saddle once more, proud and straight as an Indian as she circled the corral twice at a walk before dismounting. He saw that she had alfalfa wisps in her hair, that one of the pearl buttons was unsnapped, and that her eyes were soft and bright, and felt appalled suddenly by her careless, girlish gaiety. Mr. Peepers scuttled around the corner of the barn, and after a minute they heard the choking sound of his old pickup turning over.

"What was the matter with *him?*" Jenny wanted to know.

"Didn't he like Sennacherib? And what on earth were you doing with his *head?*"

"Mr. Peepers wasn't interested much in horses," Richardson told her. "He drove all the way over here from Idaho with a crick in his neck and I was able to straighten it out for him. Apparently they don't have chiropractors in Idaho, or anyway not the part he comes from."

She stood watching him for a while, holding the lead-rope in one hand, her head tilted pensively to one side. "I don't believe you," she said finally, "but it doesn't matter anyway," and then he was alone, watching her lead the horse away to the barn. The sun was a scarlet bow above the level blue line of the mesa, but its warmth lingered on the evening like a kiss as, with his eyes, he followed this girl-woman, monster, daughter he had never had—youth's mad, final gamble—vanish like a pink flame into the darkness of the barn's interior. Believing in her was beginning to seem a little like believing in God—the God he hadn't believed in since his confirmation in the Catholic Church at the age of ten, if he had even believed in Him then: Every other day you felt yourself distressingly let down, dropped almost. But God, if He existed, had everybody, while she had only him, for whatever that might be worth: having assumed the responsibility of allowing himself to be touched by her once, he couldn't send her away again, tell her just to go, without friends, family, or money. But, God, he thought, isn't it hell living with a teenage female! Isn't it just plain bloody hell, sometimes.

2

He had come to wonder whether there was any aspect of human life that was not at least a potential embarrassment to a small town, the psychological mainspring of which he had learned to recognize as not fear but chagrin.

Through the hot yellow-and-blue summer of his new pariahdom he drove the dinged pickup every morning into Fontennelle—indistinguishable from any one of a hundred other Western towns, with its faded lilac bushes surrounding the faded frame houses, fresh-sprinkled lawns and damp sidewalks, and seething cottonwoods—to make his regular appearances first at Ranier's lumberyard and Haggerty's feedstore, then at the courthouse; infallible as the Catholic priest trimming his roses after Mass, the Justice of the Peace in the familiar jeans, baseball cap, and windbreaker ascending the courthouse steps, or Gimp—chief among equals of his fraternity, for whom he did office—staggering before dawn from the bars toward the just-opened cafés. Officeless now, he would sit with his papers and lawbooks at a cramped desk in the rotunda, from where he could observe the static summer day with its tiled sky and geometric shadows, the houses standing livid in the white glare as thunderheads towered toward a disburdenment indefinitely postponed. At five he would drive home, sweating inside his respectable clothes and watching the clouds float on a milky haze above the mountains.

Because he considered his standing in the community to have been confirmed rather than conferred by events, notoriety had taken him by surprise. Without appearing to look, the town watched his every move; without seeming to listen, it heard every word he said. He had not known that so many ways existed to convey thought and feeling without actually expressing them. At the courthouse, requesting documents from secretaries or being summoned by them to the telephone; at the supermarket, waiting for checkout between formerly unconstrained (at times even amorous) matrons whose roofs he had repaired while they amiably served him bottles of cold beer; at the lumberyard, where the clerks seemed poised between confusion and a disinclination to appear prudish; even at the Last Chance—where, though Bill Gerhardie maintained his cool Caledonian cynicism and Bruno Bellini contented himself with lecherously knowing looks, Bob Pulasky was short-spoken and as ruffled as a grouse, as if he felt placed unfairly in an uncomfortable position—this collective, oddly self-conscious scrutiny tinged with a knowing voyeurism impinged upon him. He had even quit attending the regular meetings of the Bridger County Search and Rescue Unit, and nobody had yet phoned to remind him of them.

He understood how it looked, which was bad, and tried, by recourse to his own easy cynicism, to accommodate Fontennelle's accepted opinion. That was when he discovered that, while cynicism has its limits, disillusionment knows no bounds. He was prepared to exchange look for look, word for word, scorn for scorn, if need be. But it seemed to him an outrageous contraposition that what he had begun by defending had become the thing he needed first to conquer in order to defend. After five years he had made a sincere attempt at reconciliation of a sort, only to find himself rebuffed. Somebody, he thought, is trying to tell me something.

He was spending his evenings at home now, playing poker or cribbage with Tonio at the kitchen table until midnight while Jenny sat drawing, or retired to the bedroom he had fixed for her following Peggy's angry departure from the house. When he won, Tonio swatted cards triumphantly, celebrating his victories until they devolved finally into routs, at which point he would withdraw in a sulk; before beginning a game he took the precaution of offering fervent invocation to Our Lady for his success, a gesture that, as far as Richardson could tell, contained the sum of his religious devotion. Tonio was working part-time for him now, maintaining a slight forward momentum in the nearly becalmed roof-and-siding business, in addition to serving as a factotum around the ranch, at which he spent a large part of his free time. Between him and Jenny an intuitive—almost clairvoyant—bond had formed, forged, he thought, from something stronger than Tonio's doglike devotion and the amusement she showed at his boastful, long-winded, incoherent, and entirely fictitious tales of his prowess as a hunter, lover, and card-sharper. For himself, he suspected that Tonio's appeal lay finally in his incomprehensibility, words being somehow unnecessary to the subjective sense of what he wished to communicate. Listening to his barely decipherable babble, Richardson experienced the profound affection of one man for another when, stretched on the ground together under the stars, they lie listening to each other's breathing with only the cold guns between them.

Because he understood that even an attorney who has marked time for five years without chance or hope of anything better—probably admitting to himself that the worthiness of his clients had usually not been less than his ability to defend them—can be expected nevertheless to have his pride, he had walked nonchalantly one morning into the Office of the Public Defender, where, dropping her notarized letter on the dental school application forms that lay spread upon the desk, he had explained that, while what he called personal incompatibilities had forced his client into taking this action, he would very much appreciate the valuable cooperation of his predecessor, particularly in making available to him notes and other material. The public defender, Bob Wise—a young-ish, unprepossessing, owl-faced man with thick glasses and the round sullen eyes of an unintelligent child—had sat in his little office with its dented steel furniture, adjustable metal shelves, and ancient ceiling fixture (which lent it the depressing hue of a bad egg), holding a paper cup of coffee in his hand and wearing an expression of derisive contempt. It was the same look he had read in Judge Thurlow's face when, in granting the petition for release, he had castigated "nervous nellies of the profession who flit in and out of law cases without being able to make up their minds." The difference was, he thought, that His Honor had been just mad, while Wise had been transparently relieved.

Explaining to her that he would be acting only in a temporary capacity until a competent replacement could be found, he had proceeded immediately to file for dismissal of her indictment on the primary ground that she had herself been a victim rather than accomplice of her male companions; secondarily on the argument that the arraignment proceedings, as conducted by Bill Daniels, Justice of the Peace, had been a tissue of error and outrage—omitted advisements, mangled procedure, and bungled questioning—dominated by the hoarse, barking voice of the deaf old man who had understood perhaps one word in three, itself plaintively underscored by the strained voices of the lawyers and police officers trying to make themselves heard. (In other circumstances, he thought bitterly, Hal Pearce would have had plenty to say about that arraignment.) His move subsequently had been to obtain her release on bond—no mean feat he reminded himself grimly—posted with monies obtained by the sale of his Eastern stock as well as collateral in the form of real estate properties. Finally, he had established his client—or protégé, or *mistress:* the town had long ago formed its opinion as to which—under his own roof and at salary as a ranch hand.

He and Hal Pearce continued to meet irregularly for lunch at the Fontennelle Café (several times, too, in the courthouse rotunda he had seen Mary-Elena, who had surprised him with the cordiality of her greeting), occasions on which they would circumspectly discuss shooting and horses, save for the single instance when Pearce—tall and imposing in the wrinkled gray suit as he stood tapping the Stetson gravely against his knee—permitted his pouched eyes a parting twinkle. "You know, Chuck," he had said, "all my career I've encouraged young attorneys to become more personally involved with their clients, but recently I've been reconsidering the propriety of that advice."

He had hired in Richardson's place a brash young lawyer with political ambitions from Cheyenne; already they had appeared twice together on state television and once on a popular Denver talk show.

3

THAT FONTENNELLE HAD what were—to say the least—its suspicions did not trouble him; that it might be justified in having them did. He would lie in bed mornings for a quarter hour or more after waking, feeling himself drifting through tides of sunlight and shadow in uneasy half-sleep and hearing intermittently the cluck of the coffee pot, the fry of bacon, and the soft predatory pad of bare female feet, all the while promising himself that today for certain he would discover the solution to his dilemma.

Finally, after swinging his legs out from beneath the sheets and dressing quickly, he would stalk to the kitchen, where he would find her busy at the stove with her back to him or imperturbable at the table eating the sweet children's cereal she preferred while studying the assortment of incessant mail-order catalogues with such concentration that she would forget to remove the spoon from her mouth after swallowing. Then they would exchange circumspect good mornings and she would bring him his plate and pour his coffee, the pink chiffon robe falling loosely to disclose a plump disconcerting forearm or a soft, pale knee. She had a trick of not meeting his eyes directly; instead, supple and slender, she would pirouette toward him on long, coltish legs, brushing his face insouciantly with her gray eyes while saying in that marvelously dry, diffident voice, "More coffee?" or "Do you want me to fix another egg?"—and he would force himself not to notice the long waist, the shallow, birdlike swell of breast, the unpinned torrent of fragrant mahogany hair.

With every passing week she seemed to him to become more dryly demure and assured. It was youth he was determined to respect even more than propriety: in her presence he felt baffled, world-worn, clumsy, and old—almost, he thought, impure. And yet he was conscious at the same time of being increasingly less the instigator, agent, and director of their situation. With an astonishment that turned quickly to awe and finally to trepidation, he watched this amazing woman-child going from day to day wrapped in her grave, ghost's smile, which seemed simultaneously to reveal and conceal her being, expressed only by that composure he had begun to suspect of being intent; gathering up invisible, unsuspected threads that she proceeded to weave into a visible fabric before his eyes. For days his mind roamed frantically in search of some means of containing her, settling finally on the unanswerable expediency of Dutch uncle.

Her drawings were finding their way about the house—taped to walls, cabinets, closets, and the refrigerator door. She chose from among a range of subjects as profuse as Genesis: men and women, flowering gardens and bowls of ripe fruit, children and animals and sunrises, all of them stamped with what he mistook at first to be a simple consistency of style before he recognized it for something more basic—a coherency of vision itself, as if it were a complete articulated world she was creating instead of dozens of subjects taken at random. He could not have said whether or not they showed talent; it was the recognizable impress that struck him, as if the artist were following in the steps of some large innovator, reinventing and recreating as she went. She had tacked the portrait she had made of him in prison on the bedroom wall where he could see it every morning upon waking.

Fearing that her existence at the ranch was unnaturally, even morbidly constraining to a girl of twenty-one, he took to driving her to the movies in town one or two evenings a week. She would wash her hair and make up carefully and he would put on a clean shirt, and they would drive the ten miles at high speed with the windows down, the hot, unrefreshing air whipping at his turned-back sleeves and tearing the pins from her coiffure, while zinc-colored thunderheads lined with a coppery-green grew like mushrooms above the western horizon. Even before he could shift into first gear she would have the radio going and, like an indulgent uncle, he would sit unprotesting, tolerating the maddening metallic uproar while she sat very straight on the seat like a pointer-dog, holding her chin forward and her hands pressed expectantly between her thighs. He avoided the trailer park with his eyes now, staring directly up the highway as they flashed past the tin barrios that housed a dying empire's gathered flotsam, glancing at her from the corners of his eyes as row upon row of the dismal units spoked by; searching for some flicker of anguish to match his own. Still sweating, he would drive past the square with its lights and dark, kaleidoscopic foliage stirred by the cooling breeze of evening, and the Recreation Center, where long-haired adolescents in punk shirts groped pubescent girls across the fenders of parked automobiles and smirked suggestively at Jenny as she rode past with her nose in the air. They would stop at the ice-cream parlor to buy double-dip cones from a fat girl wearing braces and a dirty uniform who stared rudely at Jenny as she counted out the change, and then cross the road to the drive-in, where he would drink a six-pack of beer while staring glumly at the screen and they both would ignore the panting Laocoön shapes in the neighboring cars. When the feature was over they would drive home more slowly, the radio off, not speaking, not even looking at each other, while heat lightning flickered along the black line of the mountains and his flesh prickled with the electricity of gathering storms.

But when after three weeks she had made no attempt to reach her family in Mosiah he was disturbed. From the little she had told him of her parents he had constructed a sketchy portrait of unadventurous, timid, even frightened people for whom the Church of Jesus Christ of Latter-Day Saints was a defense against a disturbing and incomprehensible world; a shy, withdrawn couple with few friends whom they saw only at church meetings and for whom danger and dissolution lurked in every beckoning pleasure known to young girls of seventeen. But certainly, he thought, they were not intentionally cruel people, deserving of the unnatural contempt in which their only child clearly held them.

She had been a month short of eighteen and three months short of graduation from high school when she found herself en route at three o'clock in the morning to Salt Lake City in a car belonging to a sympathetic girlfriend, carrying only an overnight bag containing two cotton dresses and a change of underwear, a vanity case belonging to her mother, a purse with ten dollars and fifty cents in it, and her father's Swiss army knife, for protection.

In Salt Lake she found a job as a drive-in attendent at a fast-food restaurant and a room in a cheap apartment rented by a female co-worker. On the Fourth of July they bought a case of three-two beer and drove into the mountains to Heber City, where they visited a small circus that had raised a tent on the outskirts of town, and spent the day getting high and flirting with men until, abruptly, she was telling the roommate good-bye and striking the tents with the other hands. They had hired her to work with the horses, but one day, in a piquant mood, she had made a quick sketch of one of the clowns and they had dressed her in crinoline skirts and a bonnet and put her in a booth with a sign over it saying SEE YOURSELF AS OTHERS SEE YOU CRAYON PORTRAITS $1. On Labor Day she was seduced by Harry Worth, who worked as the rodeo star of Paoli Bros. and taught her to smoke hashish. It was a wonderful year under the Big Tent: the stardust glittering in the klieg lights, the costumery that looked real when you looked at yourself in the mirror, the stagey smell of greasepaint, and the dazzling roar of the crowds, which was like a gas being exhaled around you—and then, just when you were getting restless, striking the whole affair, packing and loading it into the thrilling caravan that seemed always to keep just ahead of whatever trouble might be threatening to return you to that unreal and depressing stasis in which the vast majority of people, for whom life was not a circus, lived. For the winter they went south, to California and Flagstaff, Arizona, where, in April, she discovered she was pregnant. Even pregnancy seemed like a joke, especially when Harry Worth found a doctor willing to take care of the problem for two hundred dollars. But in Durango a month later Harry was busted by the Highway Patrol and disappeared, and after that Nick Mahu began to bother her. One night, returning drunk from the ring, he tried to rape her through his ape suit from which he was prevented only by its incomplete design. Finally, in Price, Utah, while sitting one afternoon in the white-and-blue crinoline dress, she looked up to see a puffy-faced woman immediately recognizable as her great-aunt Maude Olsen staring at her, and left town that day without asking for her paycheck, hitching a ride back to Salt Lake where she took a job waiting table at the Wasatch Café. The Wasatch Café was an old-fashioned, high-ceilinged restaurant located in the downtown part of the city three blocks from Temple Square. It had heavy-plated service, portraits of the early presidents on the walls, and specialized in cheap wholesome lunches for old-fashioned Salt Lake businessmen who were rarely in a hurry, preferring to talk leisurely until one or one-thirty over dessert and coffee. At the Wasatch Café she wore a white starched dress, white nurse's shoes, and was an immediate favorite with the customers, who called her "sister," flirted with her clumsily, and left her large tips.

She made friends with a fellow waitress called Maggie, whose brother worked for a drilling company out of Bear

River, Wyoming, and drove to Salt Lake on days off "to party." He would drop into the café around eleven in the morning and sit alone at a table for four, drinking coffee and chatting with his sister until the lunchtime customers began arriving a little before noon. One week he brought with him a man about his own age, but taller and better-looking, whom he introduced as his new motorhand, Seth Weber. That evening the four of them visited the decrepit bars along South State Street, returning afterward to Maggie's apartment in Sandy, where she awoke the next morning with a hangover on a convertible bed with Seth Weber. He hadn't tried anything yet but got right to it after swallowing several Tylenols in a glass of water; he was so persuasive and she felt so sick that finally she let him go ahead. She was bored with waitressing and missed the restless transiency of the circus, so that when he described the oilpatch to her—a lurid, self-contained world of driving metal and violent men whose respite from eight- and sixteen-hour shifts of dangerous strenuosity was eight hours more of fights, liquor, and drugs—she felt a thrill in which, at last, there was nothing of trepidation. After eighteen years lived in an atmosphere of fearful distrust she had learned that fear—or whatever it was that was supposed to lie behind fear—was a lie. She was young, good-looking, and strong—at liberty in a world she had been taught to regard as a tainted oyster but which eighteen months of freedom had proved to be no more dangerous than watching an R-rated movie.

That was where her story ended and mere testimony began, he thought. For the rest of it he had only what she had told him as her attorney, or representative, or *parens in loco parentis*, or whatever capacity it was to which he owed the official account: how she had accompanied Seth Weber to Bear River, where he had introduced her to his supplier, Willie Munger, who proposed that they become partners in first a business, next a home, and finally a mistress. From the facts as he had received them—the square, hard, irrefutable bricks—he could, he believed, construct a convincing defense, or, failing that, entomb the prosecution's case in the airless atmosphere of its own circumstantiality: the trick lay in not walling himself up with his Fortunato. Because the essential mystery, he told himself, was not what had taken place that black irretrievable night but, rather, the life she had led as an integral member of a loathsome ménage à trois, first in Bear River, then in Fontennelle, where they had moved in pursuit of the drilling rigs. He suspected she had confided some—perhaps many— of the details of that existence to Tonio (a suspicion that filled him with inexplicable jealousy). He would lie in bed at night staring at the ceiling that stretched above him like a smothering sky, listening to her light snoring beyond the wall and imagining the trailer squatting on the plot of rank grass, tin cans, and bottles through which stray cats stalked to urinate beneath the unskirted undercarriage. As clearly as if in memory he would see the fetid, sour-smelling rooms with their unmade beds and flung, dirty laundry; the filthy kitchen where food rotted on the stove and in the refrigerator; the customers coming to the door—hard-faced girls, with hard-edged bodies and hair the color of mud; lank young men with ponytails, acned cheeks, and eyes as dead and wrinkled as raisins—while from behind the bit of curtain she watched the idling vehicle and Munger crouched fingering the .38 pistol he carried hidden in his armpit. Then the nightmare changed and he was watching the three of them—two men and a girl—sitting cross-legged on the burn-pitted, filthy carpet, passing a roach between them and bobbing their heads to the beat of insane music, until the gentler-looking of the men began fondling her beneath the unclean T-shirt as the other watched, sardonically at first, then with mounting, yellow-eyed passion.

Then he would be lying in the bed again, sweating into the sheets as he listened to the sound of her easy, childlike sleeping on the other side of the wall.

4

H<small>E HAD ADDRESSED</small> the envelope General Delivery, Mosiah, UT., 84532. Now he folded the letter over slowly and enclosed it; then, after a moment's hesitation, withdrew and reread it. It was a short letter. In a few lines typed single-space on one side of the page he had introduced himself as their daughter's temporary counsel, outlined for them her present status in regard to the courts, and suggested that she be remanded to the custody of her parents while he himself retained every legal responsibility. Refolding the letter, he placed it once again within the envelope, which he licked this time and sealed.

For a while after that he continued to sit at the cramped desk in the still more cramped little room in the lean-to behind the house where he had his office, staring through the wavering, fly-specked glass at the even blue-and-gold of the unequivocal summer day. At last, taking the envelope from the pile of unanswered mail, he tore it methodically into small pieces, which he afterward deposited carefully in the tar bucket he used for a wastebasket. Then, on a fresh sheet of paper, he wrote in large block letters: INDISCRETION IS THE BETTER PART OF VALOR. And anyway, he thought, it's not indiscretion, it's only temptation. He would not be a coward about it. If a letter had to be written, she was going to be the one who wrote it.

After supper that evening, before she could clear away the plates, he told her firmly, "I think it's time you wrote your folks, Jenny."

Scratching the inside of her wrist with a blunt-nailed finger, she pouted at him and squirmed like a twelve-year-old. "I don't want to," she said, and for one awful moment he was afraid she was going to put the end of her thumb in her mouth.

"That isn't the point. And it wouldn't hurt your case one bit to have them there in court, sitting up front of the jury and your mother maybe crying a little on cue."

"*Please*, Chuck. We've been through all this before, *okay?*"

"I want you to listen to me now," he said patiently. "You're not a little girl anymore, you're twenty-one years old, but you aren't going to be able to finish growing up until you learn to come to some kind of understanding with your parents."

"I came to an understanding with them three years ago."

"I don't see any evidence of that."

"That's because," she said, "I did a real good job of it."

He stared at her helplessly across the table and saw that her face, which an instant before had worn the expression of a peevish child, now exhibited the cold, womanly composure that was the Medusa mask of her other, bewildering, and terrifying self. Abruptly she pushed back her chair and began running water over the supper dishes.

"I wish you'd quit trying to act like my dad, or somebody," she told him. "You're not very good at it, for one thing, and I've already *had* a father, for another."

He left the table and for the second time that evening went outside to water the horses. A gentle breeze slapped his face as he stood holding the hose in his hand, watching the moon lurch crazily above the mesa while the cold water poured unheeded over his boots and soaked the cuffs of his pants.

"What are you looking at?" Jenny wanted to know. Her gray eyes were pale with sleep, her freckles emphatic in the early light.

"At you."

"Why me?"

"You're funny."

"Why am I funny?"

"Because you're smiling. You look happy."

"Why does that make me *funny?*" she persisted.

"Because there isn't anything funny about it," Richardson told her shortly.

When they had finished she drew the blanket over his head like a shroud and they lay still together, listening to the morning breeze through the window, warmed by the square of pale light that lay above their twined legs and seemed to emphasize a faint odor reminiscent of bruised flowers. The wind twisted fitfully in the bit of curtain, like a girl fingering a strand of hair.

Then abruptly Jenny sighed. Impatiently she slipped her ankle from his and jerked her knee up beneath the sheet. The cords of her calves felt thrillingly supple; he moved his hand to her stomach and stroked the soft bowl beneath the suspirant cage of her ribs. "Let me up!" she said.

The blanket flapped as her legs kicked out and she stretched across him like an antelope in a blur of white and tan. For an instant she stood, tall, country-solid, but flat-stomached still, her skin tawny, with an underglow like wild honey or the stored cells of the summer's sun. Her head tipped back as if from the weight of her unpinned hair. Then she was gone, and he heard from the kitchen her marvelous dry voice complaining, "I'm hungry," followed by the sudden suck of the refrigerator door.

He continued to lie motionless on his back, waiting for the smell of bacon and watching as the first rays of the sun penetrated the shifting depths of twilight, revealing a distant hill that, as he watched, flared suddenly like discovered gold.

146   *Chilton Williamson Jr.*

5

HE HEARD THE horns first, intermittent on the gusting wind, and then the voices made their entrance and he glanced involuntarily at the late-afternoon sky, a mid-August fantasia of nimbostratus, cumulus, and cumulonimbus on a depthless blue: there was no other place for Wagner to be coming from. He rode on across the creek and through the pasture, came around the barns, and drew rein abruptly at the sight of the car parked in front of the gate—a brass-colored Audi with Teton County plates. He wasn't missing a bar of music now. Christine had always been comfortable with noise.

Working deliberately, Richardson loosened the cinch and carried the saddle and blanket into the tack room. It had been six months since he had seen her last and he would be out of practice after half a year, his Christine technique gone slack. He found a brush and curry and worked the horse over for five minutes before turning it into the corral and throwing in a forkful of hay. The pickup was parked behind the hayrick, which meant Jenny was in the house with her. It made his flesh crawl to think of it.

He approached the Audi gingerly and peered through the open window. She had left the key in the ignition, and on the pigskin seat lay a Shetland sweater, the September *Vanity Fair*, a carton of Marlboros, and an oxblood portfolio by

Hermès. Richardson lowered his head like a bull, thrust his fingers into his jeans pockets, and faced resolutely toward the house, from which sound poured like water from an old bucket.

Jenny sat at the kitchen table wearing clean white Levi's, the hot-pink shirt, and a set expression that made little dents at the corners of her mouth. She glanced at Richardson with studied carelessness as he entered, and inclined her head very slightly toward the parlor, which seemed incandescent with noise. Casually he chucked his hat at the rack and crossed in front of her to the door, where he lounged for a moment on the threshold, gripping the jambs with his thumbs. The instantly ensuing silence was deafening. "Well," Christine said. "If it isn't my long-lost husband, home from the range."

A sleeveless blouse of emerald silk accentuated her deeply tanned throat and arms, against which her hair gleamed in long platinum streaks. Her legs in the immaculate white linen slacks were slender and shortish, and she held the cigarette, from which she took quick, restless puffs, at a rakish angle, shaking the heavy bracelets down her forearms. Looking at the large golden eyes, as steady and unblinking as a cat's, he felt the familiar noose retying itself in his belly. She had responded ambiguously to pursuit, with a tomboy camaraderie beneath which lay a brittle, hysterical sexuality he could not breach, and had endured only by drinking quantities of wine and brandy until she had finally asked him whether he might be developing an ulcer. "I promised your friend in the kitchen I could entertain myself," Christine said, waving her cigarette at the coffee table on which rested an ashtray, a glass, and an elaborate portable tape deck. "I never really cared for Nilsson's Brünnhilde," she added. "Compared to Flagstad, she sounds like a Swedish fishwife."

"The coyotes would probably agree with you about that. They can hear her all the way to the top of Black Butte."

"It's good for them," she replied decidedly. "It expands

their horizons. Do you want to have a cocktail with me? The sun's over the yardarm, as Father liked to say."

He walked back to the kitchen, where Jenny remained at the table, resting her chin on her hand and tapping with the eraser end of her pencil on the wood. In a coaxing voice, he said, "Come and join us, Jen; it's peaceful in there now," but she only shook her head and went on staring through the window. He set Christine's glass on the counter and, placing his hands on her shoulders, began to knead the flesh with his fingertips. "*Won't* you?"

Again she shook her head, impatiently this time, and shrugged his hands away. Richardson poured vermouth for Christine and whiskey for himself, then lifted a third glass from the cabinet. "How about a drink in here, then?"

She had started to draw again and made no reply.

"She won't bite, you know."

"She wouldn't dare," she said, and for one terrible second he found himself wondering if Mrs. Collins had seen her face like that.

He carried the glasses into the parlor and placed them on the coffee table, while Christine fumbled in the wide, capacious, hopelessly disorganized bag of the kind she had carried for sixteen years and finally produced a pack of the Marlboros and a butane lighter. From habit he took the lighter from her, snapped a flame from it, and applied it to the end of the cigarette. Her profile, with its low forehead, straight nose, and square chin, was Roman—patrician blood and assurance stamped upon a perhaps debased coinage. Once he had thought she was lovely. In fact, he still did.

Christine tossed her hair over her shoulder and blew a jet of smoke at the ceiling while the bracelets clashed violently on her smooth brown arms. "Here's mud in your eye!" she exclaimed, raising her glass. "Whatever happened to martoonis?"

"They're still around. When I'm in the mood to drink to trouble."

"You never could handle gin," she reminded him. "I re-member before we were married I used to insist on making you vodkatinis instead."

"It's possible to compromise on the little things—some-times."

Christine tapped the ash from the cigarette and ran her hand lightly along the sofa-back. "Where did you come up with *this* tacky thing?" she demanded. "Mother used to know a Jewish woman in New Rochelle whose husband was an orthodontist and had one exactly like it. She used to keep it covered in clear plastic, all the time. She kept plastic covers on her lampshades, too. It was really gross."

Richardson said, "I bought it on sale at Kay's Upholstery in Fontennelle for a hundred and ninety-nine ninety-nine." He stirred the ice cubes with his finger and considered going back for a freshener.

"I always thought," Christine suggested, "that this house was a tour de force. It takes genius to *think* of filling a log cabin with Chippendale—or maybe the word is *chutzpah*."

"Why not? It's an old frontier expression."

"I wouldn't be surprised. You meet all kinds out here in the territories. My travel agent in Jackson's name is Marty Feldstein. He's from Brooklyn. 'I should be so lucky to go to New York, Mrs. Richardson. Enjoy, enjoy!' "

"Refill?"

"Up to *here*," she agreed, drawing an imaginary line across the glass with a shapely pigeon's-blood nail. "Then I was hoping I could persuade you to buy me dinner in town. I'm broke till my check comes in from Merchant's Trust. What's that place you took me to last year—the one with the super steaks and the natural sense of decor?"

"The Last Chance Saloon."

"That's it," Christine told him. "Not a terribly appropriate name for a bar, do you think?"

He carried the glasses to the kitchen again, where Jenny continued to work at her sketch. "How are you doing, Jen?"

"All right," she said in a cool little voice, screwing up her eyes and cocking her head at the paper.

"We're going into town in a few minutes for dinner. You'd be welcome to join us, but the conversation's going to be deadly."

"That's all right. I'm not hungry anyway."

He bent his head next to hers. "You sure you're okay?"

"I guess so," she said. "Why didn't you tell me she looked like me?"

He started in surprise, but had to admit upon reflection that she was right: they *were* the same physical type. Of course, he thought. It would have to be harder than it seemed to reinvent yourself completely.

When he returned to the parlor Christine had her comb out and was stroking vigorously at her blond mane. Obviously, she had begun using a lightener. She was thirty-six or -seven now, he couldn't remember which. "Cheers," she said, accepting the glass. "Do we have time to listen to this *fabulous* Callas? I taped it last week from a record I bought in New York."

He finished the whiskey while listening to the hate-filled voice dusky with love, too, or at least regret: *Pel tuo dio, pel figlii tuoi . . .* She sat with her feet tucked beneath her thighs and her arm outstretched on the sofa-back, exactly as if they were spending a quiet connubial evening at home, her gaze yellow and even over the edge of the glass, and he thought how fortunate it was they had neglected to produce children. Outside, the prairie went from gold to lavender, fading back to a deep subaqueous blue beneath a paling sky from which the sun had consumed a frail scaffolding of cloud.

She was gone from the table when they came out; the pencils had rolled against the artist's pad and he saw that the door to her room was shut. He suspected that she was behind it, listening.

Christine leaned on her wrists across the table, craning to look at the drawing that remained attached to the pad. "Not bad," she concluded lightly after consideration, speaking around the cigarette that dangled miraculously from her lower lip. "I've always been intrigued by primitives, myself." Shrugging the bag higher on her arm, she stood looking about the kitchen, her eyes shining with yellow irony. Over her shoulder he was able to make out the picture now: a caricature of a platinum blonde with rapacious eyes and a cigarette between her teeth, looking, he thought, like a cross between a barrack-room pinup and the Mother of Harlots. "You two certainly do seem comfortable here," Christine remarked dryly.

In a too-loud, fatuous voice Richardson said, "Jenny knows that this is her home for as long as I continue to represent her or as long as she is in need of a place to live." Preceding her through the door, he hesitated for a moment on the porch, patting his pockets for the keys while two handsome Buff Orpington roosters pecked ants between the cropped yellow blades of the sun-burnt grass.

6

"PLEASE LET'S TAKE my car," Christine suggested. "I don't want to go for a nice dinner in a dirty old truck."

Climbing into the Audi was like putting on an expensive, very closely tailored suit. He tossed the sweater, cigarettes, and portfolio into the back seat, ducked his head beneath the low roof, and sat with his knees drawn up to his chin. The car smelled of cigarettes and the ashtray was stuffed with butts. He had forgotten, however, that they made internal-combustion engines so quiet, and when she snapped on the dashboard radio he was reminded of the egg-shaped stereophonic chair he had tried out for no reason whatever in a Salt Lake showroom. Christine had placed the portable tape deck on the seat between them. She had probably not got around to having one installed yet. Every car she had ever owned had been equipped with a tape deck.

"*What?*" he shouted, seeing that she was trying to tell him something.

"I said, I'm starving and I need a good bottle of wine!"

He went on turning down the volume until he could hear the rattle of gravel in the wheelwells. Fenceposts flew past in the headlights like pieces of a stick house in a tornado and the sea-green shapes of cottonwoods boiled amid clouds of white dust. "For Christ's sake, Christine. Where's the fire?"

Reaching across the seat, she slapped flirtatiously at his knee. "When you've got it, flaunt it!" she squealed. "Don't be such an old stick-in-the-mud, Chuck."

"You'll be flaunting it to the Highway Patrol if you don't slow down some."

"You mean," she demanded, "a big-shot attorney like you can't get me out of a twenty-five-dollar speeding ticket?"

Reclining as best he could in the impossible seat he remained silent and watched the plain stroke past them under an indigo sky powdered thickly with stars and washed with a faint silver-and-green stain along the horizon. In the middle distance the lights of a drilling rig made a glowworm figure against the night, and in another quarter of the prairie the long finger of a locomotive pointed. He saw the terraced benches of the coal mine's backfill, black-on-black, and then the red light of the radio tower beating like a heart above the town.

"God," Christine said. "This is the ugliest country I've ever seen—like the moon. And Fontennelle is an ash dump. How do you *stand* it living here, Chuck?"

"I like it."

"I know," Christine admitted tragically. "Sometimes I wonder whether you really deserve to be trusted with yourself. Do you know that?"

"You've been telling me about it for sixteen years."

"Is it *really* sixteen? I was thinking fourteen. No wonder, then."

"Slow down," Richardson advised her. "You're going to make a left turn at the next light."

He directed her into a space between a mud-crusted pickup and a welding truck wrapped with loops of rubber hose. "How do you suppose they chose *that* name?" Christine wondered, gazing at the neon sign over the porch. "It's a terrible name for a bar. It's a terrible name for *anything*."

Bill Gerhardie crossed smoothly to them on silent rubber

soles. "Good evening, folks!" he said. Briefly he took Christine's hand in his, then grinned at Richardson. "How's life in Jackson this summer—in the fast lane. Table for two? Right this way!" Leading them to a corner table, he gave Richardson another, barely perceptible, smile and left them.

Seated at intervals around the restaurant three other couples ate dinner. In the center of the room seven members of Search and Rescue were drinking beer from gallon pitchers. Seeing Richardson, they saluted him gravely with their glasses. Through the small window into the bar he could see Tonio standing bent over a drink.

"This is kind of neat," Christine said, looking from the stuffed elk head to the Search and Rescue party. "Why are they eating dinner with their hats on?"

"That's good manners in Wyoming—like belching after eating in Arabia."

"Doesn't one of your little tootsies work here?"

"She used to. She's going back to school next month."

"*Really?* An educated tootsie. I didn't think that was your type these days."

"I don't have types, only friends. How do you know about that, anyway?"

"Oh," Christine said, smiling, "a little bird told me." She squinted suddenly across the room. "I think someone's trying to get your attention."

Looking over his shoulder he saw Tonio standing in the door between the bar and restaurant, waggling his fingers and opening and shutting his mouth like a fish. "He looks like a strange duck," Christine said. "Do you know him?"

"It's Tonio," Richardson said. "He's doing some work for me this summer. Will you excuse me for a moment?"

Tonio's eyes were bulging slightly from his head, displaying an inordinate amount of white barely restrained by a net of red veins. His face had that almost unnatural degree of mobility it acquired when he had been drinking, and he held a glass of whiskey in his hand. "What's going on, Tonio?"

Tonio thrust the cap onto the back of his head and rubbed his face vigorously with a broad red hand.

"Almost no tar anymore!" he squeaked. "I finish job tomorrow, after that, no tar left. Maybe not even finish, Chuck!" He rolled on the balls of his feet, staring eagerly at the Search and Rescue party, which was starting to be boisterous.

"I'll buy the tar at Ranier's tomorrow afternoon, Tonio. How are you fixed for material otherwise? Need any more nails?"

"Nails?" Tonio echoed; and Richardson saw that, as far as business was concerned, the conversation was concluded.

"Tonio! I'm asking you—do you want me to buy more nails?"

Tonio removed his cap and ran a big hand over his thick chestnut curls. His blurred eyes shone moistly as he watched the men toasting each other at the big table. "Maybe," he asked, "you get me one of those Search-and-Rescue coats, Chuck? You get me coat, I work for you one whole afternoon—for nothing!" Replacing the cap, he extended a hand to Richardson. "We have deal, hokay?"

Richardson did not understand until he noticed the protuberant eyes fixed on the red-and-black shield printed boldly between seven pairs of broad shoulders. "Jesus, Tonio, I can't do that. You're not supposed to wear one of those things unless you're a member of the unit. Otherwise you'd be welcome to mine, for Christ's sake." He fished two dollars from his pocket and gave them to the waitress. "Tonio would like another Black Velvet and water, okay, Mary?" And to Tonio: "Look, I can't stand here bullshitting. In case you were wondering, that's my wife sitting with me at the table. I'll buy a hundred gallons of tar tomorrow and leave them off at Rendezvous around two o'clock, all right?" He watched the round shoulders disappear into the bar and returned to the table, where Christine was writing with a gold pencil in a small blue-leather engagement book.

"My God," she said. "You mean you actually *pay* that guy to work for you? I'd be scared to death just having him around."

"He's totally harmless. As a matter of fact, Tonio's no idiot, he's really quite intelligent—does excellent work, too. But he's like a child, in some ways. Just now he wanted me to get him one of those S and R windbreakers. He's been trying to join up for years but, like you, it makes the guys nervous having him around."

"S and R?"

"Search and Rescue. I belong to the local unit."

"I seem to recall you mentioning it. What exactly does this exclusive organization do?"

"Finds kids lost in the mountains. Unsticks stuck hunters. Recovers drowned bodies. Every few years they deputize us to help the sheriff's department out. Last fall a plane flew into a mountain fifty miles north of town. We found two pairs of shoes with the feet still in them in what was left of the cockpit and shot a couple of magpies that were eating pieces of brain tissue out of the trees. Gathered it all up in body bags and took it to the coroner's. Last year we got called out twice, the year before twenty-three times. Hunting season's the busiest."

He could not remember seeing her pale before. "How *awful*, Chuck. Don't tell me any more." She shuddered, then looked with sudden interest at the uproarious men in their red-and-black jackets. "So those guys are part of this—this organization?"

"Uh-huh. Probably just come from a meeting. I haven't attended myself for a couple of months."

Again he saw her shoulders quiver before she turned away. "They *look* like normal people," Christine said. "I hope they wash their hands well before eating."

They ordered drinks and sat silently over them for a while. Then Richardson said, "Now that you've mentioned Hal

Pearce, perhaps you don't mind explaining what the hell the idea was sticking your nose into my business again."

"You didn't *have* any business at the time," Christine told him. "Can't we have a nice dinner tonight without squabbling, Chuck? I haven't seen you for six months."

"Okay. I'll say what I have to say better after a bottle of wine, anyway."

"You always could, couldn't you."

Setting his elbows on the table, Richardson stared at the dead stove in which the ashes of spring lay cold. Then he lifted his head and stared for a long while at the glass eyes beneath the spreading rack above the door. The girl returned carrying a bottle and two glasses on a tray. "Hi, Becky," Richardson said absently.

When she had gone he poured the wine and Christine raised her glass. "Cheers," she suggested.

"You bet."

They drank. "You'd never be guilty of learning from experience, would you?" Richardson said.

Rakishly she lifted her chin and blew a jet of smoke toward the elk. "LeRoy was just bad *karma*," she said. "It was you who screwed up this time, darling."

"Bad *karma?*" He set the glass down with a clatter and looked at her in disgust. "Jesus Christ!"

"Anyway," she added, "that was four years ago, Chuck. What kind of an attorney would let a bad case bug him for four years?"

"The kind that doesn't take cases anymore."

"What do you call what you're doing for *her?*"

"Which brings us back to square one, doesn't it." He felt overwhelmed by an iron, a hopeless weariness—the kind that makes drunkards of rakes, crusaders, and philosophers. Timidly, the little waitress offered menus and fled.

"No matter what else," Christine said, "at least you're working at your profession again. You're not a boy any longer, Chuck. Whether you're willing to admit it or not, you sound—look—in better shape than I've seen you since we came out here."

" 'Here' meaning where? And you actually think it's because—" He stopped then and began rolling the stem of the empty glass in his palms. Christine was sitting rigid and straight, her lips slightly parted from her large but very white and even teeth.

"Then *what?*" she asked in a soft, deadly, encouraging voice.

He had been expecting the trap, eager to let himself be taken and to fight his furious way out. Only not quite so soon, he told himself.

"Don't sit there," Christine hissed, "a grown man nearly forty years old, and tell me it's *her.*"

He smiled at the little waitress, who had been standing on one foot gazing importunately at him across the room; she came over quickly and waited with her pencil poised tremulously above the order pad. He ordered for the two of them—twenty-four-ounce New York-cut steaks, home-fried potatoes and tossed salads, and another bottle of the red wine—and returned the menus to the girl, absently maintaining the reassuring smile as he watched the solid brown calves pumping away above the low flat-soled shoes. How many dinners like this had he eaten with her, he wondered. He had loved this woman once; only *had* it been love?—that mad, hysterical dependency upon a projection of his mind, in which she had figured not as the subject but merely as a supporting figure in a tableau, like an expensive advertisement or a frame from a cinematic romance, full of money and what his prep-school imagination had conceived of as beauty. Looking now at her stiff, angry face, he felt like a boy of seventeen or eighteen who has barely avoided a mistake he would have spent the rest of his life paying for.

"What did you *mean?*" she demanded, "taking out that mortgage without consulting me?"

"The ranch is in my name. The Jackson property is yours."

His voice, to his own ears, sounded patient and calm—the patience and calmness not of fortitude but simply of having nothing to lose.

"You know *fucking well* that I wouldn't *dream* of doing anything with that property without talking to you about it first."

Reaching suddenly beneath his chair, Richardson retrieved his hat and placed it firmly upon his head.

"Where are you going?" she demanded.

"I'm going to wear it as long as you keep using four-letter words."

"*Oh, shit*," Christine said. She thrust a cigarette between her teeth and sat holding the lighter in her hand, not thumbing the flint. The waitress came with the new bottle, looking scared while he bit the cork, and poured out wine.

"You fool," she told him after the girl had left them. "Everybody in the state of Wyoming knows she's guilty as sin, just from reading the newspapers. Maybe you didn't know it, but men aren't the only ones who can recognize an easy score when they see one. She spotted you from the word go, buster, and you were dumb enough to fall for a lot of pretty hair or good legs or a nice ass or whatever it is that's given you hot pants. I'll grant you one thing—she's not stupid. I saw *that*, in fifteen seconds."

He had emptied the glass in a swallow and sat now staring at the bottle, holding his head drawn slightly in between his shoulders.

"I absolutely *refuse*," Christine said in a shaking voice, "to sit up there in Jackson while you fritter away our hard-earned money on that murdering little doped-up tramp."

He said, "Like you did on LeRoy?"

He thought she would hit him then, rising from her chair and making a long, slow-motion lunge at him with her arm across the table. But she sat back and took up the wineglass, which glinted, a ruby cyclopean eye, between the shine of her two yellow ones.

"I want a divorce," she said slowly. "They're never going to let us have that annulment."

"I kind of suspected you were leading up to that."

"Well then, *darling*, you shouldn't have. Because, until five minutes ago, I *didn't* want it."

"What did you want?" he asked, and wished immediately afterward that he hadn't.

Christine pushed away her glass, letting her head sink slowly toward the table. "You *idiot*," she whispered. "I wanted us together again."

They ate deliberately, without tasting the food but drinking a third bottle of wine for compensation, and finally Richardson excused himself and went around the corner to the phone booth, where he sat with the door pulled shut, gripping the quarters tightly in his damp fist. *Are you all right?* he would ask; and could almost hear the answer, spoken in her dry, reassuring voice: *Yes, I'm all right. I'm all right. I'm all right.*

7

As soon as he woke he knew that there was something in the world worse than hangover and that he had had the rotten luck to get hold of it. He lay very still in the bed, feeling his body at the center of its cool loneliness and listening to the roosters crowing out of the chill dawn in which the perfume of sage was congealed like wax: vaguely alert to some dim, impending disaster he must identify before it took him unawares. It had, he supposed, something to do with his wife, or ex-wife, or soon-to-be-ex-wife, and he began a slow, queasy search among the events of the past night. After eating, they had had drinks at Al's Supper Club and she had driven him out to the ranch before returning to the motel. He recalled staying silent as the Sphinx for the rest of the evening, while Christine, having committed all of her firepower in the initial assault, had retreated into a cold, brittle politeness.

His mouth was parched, as if every drop of fluid in him had drained into the fragile, throbbing beaker of his brain. He raised himself delicately into a sitting position and swung his feet onto the floor, wincing as he paused for the sloshing pain in his head to subside. Then, very carefully, he stood and commenced a cautious forward shuffle, holding his tremulous hands before him like a stroke victim in search of his cane. After three glasses of water he felt better and thought he would try some coffee.

Her door—flimsy and unpainted, the thin, tympanic panels vertically cracked in silver threads of light—stood partway open, and he had a vision of her the evening before, sitting still as a statue on her bed from which she need not have stirred to hear them. Her presence lay everywhere: heavy, soft, and white as snow; pervasive, unquenchable, and inevitable as dawn itself. It was too late to go back, so he went on.

She was sitting at the end of the parlor in one of the Chippendale chairs, holding her knees under her chin, her pink toes curled owlishly over the seat-edge. The white cotton nightgown was tucked modestly around her thighs and she had cloaked herself further in the dishevelment of her oxblood hair. Dark half-moons lay under her eyes, but her face, though pale, was calm. She gave him a long, tragic look as he entered, and glanced soulfully away.

"How long have you been up?"

"Most of the night."

"Doing what?"

"Thinking."

"About last night?"

"Um."

"It isn't anything to brood about, honestly."

She gave him another long, even look and twisted one finger into her hair.

"Let's have breakfast first, okay?" From the corner of his eye as he left he saw her enfolded in Chippendale, cold and still as the Bride of Lammermoor, wrapped in her blood-red hair.

He cut circles of meat from a roll of antelope sausage and placed them in the frying pan; when the bottom was thoroughly greased he removed the sizzling half-cooked pieces and broke four eggs into the hot fat. He turned them easily, slipped them onto a plate, and placed them in the oven to warm. When he was ready to return the sausage to the pan he discovered he had forgotten the coffee. He emptied the sodden grounds into the sink, added fresh ones, and filled the pot with water. Then he cut two potatoes into slices with his pocket-knife and laid them with the spattering meat. He worked with elaborate concentration, as if his mind were a shallow, overful bowl balanced on the top of his head.

Her presence at his back was like a hovering ghost, but he went on working, vigorously stirring the potatoes with a fork. Finally, without facing her, he said, "Breakfast's ready. Time to chow down."

She did not say a word, but he felt her eyes striking between his shoulder blades. "Come on, Jen," he said, holding out the plate to her. "Let's eat now."

She stood behind one of the tall kitchen chairs, gripping its spooled tops with her hands—staring while he carried the plates to the table and sat. Picking up his fork he began to eat quickly. "That antelope sausage hits the spot," he encouraged her. "Sit down, Jen, and eat, before it gets cold."

"I'm not hungry," she said, pulling out the chair. Tossing her hair over her shoulder, she sat with her chin on her fist and began toying with her fork. "Did you have a good time last night?"

"Christ, are you kidding?" Laying his knife and fork across the empty plate, he shoved the pot toward her. "Coffee?"

"How much did you lose?"

"Lose?" he said, not understanding at first. "Not a red cent, yet. But she asked for a divorce, so we're going to have to work out some sort of settlement soon." He tried a laugh. "I'll end up handling my own divorce case, I suppose. The ABA hasn't got around to classifying do-it-yourself divorce as a conflict-of-interest problem yet."

She said, carrying her uneaten breakfast to the sink: "You make out pretty good with this conflict-of-interest thing, don't you?"

He started to tell her, "You know that's a rotten, unfair thing to say," and choked on it. The worst thing, he thought, about being half a decent person was that it was impossible to be certain at a given moment which half of you was doing the talking.

He heard the door to her room slam as he went to rinse the dishes. When she came out again she had on her riding outfit—jeans, cowboy boots, and the new straw hat he had bought her—and walked straight past him onto the porch without a look. Elbow-deep in hot water, he watched her cross the yard in long, boyish strides, striking the leather bat impatiently against her leg, her body slightly rigid with an uncharacteristic stiffness. After she had ridden out in a spool of yellow dust he returned to the bedroom and lay on his back with his eyes shut, waiting for the headache to break before driving into town for tar and roofing nails.

When he woke the window was filled with the white glare of midday, but his head felt fine. The sun-burned prairie rolled in harsh yellow folds to the horizon, where an equally harsh sky met it without gap or buckle, impervious as the boundary between irreconcilable countries. There was no sign of Jenny and, after standing for a time with his hands in his pockets squinting against the light, he went out to the pickup and drove off slowly. It seemed appalling that this vast emptiness could be as much a witness as Cambodia or Westchester County, but in that, at least, Hal Pearce had hit the nail on the head. He had not, after all, run far enough.

8

CONTRAILS CROSSED AND recrossed overhead like packing cord as he drove into town past the cemetery, which appeared with the suddenness of an apparition from behind the cutbank, gay with its bright flowers, well-watered lawn, and neat graveled paths among which the two fresh graves, conscientiously decorated with paper flowers twined on wire frames, awaited headstones. It had occurred to him that he should visit them, but each time the fear of meeting relatives had dissuaded him. He passed the cemetery now without turning his head and drove directly up to the loading dock behind Ranier's Lumber & Building Supply.

Richardson enjoyed hardware and supply stores, where he could savor the dangerous odor of new steel, the pungent springtime smell of paint and shellac, and the faint, dying one of grain dust and old flypaper. He liked discovering ingenious modifications made in gadgetry in whose design the most primitive of human artifacts were discernible, experiencing, as he handled these implements of rudimentary human competence, a gratifying sense of solidarity. The warehouseman was a fat, sweaty, red-faced youth with bristling nostrils. Wiping his flowing nose with a wadded bandana handkerchief, he goggled at Richardson in rheumy curiosity. "Ain't seen you around town in a dog's age," he said. "Been keepin outa trouble?"

"More or less."

The fat youth nodded sagely, as if his discretion were something to be counted upon. "Well, you have a good one, now."

For weeks the dry, parching heat had been rising. Now, at midday, the town lay suspended in a still white glare through which occasional traffic crawled beneath the motionless cottonwoods, heavy with dust and fatigue, trailing their listless branches over the gray frame buildings. He drove on to Rendezvous Motors, where he offloaded the tar and carried it up to the roof, setting his teeth against the wire handles cutting his palms and the black sticky residue which, after eight weeks of clean, untarred hands, had become positively offensive to him. When he had got rid of all of it, he sat in the pickup for a minute to watch a dust-devil whirl down the adjacent alley like a beckoning yellow wraith. Then, releasing the clutch, he let the truck roll very gently downhill, in quiet pursuit.

Gravel popped beneath the tires, and he could smell the mingled odors of roses, cut grass, and creosote. This gridwork of narrow bisecting lanes was Fontennelle's bid for an historical past: a charming, almost eerie, remove from the modern facades and manicured lawns fronting the wide paved streets. It was a town within a town, a rich compost of unpainted, dilapidated outbuildings built long ago to accommodate horses and buggies and Model-A Fords; sections of collapsing board fence alternating with iron railings and gates hanging by a hinge under the poignant heart-shaped leaves of ancient lilacs and leggy untrimmed roses; scrappy gardens of lettuces, onions, radishes, Swiss chard—whatever flourished in a growing season of eight or ten weeks and a soil compacted of clay, coal-dust, and rotting scrap-iron—planted between borders of old railroad ties; the humped backs of rusting automobiles; and, now and again, a retired sheepherder's wagon, its tongue dragging and toy chimney bent in dismay, oxidizing like an outsized tin can set in a warped bed on broken wheels.

Richardson drove slowly along the alley, occasionally raising from behind a sagging gate a dog whose outraged barking could not dispel the peace that had settled so strangely and suddenly upon him. He reached the cross-street, paused, and glided across to the next corridor of gravel, lilac, and weathered board. Above him thunderheads were piling, their flat bottoms turning quickly from copper-green to livid purple as they built upward toward the climax that for four rainless weeks had proved elusive. Smears of moisture hung from them like nets lowered slowly toward the ground before being snatched back abruptly, leaving only the murmurous thunder and the scent of rain. In one of the crabbed back yards an elderly lady, gray-haired and petite, was filling a marble birdbath from a garden hose. He recognized her instantly: Why, that's Mrs. Collins, he thought.

He hit the brake-pedal so hard he stalled the engine and had to fumble madly, jerking the shift-arm and pounding the accelerator with his boot, to put it back in gear. She came toward him, drawing out the serpentine hose behind her, as, paralyzed, he stared in horror from the truck. Her eyes were round and very blue, calm and farseeing as a nun's. "Aren't you," she asked, "the young man who is defending the girl who killed my sister?"

It being not only painful but supremely unnecessary to do so, he did not answer her.

"I've been considering writing you a letter," she added, "but perhaps this way is better. May I give you some coffee, or a little tea?"

He left the truck in the long grass against the fence and followed her, obedient, across the beautifully tended yard—like an oasis, he thought—and through the back door.

"Sit down," she invited, pointing at the kitchen table, on which a cut-glass vase filled with yellow tiger lilies rested in the center of a cloth of spotless filigree. "I just stepped into the yard while I was waiting for the water to a boil. Will tea be all right?"

"Yes, thank you, ma'am," he told her.

He watched as she poured water from the kettle into a round pot patterned with blue cornflowers and took a matching sugar bowl and creamer from the shelf, moving with quick, dipping, birdlike motions: a trim little woman with a tiny waist, wearing a well-cut lavender dress, rather low at the neck. The kitchen, he observed, was spotlessly clean. Geraniums grew in pots in the windows and a cage containing a pair of blue parakeets hung on a hook from the ceiling. On the wall opposite, a statue of the Virgin, made of plastic so yellowed with time it looked like ivory, stood on a little wooden platform.

"I'm sorry," she said, placing the pot and two cups and saucers on the table. "I shouldn't have said 'killed.' I'm afraid I have anything but a legal mind."

"I understand."

"After all," she added, "it wouldn't be a world if everyone thought the way lawyers do, would it?"

She poured the tea, then reached on tiptoe for a box of cookies on the shelf. Making a circle of them on a blue-and-white china plate, she placed them before him. "Please take several," she encouraged, as if he were a child of ten having afternoon tea at a maiden aunt's. Through a door that opened into the parlor he saw the curled arm of a Victorian sofa and a bookcase filled with heavy dark-blue and plum-colored volumes stamped with rubbed gilt lettering.

"You are a courageous man, Mr. Richardson," Mrs. Collins's sister said. "Perhaps a wrongheaded one, we shall see. Or then again, perhaps we won't see."

"Your name is Mrs.—?"

"Tyrrell—Miss Tyrrell. Lisa Tyrrell. I'm sorry, I should have—"

"No," Richardson corrected her. "I should have. I would have remembered in another minute."

She poured the tea, gripping the handle of the pot with a blue-veined hand that looked itself as if it were made of the same old porcelain. The steam seemed to him to enhance the odor of lavender that hung like a color—like twilight—about her. "I know it's early," she said, "not to mention hot. But would you care for whiskey in that?"

All at once he felt at ease—almost pleased to be there. "Am I going to need it?"

"Mr. Richardson," she said, looking at him severely over the rim of her cup, "you are a guest in my house this afternoon. Please remember that, as I shall. If you would truly care for whiskey with your tea I'll be happy to oblige you. I myself have a double whiskey-soda every afternoon, but never before five o'clock."

"No thank you," he told her, sipping the tea, which was gold rather than red in color and addressed itself, palely, to his olfactory senses. "Just plain will be fine." Tasteless as it was, the hot drink emboldened him. "How is it you happened to recognize me?"

"Oh," Miss Tyrrell said, raising her eyebrows, "I've been noticing you around town for the past two months. I've been keeping a scrapbook, you see."

"A what?"

"Wait," she said, rising, "and I'll show you."

He heard the sound of a drawer coming open in the next room and then she returned carrying a discount-store album, which she placed before him on the table. The cover was printed in yellow and blue and had a church steeple on it surrounded by wreathed flowers twined with bells, above which the slanted looping letters read: *A Very Special Day*. Opening it to the first page, he started violently, spilling tea into the saucer and over the pristine cloth.

"Take this," she said calmly, handing him a paper napkin, and he dabbed violently at the spreading stain the color of thin blood, casting as he did so a desperate glance through the window, where the afternoon light was like smoked glass behind which swallows plunged along the level of the roof-tops.

"Look at it," Miss Tyrrell said, and he began slowly turning over the pages, which appeared to contain every photograph, every news article, he had ever seen or read about the murders. She had pasted in the *Time* clipping, too—that column of print broken in the middle by the terrible AP photograph of the three of them being led in handcuffs from the arraignment, their hair of nearly equal length, and hanging stiff and straight as icicles about the haggard faces.

"I believe I would like some time to meet the girl," Miss Tyrrell remarked.

He stared at her almost beseechingly, but she seemed not to notice.

"Don't you see?" she demanded. "We are skeptics, you and I, but we are wagerers as well: perhaps we are wagerers *because* we are skeptics. If I were a man, professionally qualified and not both a sister and an aunt, I would do as you are doing—I think. That is why I would like some time to meet her—not to see whether I am right but just in the hope of maybe finding a clue. That's all we can ask for, you know—only a clue."

He could only stare at her, as she continued:

"It's because women are before evil, which they have never really known, experienced, since they are the carriers of evil rather than its instruments. Women are like organisms that transmit disease without ever developing it themselves. They receive it like mosquito bite or by impregnation, and eventually it passes through and out of them as a parasite passes through a horse and for a while they are clean again, until the next time. That doesn't make them less dangerous, of course. Probably it doesn't even make them what we would call innocent. It just makes them—shall we say, impervious?"

He had been holding the rim of the empty cup against his teeth, and she interrupted herself to extend the teapot.

"Because," she continued, "why else would women exist?

What use do you think they would be? When anyone can tell simply by looking at them—those sagging, wide-hipped and narrow-shouldered bodies meant for pain and afterward, if there is anything left over, for love—that they are good for nothing else but to preserve—I don't say propagate—the species?"

Turning halfway around in the chair, she pointed to the yellow Virgin on Her cracking, desiccated platform. "What use are we told *He* made of them? In fact, perhaps it is not *He* at all. Perhaps, from the very beginning, it was *Her*." She paused, holding her head to one side as if listening to a playback of herself. "It horrified my poor sister to hear me talk like that," she added. "Catherine was a devout woman— very orthodox. I'm sure she considered me some kind of theological feminist, as if what I was talking was politics or theology instead of just plain endurance—the promise of a human future with or without God." A smile came onto her face and she glanced at him archly—almost, he thought, flirtatiously. "When I lived in France the men would describe an attractive woman this way"—as, giving a long, astounding wolf-whistle, she described with her hands the voluptuous outlines of an imaginary urn.

"You lived in France?" he asked, desperately seeking pause in irrelevancy.

"Yes," Miss Tyrrell replied. "I lived in France and Italy for many years and a while in Barcelona. I went to Europe to become a nun and stayed to become a doctor and returned to Fontennelle without ever becoming either when an uncle died and left me this house. Now I do not try to be anything. Have you noticed how out here, where the state boundaries were surveyed like enormous picture frames that seemingly frame nothing, how everything is magnified by a quality of light until it expands beyond the picture to contain the entire universe? Or, perhaps, like those paintings in which the picture is actually a reflection of itself, the subject receding in infinite planes toward the infinite center of the canvas?"

"Yes," Richardson—whom Christine had taught nothing at all of painting—said.

"I suppose," Miss Tyrrell continued, as if the idea had just occurred to her, "that is why I returned after all to Fontennelle—because I was tired of looking at the woods and just wanted to stand still and take a long look at a single lonely tree. Of course I regret," she added dryly, "that two of those trees had to be my sister and favorite niece."

"I'm sorry," Richardson said, staring at the tea fragments that were settling at the bottom of his cup like leaves in a shallow grave.

"That's all right now," she told him, in a harsh, startling voice. "Don't be sorry about *me*—don't even be sorry about *them*. That isn't your business, not your burden. Worry about *her*—and after that, yourself.

"Well," she finished after a silence, rising from the table. "There's more tea if you want it, but I suppose I ought to be offering you the opportunity to make your escape." The sky had lightened to the color of a bad lemon and the humped black clouds marched down the horizon like a herd of surly disappointed elephants.

"Thank you, Miss Collins—Tyrrell. I've enjoyed our conversation, and you were right about the whiskey. It would have been overkill. Perhaps we can talk again sometime."

"Of course," she said. "Come anytime. I do very little but read and watch the sky, which in this country is like reading one of these big Victorian novels with all the characters subtracted from it. Or like listening to the music of Herr Wagner. Do you like Wagner, Mr. Richardson?"

"Not particularly."

"Well, I do," she told him. "I used to go to hear his operas when I lived in Europe, but they don't seem to have meant anything to me until I was home in Wyoming again. I don't own a phonograph, so I have to hear them in memory now. I have an amazingly good memory for music."

"Yes," he agreed. "They are better that way."

"Well," she said again, and moved toward the door. "I mustn't keep you any longer. But the weather at least has improved while we've been talking, hasn't it?" She laid her little porcelain hand on the knob, standing erect before him but very small, so that abruptly he found himself looking into a gray mottled runnel between dry shriveled paps haltered in pale silk and between which a silver crucifix rested. Recoiling a step, he felt his cheeks burn with shame, or revulsion.

"Yes," she said simply, taking his eyes with hers. "I'm short on Faith perhaps, and more so I'm afraid on Charity, but somehow I've managed to hold onto Hope."

He felt embarrassed still, but she was not even thinking of him now, he saw, as she gazed over his shoulder and beyond with the pale, farseeing eyes that seemed the reflection of the world in two drops of blue water. "Do you know," she said to nobody in particular, "she *fascinates* me?"

He started the truck and continued on at a snail's pace down the alley, not looking back until he reached the cross-street. She had come into the back yard again and stood holding the hose above the parched lawn, gazing at it intently, as if examining it one blade at a time.

9

Judge Thurlow sat behind the ample desk, holding a sheet of paper in his square, rather small white hand as he stared through the window at the pointed black tops of the fir trees: from his third-floor chambers he had the impression of being able almost to walk on them. The law, somebody—some writer—had said, is an ass. Whoever it was that said it had had his head screwed on straight. They should have made him a Federal judge. The morning sun on the glass front of the high walnut bookcase that housed his library shone with the limpid, outrageous purity of light reflected from a mountain spring and offended him mortally in his present mood of black and hopeless despair. Many years ago he had discovered that the antidote for despair was mortal despair. Well, he assured himself coldly, he possessed the means of spreading it around.

Of course the law was an ass—from Justinian to Blackstone, from Marshall to Holmes to the bitch they had appointed to the Court for the absolutely sole reason that she divided below the belly. Trust the English—it was, he seemed to recall, an English writer—to make of a platitude a pearl of wisdom. He had hated the months he had spent with the army in England during the war—hated the warm thin beer and the cold gray rain and the women, whose calves were perpetually red from backing up to coal grates and who called you "Yank" after eating up your bundle from home. Women were bitches, but English women were the greatest bitches of all. A man could forgo liquor, tobacco, tea, and coffee, but Brigham Young himself couldn't forgo women. Now they were telling you from East North Temple to have twelve kids, all of whom might just as easily be female. Jesus Christ, the judge thought. They must be crazy in Salt Lake these days.

The red light on the telephone winked silently. He ignored it and continued to stare through the window as if he were trying to face down the sun, which continued, nevertheless, to mount buoyantly into the sky like a child's balloon. The telephone stopped flashing and then the buzzer on the corner of the desk went off. He laid the sheet of paper—which he had just finished reading for the third time without having understood a word of it—on the crisp leather-edged blotter and brought his fist down on it with a crash that rattled the glass panes of the bookcase, causing the sun behind him to ripple and flash in liquid mockery. He pushed the button with his thumb and barked, "What is it now? . . . . No, I do not wish to speak with Mr. Bates this morning. . . . Tell him I have court in exactly one hour and if he wants to talk to me he'll have to get off his butt and come in this afternoon." Court was scheduled to convene in less than an hour now and he still had this son-of-a-bitch motion to decide on. He took up the paper and, holding it close to his face, tried again to read. The sun glared in the corner of his left eye like a klieg, focused by an outrageous conspiracy of heaven. The journalists and the politicians talked as if the judicial complexity of a case were in direct proportion to its notoriety, which might or might not accord with what they honestly believed. One way or the other it was crap, not a judicial approach: justice was a qualitative, not a quantitative, matter. It was also a simple one: either people deserved to get it, or they did not. More and more he was coming to understand that they did not. Not only was there no justice, there was scarcely a human being alive worthy of it.

With an effort, he steadied his trembling hand and squinted once more at the page. The pills the doctor had given him seemed to exacerbate his nerves instead of soothing them. Wadded in cotton, they came two to the bottle, an outrageous extravagance the cost of which the pharmaceutical companies naturally passed along to their customers. It would be gratifying, he reflected, to preside over an unfair-pricing hearing and throw the book at them.

"IN THE DISTRICT COURT," he read: "FONTENNELLE, BRIDGER COUNTY, WYOMING, STATE OF WYOMING, Plaintiff, vs JENNIFER GRACE PETERSEN, Defendant, NOTICE OF MOTION TO DISMISS. . . ." Impatiently he rifled the pages, scanning the arguments which seemed to him this morning to have even less plausibility than he had recognized the previous evening when he had read them through quickly in his study, shading his smarting eyes with one hand and pressing the right pinna with the forefinger of the other to shut out the sound of his wife's stifled sobbing from the next room. He read, but did not read, caught in the thrall of concentration's opposite, as if the brain's electrons, rather than focusing in a single laserlike beam, were instead spreading outward in a shotgun pattern. At the bottom of page four he read: "By (s) Caleb North Richardson, Attorney (Acting) for Defendant, R.F.D. 7, Fontennelle, WY 81090."

He knew the man for a fool if not worse: an aging hippie from somewhere back East. He didn't like the fellow, didn't trust him. There was an indefinable arrogance about him that made you itch to have him up before you in court. He was the sort of person who might never commit any actual breach of law or the public morals beyond earning a few DWI citations, yet would nevertheless, by the simple fact of his presence, undermine the decency and wholesomeness of whichever community he might elect to confer it upon.

He was himself, he recognized, in no small part to blame. He should not have relented—not have let the fellow off the case but held his feet to the fire instead. But who in the *hell*, he thought, with a feeling of outraged astonishment nearly as fresh as when he had first learned of the fact—who in the hell would have guessed that, once released from the case, he would walk straight into it again by the back door, with the murdering little bitch on his arm?

He dropped the document on the desk and rested his elbows upon it, pushing his spectacles onto his forehead to rub the chafed place over the bridge of his nose. Life was so damned unfair—so cruel, so without scheme or reason both, forcing you to doubt at the age of fifty-four all that you had ever been taught of hope, faith, belief. He sat thinking of this Jennifer, runaway from a decent, law-abiding family, and of his own daughter. My God, he told himself, but they're nasty little animals. And yet he had trusted, refusing to believe when his wife met him in hysterics, until he had actually read the crumpled sheet she thrust at him—promissory note of her shame and their own.

The phone flashed silently again but he continued to ignore it. His robe hung on a peg in the corner: in twelve minutes he would have to wear it into court, like a corpse presiding at its own funeral. He opened the bottom drawer of his desk and took from it, facedown, a framed photograph of a girl of about twelve. In the bland, smooth face there had been no clue, he thought, of the young woman to come—of the future tucked within the childish soul like a cancer seed. Perhaps the cells of the heart were like any other cells: growing, dying, being replaced by new ones that both were and were not coidentical with the old. Perhaps that was well enough for mere flesh and bone. But not for the heart, which, as guardian and guarantor of human hope, was—or ought to be—changeless, invulnerable, and inviolate.

Selecting a pen from the walnut-and-brass holder before him, he wrote across the top of the first page in even block letters MOTION DENIED. Then he rose slowly out of the deep leather chair and, crossing the room, took the robe from its peg and began pulling it over his shoulders. The sun had climbed above the window, and gradually he felt something of peace returning. If he had decided wrongly, there was always time to reconsider. Smiling, he recalled a session five or six years previous in which he had begun by ruling against everybody, creating such havoc that it had taken the rest of a week to undo—by the simple expediency of self-reversal —the damage he had accomplished in six hours.

10

THE OFFICIAL EMBOSSED lettering at the top left corner was like braille under his thumb as he tore the envelope and removed the long legal sheets, neatly folded and stapled at one corner. Sitting behind the wheel with his elbow out the window, he read them quickly through before refolding them into the ragged envelope, which he thrust into his shirt pocket. Then he closed the mailbox and began driving at high speed toward town.

Black-eyed daisies threshed above an endless border of green beside the highway, and the prairie undulated in long russet waves as the redtop grasses bent before a yellow wind. By the time he reached the outskirts of Fontennelle the sky had hardened to a smoked-glass opacity and thunderheads like ice castles were driving down from the west, billow over-thrusting upon billow. He swept into the speed zone at seventy-five, cursing in his heart the square, shabby houses clinging to the hills like cats to a pitched roof, the storefronts with their blank, impenetrable windows that seemed to dare whatever smug paterfamilias brooded over them to assert himself now against the alien, the incorrigible outlaw he was and ever would be. Uniform in frowning limestone, the bank, city hall, and post office stood shoulder to shoulder against him, while behind and above them all Lady Justice—whore, idol, witch—trod as serenely as if it were not spiked iron she walked on but a path of gold and onyx stone through a garden oasis. Going up the courthouse steps three at a time, he could see the storm clouds standing like whorled marble at her back, while the wind hurled gouts of dust into his eyes and mouth.

He burst in on the secretary without bothering to knock. "I need to speak to the judge as soon as possible."

Coldly she took in the tar-stained pants (supported this afternoon by a length of rope), the faded denim shirt with its frayed collar, the fierce eyes beneath the thick gunmetal hair. "I'm sorry, Mr. Richardson," she told him, "but Judge Thurlow is in court now. Would you care to leave a message for him?"

Drawing the envelope from his shirt, he waved it under her nose. "It's about this—this *obscenity*. What does *he* call it—frontier justice or rustic chivalry?"

"The judge feels he had no choice other than to decide as he did, Mr. Richardson. If you wish to make an appointment to discuss it with him that might be arranged—perhaps. Meanwhile I can assure you that he has conscientiously considered the points listed in the motion—as well as, of course, the ones Mr. Pearce offered in his argument for denial."

Contemptuously he stared at her—a plump little woman of perhaps fifty-five with gray hair, a large bosom, and ridiculous spectacles on a black silk cord: a woman who doubtless had shuffled between clerical jobs in that same courthouse most of her working life and considered the judge more a son than an employer, despite the fact that the difference in their ages could not have been greater than five years.

"Of course," he said bitterly. "Mr. Pearce's brief makes it chivalry, then."

He left the building and ran through a rattle of hailstones to the truck, where he sat with the motor running, watching ice ricochet from the hood like BB pellets. Overhead the sky was a livid fuchsia, and the hills beyond the river were veiled in clouds of yellow dust. His watch said twenty past two— a little early as yet for a drink he thought, before it occurred to him that, after five years, he was a failed lawyer again and that failed lawyers have only two choices: drink, or politics. That settled it then: he would drink. But damnit, he thought, if I'm going to get drunk in broad daylight, I'm at least going to be honest about it and not hide out in the dark like a badger at the end of a tunnel. Three minutes later he had parked the truck outside the plate-glass windows of Al's Supper Club, a modern single-story restaurant built to the specifications of an automobile showroom, and found a place at the bar between a frail, white-haired man with scarlet-threaded cheeks, and a much younger man in jeans and a motorcycle T-shirt whose sharp hostile features showed, beneath the submerged expression, every sign of meaning trouble once the insulation of alcohol should wear off.

Because he had to break through the stale, guilt-laden atmosphere all bars have by daylight and that only drunks ever learn to ignore, Richardson drank the first martini quickly, watching the bartender—a heavy bald man in an Hawaiian shirt whose name he could not remember—follow the ballgame on TV, while the cocktail waitress stood on one foot at the service bar, sucking Coca-Cola through a straw. When he finished the drink he ordered a second one, which the bartender mixed and shook slowly, without taking his eyes from the screen.

"Jesus Christ!" he said, shaking his large head vigorously so that the Hawaiian shirt rotated a full quarter-turn on his belly. "What a run—what a *run!* Looks like they got 'em clobbered now, all right. Who're you bettin on?" he asked.

Richardson said, "On the clobberers, but I'm rooting for the clobbered." Turning his back abruptly, he rested the glass on his knee and watched the storm: a purplish-black mass in violent downward eruption, brilliantly stitched with lightning, through which raindrops plopped monstrously to raise small explosions of dust that the ensuing drops dampened instantly. Like weeds in a river the aspens streamed upon the wind, in which birds also whirled, and twigs, and bits of paper; while through the sealed glass the thunder crashed remotely as if it were no more than part of the afternoon's entertainment, carefully monitored for his listening pleasure.

He drank until the storm cleared and the day outside grew mellow with five o'clock, as the gin replaced the darkness of the bar with a glare that filled his head like white sound. Above the hills the sky showed a washed blue with a faint pattern of high cloud like the fading wake of a great ship, while the round leaves of the aspens glittered tremulously. Beside him a wizened man with a grizzled beard and a straw hat pounded his fist on the wood and yelled "Bullshit!" at the television, where the ballgame had been replaced by a commercial showing a woman rubbing baby-oil on herself after showering. For the first time that he could remember, wormwood and gall had let him down—badly. On the spur of the moment, Richardson decided that it was time to leave now.

He walked straight into her on the way out—or, rather, into her table, where she sat holding a glass and facing an empty chair. She wore the same sharply severe expression that was as material a part of her features as her nose and chin, the same black-and-white outfit set off by the same coral necklace she had worn last May, and it occurred to him that, while it must be rather warm for mid-August, it was exactly like her not to have noticed.

"Hi," Mary-Elena said, looking at him over the glass. "Do you have time for one more drink before you go?"

He sat obediently opposite her, too dull and astonished to offer an excuse.

"What are you drinking?" she asked. The evening light from out of doors made a halo of fire around her dark head, and he saw by her eyes that she was a little drunk. Lifting her arm in a classical gesture, she signaled with a scarlet-tipped finger to the cocktail waitress. "He'd like a Tanqueray martini very dry, straight up with an olive," she ordered; adding, after the girl had gone, "How's that for a memory?"

"Not too bad."

"You see?" she said knowingly.

He didn't see and so he said nothing, staring morosely past her at the door. The waitress came with the drinks, and Richardson laid a five-dollar bill on her tray. "Thank you!" the girl brayed, moving on to the next table.

Smiling, Mary-Elena raised her glass in a toast. It was not a bad smile, he thought, for somebody so out of practice.

"Cheers!"

"Cheers."

This time the drink tasted better. "Where's Pearce this evening?" he asked.

"He's in Cheyenne until tomorrow night. I took the afternoon off. My first since June."

"I see."

"It's been terrible," Mary-Elena said. "You know about Willie Munger, don't you?"

"I don't think so. What?"

"They were supposed to take him to Bear River today for further observation. He's been acting completely off the wall for several weeks."

"That part I was aware of. I didn't know Thurlow had ordered a second examination."

"He did yesterday morning, at Wainwright's request. Hal couldn't talk him out of it. He's convinced that Munger is 'dangerously sane,' as he puts it. Last week someone at the jail let him make a phone call, and Hal hit the ceiling. He's been reading the papers in his cell and talking about how he's going to get the people who are trying to do this to him. Hal thinks he still has plenty of contacts outside he's trying to get through to."

"I didn't hear about that call." Something at the back of

his mind stirred faintly as he took a long pull at what tasted like raw gin.

"I suppose you heard from Thurlow today," Mary-Elena said after a pause. Her voice, he thought, sounded ever so slightly smug.

"Uh-huh."

"I called Hal in Cheyenne this morning and told him about it."

"He must have been very pleased."

"Yes," she said. "He put a lot of work into that brief."

"Good for him."

After another pause Mary-Elena said, almost gently, "You must have been prepared for it to go that way, Chuck."

"An attorney is always prepared to see the law turn against an innocent client."

"You know," she told him, "it took me a long while to realize that the tough-guy, cynical pose was really just an act. At heart you're even more of a crusader—a believer—than Hal. The trouble is you've denied your own nature so long you've been unable to develop your best instincts, which makes you a pushover for people like Jenny Petersen. Of course Hal believes you're just what he calls *susceptible*, but I've come to the conclusion it isn't as simple as that."

"That's sweet of you."

"I probably have no business telling you this," Mary-Elena said, "but what you need to do is find one of these feminist lawyers to represent her. She could work a lot of psychological angles you probably don't suspect even exist. I suppose Hal would fire me if he could hear me talking to you like this," she added.

"I would if I were he."

She leaned toward him on her elbows, her long back curved tautly like a big cat's. Alcohol had loosened her face without softening it, and her eyes were black and ferociously alive. He felt her palm, dry and light as a cat's paw, on the back of his hand.

"Would you?" she asked quietly. "Among other things, Chuck, you *are* susceptible."

For an instant he thought, Why the hell not? As a means of sticking it to Hal Pearce the idea had a diabolical ingenuity worthy of a Renaissance prince. He smelled her hot liquorish breath on his face, and he drew his hand away. "Time to quit now," he said, swallowing the last of the gin and pushing back his chair.

"I'll leave with you," Mary-Elena said, reaching beneath the chair for her pocketbook. "My God—do they have a zoo like this in here every evening?"

The bar was crowded with loud, jostling men, and she seized his hand as he plunged among them and fought toward the door through which more customers were arriving. When they reached the foyer Mary-Elena said, "Wait!" She placed a light hand on his shoulder while, standing on one foot, she ran a finger along the instep of her shoe as he stood helpless under her fragile weight, watching the evening light like pink champagne drain from the sobering hills. Abruptly she gave a little shriek and came down hard on his foot. "That *animal!*" she cried. "That one in the red shirt going into the bar. He just . . . *patted* me!"

Richardson closed on him in three steps. "A word with you, my friend," he said; and, when the man turned, swung. It had been a long time since he had hit anyone, had felt human weight on the end of his arm; and it was a good feeling, he discovered, a wonderful feeling—better even than the exaltation of gin. He had taken an easy step backward to admire his handiwork, which lay broken at the waist against the cigarette machine with its hat knocked off and its chin on its breast, when he became aware of a gathering presence behind him and after an instant's hesitation turned gamely to face it. He came to lying on his back on the floor, surrounded by a crowd of people with drinks in their hands and straddled by a pair of khaki legs against which a sturdy, hand-polished stick swung easily from a leather thong. Somewhere he could hear a woman, who might or might not be Mary-Elena, sobbing quietly.

Its tires hissing faintly and intermittently over the damp patches of pavement left from the storm, the patrol car bore him rapidly across town through an indeterminate twilight that could have been equally the harbinger of dusk, or dawn.

11

THE STARLINGS WERE making their final settling sweep as they approached the courthouse, swooping upon clouds of insects circling the streetlights which reflected in still yellow ripples across the black windows. The patrol car came around the square and made an abrupt stop before the jail, which, with its long cream-painted decks separated by bright intervals of glass, resembled even more at night a cruise ship immobilized in concrete. Across the street other patrollers idled by the curb, their light-bars lashing the twilight, while on the sidewalks khaki-suited deputies sauntered over a litter of damp leaves and twigs, holding walkie-talkies clapped against their ears. The blow he had received seemed to have cleared his head, and it occurred to Richardson that the reaction on the part of the sheriff's department was somewhat incommensurate with the simple, time-honored act of one man using his fists against another in defense of female modesty.

Deputy Smith slid from behind the wheel and, after pausing briefly to remove his cap and pat casually at his pale yellow hair, unlocked the rear door. "Get out," he said in a hard voice; and, gripping him tightly by the elbow, hurried him past the gawking bystanders into the lobby with its flat lighting that seemed to pervade everything while illuminating nothing. In one corner a wiry little man with long mustaches was calling the Cowboy Bail Bond, and beside the soft-drink machine a covey of grim-faced officers made change for each other and fingered their guns.

"What's going on here tonight?" Richardson asked, looking at the nervous deputies.

"Don't you worry about it," Deputy Smith told him harshly. "You better tend to your own troubles tonight, mister. It looks like you got a whole bunch of them."

Of course, he thought: There's nothing nastier than a toady when he discovers he doesn't have to kiss ass anymore. "What exactly are you holding me for, Deputy?"

"You're a lawyer and you can't guess, huh? Assault and battery for one. Public intoxication for another. Not too bad of a night's work, Richardson. Maybe seven-hundred-and-fifty bucks' worth."

The handcuffs chafed painfully the insides of his wrists; he wanted to ask Smith to loosen them but decided against requesting favors. Beyond the bulletproof glass of the dispatcher's partition an enormous woman with the hips and belly of a Texas cop, snake's eyes, and cropped, mannish hair was smoking a cigarette from the corner of her thin-lipped mouth as she answered calls.

Deputy Smith escorted him past security and into a sound-proofed room furnished with a desk and two chairs arranged beneath a bulletproof window and a speaking-grill installed with headless screws. The soundproofing was scarred by sets of initials carved in block letters belonging, he supposed, to bereft wives and girlfriends.

"You want to call an attorney, or you goin to handle this one yourself, too?" Smith demanded.

"Neither of the above. I guess I'll just ask the jailer for a set of those nice gray pajamas and sit this one out."

"That mean you want to plead guilty?"

"Why the hell not?" he asked, thinking: Why do we middle-class folks experience this feeling of crushing humiliation when the law catches up with us at last? Is it perhaps because we, having written the law, are the only ones who actually believe in it? But Deputy Smith's weak blue eyes were staring at him suspiciously now.

"It's your funeral, buddy. So you want to pass on the sobriety test?"

"Christ yes. I'd probably blow your lousy equipment clear through the roof."

Shaking his head, Deputy Smith rose ponderously from the chair. "Let's go, then," he said. "I got to have you fingerprinted, get a mug shot, do some paperwork on you. I hope you ain't in a hurry because everythin's in total chaos now with—" He caught himself then, and gave Richardson a stealthy look. "We're just kind of all balled-up here tonight," he finished lamely.

"No," Richardson said. "I'm not in a hurry." Discovering that he still had on his hat (somebody, he recalled, had retrieved it from the floor of the lobby and, after carefully brushing it, returned it to him), he performed the courtesy of removing it now. "Unless you want it for the picture."

But Deputy Smith only grunted, without amusement. "Any way they take you's okay with me, Richardson."

While they were brushing his fingertips and splaying them on the chemically treated paper, and afterward readying the camera and taking their shots—left, right, front—he was observing the activities with the clinical detachment with which a dying priest might follow the exertions of his soul under extreme unction. At last, having taken away his street clothes and replaced them with prison ones, they placed him in a cell and, after asking whether he required anything, left him.

The jailer was a dark-complected man with black hair combed to a wave above his forehead and grading to a crew-cut at the back of his skull. He had sad, sloe eyes heavily pouched and a voice that was gentle and full of regret, like that of a man who has given up all hope in this life. When he had gone, Richardson lay on his back on the bunk, watching the leaf-broken light play on the ceiling and listening to the peaceful, reassuring sounds of the late-summer night—

of crickets, radios, the slow stir of branches, and an occasional passing automobile. They had removed his wristwatch, but he guessed the time to be not later than ten-thirty. Prison, he was relieved to discover, was one of life's few experiences that in the event did not disappoint. . . .

Suddenly he was wide awake, hearing the jailer's mournful voice through the door: "Your wife is here for you, Mr. Richardson. She's already paid your bond."

Richardson sat up from the waist like a dead man revivified. "But how would she—?" In desperation he tried to remember whether he had asked them to telephone. "You didn't call out there, did you?"

"No, Mr. Richardson," the jailer answered reassuringly. "She's waiting for you at the front desk now."

Then he thought of Mary-Elena. "Tell her I'll be with her in a minute," he said. "It won't take long to get me out, will it?"

"Won't take but a jiffy, pardner. I got your clothes with me. You can be dressed and ready to walk in five—hell, three minutes, depending on the kind of hurry you're in."

He dressed deliberately, stripping away the cheap flannel that had not had time yet to absorb the sweat and heat of his body, and replacing them with the tired, familiar cloth that bore all too much of him. Returning, the jailer unlocked the door and led him past cells in which other men, more fortunate than he, read or played cards or slept in peace, past the soundproofed visiting room, through the heavy security door, which closed behind him with a soft regretful cluck; and then he was on the outside, a free man once more.

Perfectly composed, holding a magazine outspread upon one slim, elegantly crossed knee, Christine was waiting for him. "Hi there, Tiger!" she said.

She put aside the magazine and came toward him, placing her arms lightly around his neck and holding her body a little apart from his. "You don't mind if I'm a little shy?" she asked. "I don't think I've ever kissed an ex-con before."

12

"Remember, ma'am," Deputy Smith warned her, "he's legally intoxicated as far as we's concerned. He drives, we bring him in again, on a DWI this time."

Christine gave him a charming smile. "Don't worry," she said. "If he gives me any trouble I'll throw him right back to you." Her eyes widened, as if to express some special understanding between them, and then she turned again to her husband. "Ready to go, sweetie?"

He followed her to the Audi, which stood parked between two police cruisers. For a moment he lingered on the pavement, smelling the damp clay and the rain-moistened bark of living trees. Then he got in beside her. "Why didn't you go back to Jackson?"

"Because I decided I still had a few things to take care of here."

"Such as bailing me out of the drunk tank for three hundred and fifty bucks?"

"That was a coincidence, actually. I was sitting in the restaurant eating dinner when the fight started. I don't think that cop cared for you particularly to begin with."

"Smith is a real asshole—what Tonio and I call an apple-ass."

"I bet he hasn't had that shirt washed since Memorial Day."

"It's in the regulations book. If they can't draw in time

they're supposed to flap their arms and you're out cold anyway. How The West Was Won."

"Why is it," Christine wanted to know, "that all lawyers hate cops so much?"

"Maybe," he offered, "because they're the ones that get the first licks in."

The traffic light flashed red on the bull's-eye windows of the prostitutes' vans parked around the square. "Circle the wagons, folks," Richardson mumbled.

"*What?*"

"Nothing. Don't forget, my truck's still parked at the supper club."

"You heard what the man said, Chuck."

"What the hell, I'm sober as a bought judge."

"*No!*"

"Then where are we going? This isn't the way out to the ranch."

"I'm taking you to the motel with me," Christine said.

He recalled hearing of a case in which a woman had escaped rape by jumping from a moving car at eighty-five miles an hour. "At three hundred-fifty bucks that makes kind of an expensive one-night stand, at least in this part of the world." That driver, he thought, must have been a real Houdini—or perhaps there had been a second man in the car.

"I'm certain if your little cookie were to add up what you could be charging her in legal fees she'd be owing a lot more than that."

He thought of something then, and asked, "Would you mind stopping at the Seven-Eleven? I want to buy a box of cigars."

"Those awful black things? They'll eat the upholstery, Chuck."

"I'll save them until I get home, I promise."

He bought the cigars from a plump girl with dyed yellow hair and raccoon eyes wearing a candy-striped coat, and, keeping out twenty-five cents from the change, went to the pay phone at the back of the store and dialed the ranch. She answered at the eighth or ninth ring, her voice as dry, light, and noncommittal as he remembered and with none of the thickness of sleep, though his watch said almost eleven-thirty.

"Where are you?"

"At the Seven-Eleven, in town. I'm on my way home now."

"Where have you been?"

"I'll tell you about it when I see you."

"Okay," she said.

When he returned to the car he found Christine smoking a cigarette and tapping her finger on the steering wheel. "What took you so long?"

"Just slow." He thought how her manner had been exactly like that of a wife of ten years whose patience at a distance can be stretched to any length merely because she knows that the moment the front door closes retribution will be hers. How do they *know*, he wondered—when apparently half the adult male population needs to read a book by an author with the initials M.D. after his name just to arouse a female sufficiently to get her with child?

"Okay then," Christine said finally. "I'll drive you out to the ranch, if that's what you want."

"No," Richardson told her. "Don't do that." Two men, resembling Jack Blake and Bill Erikson from Search and Rescue, were gasing a pickup truck at the center island; under the pump-light the scarlet-and-black emblem showed plainly behind the front wheel. It had been weeks since he had switched on the radio to the S and R frequency. "I have another idea."

He directed her through town to the Sundance Trailer Court, where the house-trailers slept like pale coffins in the starlight. Tonio's truck idled at wait in front of his place with both doors open and the cab light on. "For heaven's sake," Christine said. "Who do you know here? If I'd thought you were planning on spending the night at a dump like this I'd have left you in that nice clean jail."

Through the narrow window at the end of the trailer he could see a figure in agitated motion. "It's Tonio," he told her; unable to explain what urgent business he might have at a quarter to midnight. "Just let me out here. He won't mind driving me home."

"If that's what you want."

Compelled by some unexpected quality in her voice, he turned to see her holding out a hand to him across the seat, her eyes bright in the dashboard lights, her chin tremulous. He hesitated, then accepted the hand and shook it to the accompaniment of silver chimes. So that was it, he thought, that was what made her so different tonight. He had never known her to be quiet before.

"I suppose it's good-bye then," Christine said miserably.

He let go of her, overcome in spite of himself by the sadness that attends every ending, and by pity. "I'll mail you a check Monday morning for the three hundred and fifty."

Behind him he heard the gears engage and the sound of the Audi slipping away into the night. Then the trailer door opened and a man stepped onto the little porch. He shouted: "Tonio!"

"That you, Chuck? Jesus Christ!"

In the starlight Tonio's face was a moon in which a tiny red fire jerked spasmodically. "I look all over for you, Chuck—where the hell you been? Munger—he escape tonight! Get in the truck now: I drive like hell!"

13

IT WAS EXACTLY like opening morning he thought as he sat in a condition of nerveless fatigue, the window up against the rushing air that carried the chill of fall, clear and sharp as Persian ice, watching the staggered procession of taillights to the north crawl higher on the treeless bench toward the mountains. "I tell you what!" Tonio kept shouting: "I shoot heem *bang* in the neck, like I shoot the deer, the antelope, the bear, Chuck! I do not miss, no? Not from six hundred yards even!" But Richardson sat unresponsive, seeing the Other stealthily traversing the luminous topography, the two of them unreconciled, incomplete, the hunter and the hunted, until the moment of closure that he had expected and feared since their meeting almost three months ago at the jail. In his lap Tonio's revolver rested with the weight of every undischarged obligation he had ever known, or suspected.

Up the highway the flashing blue-and-red lights came into view—only seconds, it seemed, before they had already overtaken and passed them, so that he had to twist around in the seat to see Jim and Pat Thomas's new wrecker with the white cruiser belonging to the sheriff's department hoisted behind it, its front shoved in by the deer's impact, the top crushed where it had rolled, the doors sprung and the windows—through which Willie Munger had crawled past the two unconscious deputies—shattered. Beside it sat a second cruiser, the three khakied deputies standing aimlessly on the shoulder. "When was it you last tried to call?" he asked.

"About ten minute before you come! First, I try on the telephone but nobody answer! Then, I try again and she is busy! I try once more—five, maybe ten, minute later—and *nobody answer!*"

Richardson said, "She must have gone to the barn for something. I talked to her from the Seven-Eleven on my way to your place and told her I was on my way home." After a pause, he added, "It's almost exactly three point five miles from where they rolled to my place."

"*Goddamn!*" With a trembling hand Tonio lit a cigarette; by the light of the match Richardson could see the shine of moisture on his face. "I drive like hell now, Chuck—for *her.*"

Craning at the diminishing lights of the posse, he wondered by what postulate or faith the quarry is assumed always to flee uphill. Appalled by a renewed appreciation of her peril, he bent forward on the seat, clasping and unclasping his hands between his knees. *Yes* he could hear her cool, dry voice assuring him. *Yes, I'm all right. I'm all right. I'm all right.* Then, remembering suddenly the snub-nosed .38 he kept in the top-left drawer of his desk: *Godammit—I wonder if she knows how to handle a gun?*

14

Toward suppertime, having observed that the truck was gone from the yard and the door had been pulled shut behind the screen one, she rode up to the corral and dismounted. She filled the grain buckets and hung them on their nails, filled the water troughs, and afterward stood leaning on the fence rail, watching the starlings flirt for spilled oats between the placid hooves and hating him. At last, pushing herself impatiently off the fence, she went on down to the house.

She noticed the man-smell at once tonight, as a horse smells bear. The oilskins, canvas dusters, and denim coats hung like shrouds in the entry, exhaling a foetid odor as she brushed past them. In the kitchen the scent was fainter but still pervasive, mingled with the acrid odor of the filthy cigars he smoked and the heavier one of neetsfoot oil; and suddenly, drawing back a chair and stretching her arms across the table, she began to cry. She cried for a quarter of an hour, drawing out her sobs in long convulsive breaths, and when she was finished she went deliberately to the cupboard, poured three fingers of whiskey into a glass, and downed them with a swallow. Then, hiccuping and dragging one hand along the wall for support, she went to the bathroom, where she undressed slowly out of her storm-drenched clothes, and filled the tub.

Lulled by the whiskey, hot water, and steam, she began

to feel better. Rubbing herself with the washcloth, she admired the healthy glow of her own young flesh under the tan, the long lines of her legs and arms floating just under the surface of the water, and the round, pinkish-brown aureoles of her nipples. It was a beautiful body, she thought, a mysterious vessel for some promised accomplishment. The too-full bowl of her belly protruded roundly above the soapsuds, and she decided she would have to do something about that. Still, she assured herself, it *was* a lovely body, and if he was too snooty to appreciate it—staying away nights, avoiding not just their bed but the supper-table, forgoing their evenings together—she could find other men who would. When she had acquired a livid, boiled color she climbed out of the tub, splashing water over the floor.

She decided she would dress up just for herself and prepare a nice supper of half a cold chicken and salad: when *he* got home late, and probably drunk, from the bars he could fend for himself. When the phone sounded peremptorily in the next room she let it ring—seven, eight times. Choosing a candy-striped blouse and a pair of jeans from the closet, she laid them across the bed, took up one of the monogrammed brushes, and worked vigorously at her hair, pausing now and then to inspect the strands for split ends. She hated—loathed—the heavy old furniture with its elaborate carving, its scarred, cheesy finish and its accumulated layers of dirt and polish; though at first it had intrigued and even awed her, now in some indefinable way it weighed upon her oppressively. In the haughty sculpturing, which seemed to reproach her with an innocence for which she bore no responsibility, she sensed the explanation of that impenetrable mask that hardly ever slipped and which she was beginning to despair of ever displacing. He spent nearly all his time in town now, and when he spoke he appeared not to be looking at her but instead at some imaginary object behind her: It was as if she thought he was wary of some ghost perceptible only to himself. At his implicit suggestion they were sleeping again in separate rooms, and she had noticed when they were together how he flinched even from the touch of her hand. She was no longer jealous of Mrs. Richardson, she was no longer jealous of anyone; she was only disappointed. She had begun to wonder whether she might be merely the necessary implement of some sophisticated professional sport belonging to the rich man's world, a sport he was playing thrillingly and against all odds.

Widening her eyes exaggeratedly in the mirror, her reflection wreathed gracefully by carved vines and clustering grapes, she applied a touch of liner and lipstick and smiled approvingly at herself. Then, pulling the blouse over her head and buttoning the jeans that were recently starting to pinch, she took the hairpins from between her teeth and pinned her hair above her damp neck. She was, she discovered, suddenly and ravenously hungry. While she was fixing supper the phone rang again, maddening and insistent.

She made herself eat slowly, propping a tack catalogue against the plastic milk bottle and tucking back strands of her drifting hair. There were, she had found during the past several weeks, ways of being alone she had not experienced since childhood, and she was learning again to appreciate them. When she had finished eating she sat for a while above the plate, enjoying this measure of peace. She thought about getting out her pencils and paper, but rejected the idea; drawing seemed incompatible with her mood of quiet placidity.

When the telephone rang for the third time she hesitated a moment and then answered it. It was *him*, calling to say he was on his way out from town, and she got off almost at once, not minding if she had sounded cool and telling herself she hoped he would not be in too big a hurry even though it was already nearly eleven-thirty. Actually, she had had no idea it was so late: she must be learning to make time pass on her own. Perhaps, she thought, as she cleared the plates from the table and ran cold water over them, it would be better if I tell him everything: perhaps we should have a fight! The idea frightened and exhilarated her at the same time.

Hearing a quiet step on the porch, she glanced involuntarily at her proud reflection in the bit of mirror over the dry sink, then fled on bare feet to her room where she shut herself in. She considered locking the door but decided not: If that's the way it's going to be she thought, I might as well have stayed in jail. So she waited, rigid with expectation beside the bed, listening—wondering why he was so quiet, why he hadn't made a sound yet. Then she heard it, knowing in the same instant that it was not him at all and trying to summon a scream against the sudden inward pressure of the door. "Hello, baby," the voice said tonelessly. "Say you ain't surprised to see me."

She went on backing slowly across the room until her calves struck against the edge of the bed and she collapsed upright upon it, staring at Willie Munger as he closed the door behind him and set a chair against it. "Maybe more surprised than pleased, what?" His lips were thin and straight and gray, like a knife-wound that has not had time to bleed.

Pressing her arms against her sides, she squeezed her hands between her knees, while her tongue began to make sharp clicking sounds against her teeth.

"I been reading all about you in the papers," Munger said. "There ain't a hell of a lot to do in jail but read the papers, so I been reading them. You're some kind of a lady now, I guess. I met your old man once, too. Thinks he's pretty much of a cool dude, don't he?"

The clicking stopped and was replaced by a long whistling noise that wracked her body like a cold wind.

Munger nodded—exactly as if his small, square, head were being worked by a string. "Got him a nice spread—ranch, horses—I been admiring it from the highway for a year. He's made out like a bandit, all right.—Get up now!" he told her abruptly.

She went on staring at him, the same harsh whistling noise

coming from the little gap in her front teeth, and he started for her then, keeping his half-crouched body between her and the door. Grabbing her wrists, he jerked her roughly to her feet and held her hard against him, her head hanging limply backward, her legs stiff as wood at the knees. "Lookin good," he said in a voice that was like a cold finger on her spine. "Nice tan. Gettin fat, too." He prodded her ribs with a waxen finger, and she felt his breath cold on her upturned face. "Could be the livin's *too* good."

When suddenly he let go of her, her knees went and she fell back onto the bed. In a voice like the rattle of wind through October corn she whispered, "What do you want?"

He did not answer her, and began to prowl the room, stooping and straightening, his body flowing in swift, supple, anthropoid motion. Taking up a pencil sketch mounted on pale-blue cardboard, he held it at arm's length, and squinted. "Where'd you get this at?"

"It's a self-portrait I drew in prison."

He ripped the picture from its mounting and tore it down the middle between the wide, exaggerated eyes, and went on tearing until the tiny fragments lay scattered like pieces of a rainbow across the floor. "That ain't how you look," he said. "Who taught you how to draw, anyway?"

"What do you *want?*" she breathed.

For an answer he jerked the chair away from the door and sat on it, his shaved stubble like a skullcap above the black, bottomless eyes. "Money, for starters. You got any?"

"No," she whispered. "We—he don't keep it around the house."

"What about guns?"

She did not answer.

"He own a pistol?"

"In his truck."

He jerked his head, sharply and contemptuously, and she almost cried out as the mask seemed to slip sideways. "If they's anything I can do," she cried, "you know—"

"Shut up," Munger told her casually, and she stopped as if he had struck her across the mouth. "You never was much use but for the one thing. Hey, you heard about that judge yet?"

She shook her head at him and went on shaking it as if she would never know anything again.

"That dude ain't goin to save your ass," Willie Munger said. "He ain't going to be able to fix it. You ain't going no place except back to jail."

She began again to shake, and stared at the floor.

"Guys like him ain't interested in chicks like you," he went on. "They's interested in only the one thing and afterward they'll sell you out for thirty cents and swear they never had a thing to do with you."

"*No*," she whispered.

"That's right," he repeated. "I ain't trying to tell you nothing because I ain't got any interest in you anymore. I showed you the whole goddamn world—anywhere you wanted to go, anything you wanted to do. It's *you* now, baby, you get what I'm trying to say to you? You ain't got no chance with him."

He rose from the chair and began weaving in a slow, trance-like motion on his rubber-soled convict's shoes, as if in response to some unearthly music. "Thirty cents," he repeated in a hissing, singsong voice. "Sell you out for thirty cents, swear he never laid eyes on you."

"I'd die for him," Jenny whispered. "I'd *die* for him."

A sword of light cut suddenly between them and she heard the violent spray of gravel in the yard. She didn't see him go—only the chair flung aside, the bedroom door standing open on the quiet half-lit house beyond. But she did hear the shot, loud as a cannon and fading into silence upon which voices gradually obtruded like smoke, and the sharp, faint odor of cordite.

15

HE DISCOVERED HER sitting decorously on the edge of the bed wearing her newest blouse and a clean pair of designer jeans, staring at the overturned chair that lay in front of the door and a scattering of paper bits across the hand-woven rug. When he raised her by the armpits her body felt as light as a feather against his own, as if the terror of which she was emptied had been all that was mortal about her.

"I'm all right," she said, but he went on holding her, feeling her heart beat more smoothly and unhurriedly against his ribs while her throat pulsed like a bird in the hollow of his shoulder. At last, bracing her hands against his chest, she pushed herself away and looked toward the truck, idling with its lights on just beyond the window. "Where is *he?*"

"Would you like a drink?" he asked. "If I fix the pillows and bring you a little—"

"I know, you don't have to hide it from me. I heard—"

Her look was even and direct, but he could only nod.

"I want to see," she said.

"Jenny—for God's sake!"

"It won't upset me," she replied in her dryest, most sensible voice. "I just want to make sure—that's all."

She walked ahead of him, her legs slightly rubbery, over the porch, down the steps, and across the patch of burnt grass through the darkness to where Tonio stood smoking a cigarette above the crumpled figure. As she approached he grinned and, removing the cigarette from his mouth, nudged the shape with the toe of his boot. "*Don't!*" she said.

Seized with an exhaustion greater than any he had ever known, Richardson dropped to one knee and for a while they remained in silent tableau: Tonio standing with one foot placed contemplatively in advance of his body and holding the butt of the deer rifle in the crook of his arm; Jenny rigid above the corpse with her head slightly bent; himself holding Tonio's revolver on his knee and thinking *Now I* have *killed a man* with the uncomprehending astonishment of a man actually experiencing for the first time what he has only experienced in imagination before.

"See!" Jenny said.

"What?" he asked her warily, advancing within five feet of the thing.

"*There!*"

Leaning out as though above a precipice, he craned his neck in the direction of her pointing finger toward the thin, hairless chest upon which a trickle of silver lay, pulled sideways over the left breast by the weight of a small crucifix that he recognized at once as Miss Tyrrell's. Or rather, his brain corrected itself, as the exact, identical correspondent of Miss Tyrrell's.

"He took it," Jenny explained, sitting back on her heels and staring indignantly at the eyes that looked in the starlight like twin wells gone dry. "She gave it to me and I must have dropped it and he found it and took it."

Giving the corpse a last scornful look, she rose and began walking quickly back to the house. "I was starting to think I must be going crazy," she remarked over her shoulder, to no one in particular.

BOOK

4

1

THE LOWDOWN SEDAN with its discreet spotlight mounted over the fender bore menacingly upon them and passed in a rush of furious air, the driver's face a blur above the beehive emblem on the side panel. "What happens if they stop us?" she had asked, to which he had replied honestly: "Run; or apologize." After five more or less desperate years, he still held the old, depressingly familiar, hand.

Parched by the hot wind, he drove on at a prudent fifty-five into the glare beneath which the desert was a vast, motionless sundial studded with tortured gnomons colored brick-red in the foreground and lavender in the distance. Beside him Jenny sat with her legs tucked under her, patiently replacing strands of hair torn loose by the slipstream as she stared calmly ahead. Preoccupied by the thing he was preparing to do to her that, terrible as it was, was still less dishonorable by far than the thing he had already done, Richardson had said hardly a word to her for the past few hours, answering only when spoken to. Crossing this flayed, pulverized, sun-scorched country was, he thought, comparable only to traversing one of the numberless eons that had created it.

For a fortnight he had imagined them, good country people, accepting the letter at the post office in Mosiah and carrying it home to read at the oilcloth-covered table after having searched for and found the matched pairs of wire-framed spectacles; slitting the envelope with the penknife her father would inevitably carry on his keychain before drawing the paper out and unfolding it; reading it through finally, two or three times, from salutation to closing, before laying it with shaking hands between the steak sauce and the butter dish, and staring helplessly at one another with frightened, confused eyes. One week later to the day, he calculated, the second letter would have arrived.

Of course, he assured himself, they wouldn't—they couldn't—have known how to answer those letters from a complete stranger who was also the self-appointed guardian of their daughter's fate: his unpardonable mistake had been to believe that what he had to say could be said in writing across a distance of four hundred miles and in the absence of her own irrepudiable flesh-and-blood presence. Against that presence was not only her stubbornly expressed antipathy to a meeting, but the certainty of Judge Thurlow's retribution should they be discovered in violation of His Honor's interdict against Miss Petersen's leaving the state; in favor was the strategic necessity of attaching her family to the defense effort. But was it really, he had asked himself, a necessity? Perhaps necessity was only one of those words behind which a coward such as himself found refuge. Was it cowardice, then, that had been gnawing at him all summer, or rather—as he preferred to think of it—conscience? Whichever it was, it made no difference as far as *she* was concerned, he had decided, no matter what the inferences regarding his own character might be. What counted was that, so long as their exclusive dependency existed, the immorality existed also—an albatross in which (especially considering her own past) he could discover no justification for hanging upon her. From this conclusion a solution had easily followed: he had simply informed her, in a direct, no-nonsense manner, that he was taking her to visit her parents in Utah and that she should pack an overnight bag to bring with her. Then he had asked

Tonio to box the rest of her things after they had left and ship them by United Parcel Service to the Petersen address in Mosiah.

He had expected her to sulk, perhaps to balk or even to refuse outright, but she had merely looked pensive and remained silent. Only later, when he was preparing for bed, had she left her bedroom and stood leaning against the doorjamb, her hair falling over the cotton nightgown and her arms crossed upon her breasts. "They aren't going to recognize me," she had told him in a quiet voice.

"*Who?*" he had asked stupidly, drawing the sheet up apprehensively to his chin.

"My folks."

"Of course they'll recognize you. It's been only—"

"No," she had answered with grave certainty. "You don't know my mom and dad. They don't like surprises."

He had lain awake after she had gone to bed, thinking: If a house divided cannot stand, how much less a man? But perhaps that was the nature of courage: to accept dividedness and insist on standing anyway. He had slept badly, and wakened into the gray dawn that came later now and carried with it the hard, foreboding chill of autumn.

A line of fabricated silhouettes appeared on the horizon, which he took for the outskirts of a desert town until they made out the house-trailers strung like lawn ducks behind a whitewashed adobe building with twin red gas pumps set in front.

"I think I'm getting hungry," he told her in an attempt at jocularity, "and I know you are."

She gave him a half-sour, half-wistful look. "Is that a good idea?"

"Why not? We haven't done a thing that's illegal today, except to cross the Wyoming line."

He drew off the highway and parked the truck between an ancient Chrysler with a Venetian blind across the back window and a tilting water-well rig propped on wooden blocks. One of the pumps, half-torn from its pediment, leaned from the crumbling cement island and a pile of broken, manure-crusted chicken crates stood against the sun-peeled walls.

Inside it was cool and dark. The proprietress was an obese old Indian, with cheeks like dried apples and a coil of black hair streaked coarsely with silver, who had been sitting with her broad knees apart and her feet turned in like a child's, watching the highway through the window-film. Upon seeing them she rose immediately and began waddling toward them, her protuberant chin lifted as if in support of a heavily determined expression.

They ordered tacos and fries, and the old woman, without having spoken, hobbled indomitably toward the kitchen and through the grease-blackened door. Jenny asked him for a quarter for the jukebox, where she spent minutes making her selection while he watched with a profound, sinking feeling of the heart. She looked particularly childlike today in new white Levi's, tooled Western belt, white blouse on which her bare arms showed in streaks of tan, and blue-striped running shoes; he noticed the way she wrinkled her small, slightly turned-up nose in concentration and the plumpness of her dimpled elbows, as if the baby fat were trying to come back. When the first song came up he realized what it was he had been missing—she hadn't played the truck radio once all day. Returning to the table with a demure smile, she sat bobbing her head and tapping out an accompaniment with a neatly manicured forefinger. When she noticed him looking she reached, without losing the beat, for his hand.

"What are you looking at me that way for?"

"What way?"

"So kind of—tragic. Like a father giving the bride away."

He thought he was going to break down then, but recovered himself with effort. "Because you look happy," he managed to say.

"As a matter of fact, I'm so nervous I'm ready to scream."

"Because of your parents?"

"I guess. I just have this feeling like I'm about to lose my best friend. Maybe I'm getting ready to start my period. I've lost track of the days."

The old woman came out of the kitchen carrying the food on a dirty tray. She served them silently and, after fetching a bottle of jalapeño sauce, returned to her place at the window where she sat staring with a self-satisfied look at the highway. Outside they could hear the occasional whip of a car going by and once the heavy crunch of tires, followed by the sound of rapid acceleration and the spray of gravel.

The food was heavy and rancid. Jenny tried a potato, said "Uch!" and finished it, then ate several more in a finicky manner.

"Don't eat any more of those," he told her sharply. "They aren't good for you."

She shrugged, and pushed away the plate. "Let's go, then."

"In a minute," he agreed, as if he were pacifying a restless child. "Just hold your horses, okay?"

The old woman—who, he noticed, had been glancing covertly at them while they ate—had moved from the window to an alcove containing a cash register, an antique curved-glass-and-wood display case filled with candy and cigarettes, and a shelf of cheap souvenirs, where she awaited them leaning on her elbows and gumming a stick of peppermint candy. Counting the money from his billfold, with Jenny tagging behind him, he went back to the alcove and paid for the meal.

The old squaw snatched the few dollars and threw them unceremoniously into the tray. Then, jerking her thumb at the souvenirs: "You want to buy, maybe?" she asked, glancing inquisitively at Jenny.

"No," Richardson said, having looked at the shelf on which an assortment of ashtrays, tiny beaded baskets, and Indian dolls rested under a coat of red dust.

She stuck out her chin at him, her eyes black and disdainful under the heavy brows, and, reaching awkwardly, took down a doll and thrust it across the case at Jenny. "You take. Maybe bring you luck. I no sell anyhow."

"Thank you," Jenny told her politely, holding the brightly clad figure, from whose tiny brown face she stroked the dust with a careful forefinger, against her chest. "He's cute. I'll take real good care of him."

In the truck she made him wait until she had spread the leathern loop that fastened behind the doll's shoulders and fitted it over the rearview mirror, from which the homunculus commenced to swing in gentle pirouettes. When he started the engine, she looked at him in astonishment. "*You* turned the *radio* on?"

"Why not?" Removing his hands from the wheel, he held them toward her, palms out. "Look, Ma—no quarters!"

The country was changing now, and suddenly she began to talk, her dry, light voice riding above the harsh sound of the engine. She talked of how her great-grandfather had been converted by two missionaries outside the Union Pacific station in Salt Lake City less than a week after he got off the boat from Stockholm in New York, and how he had worked for the Union Pacific Railroad for the rest of his life. She talked about her Uncle Ted, who lost his money in a uranium mine and, blaming God for the disaster, quit the Church in an outburst of blasphemous rage. She described her first waitressing job, serving breakfast in Willis's Luncheonette behind the Chevron station in Mosiah, where he imagined her moving briskly between the tables on strong, well-shod, girlish legs, wrapped toothsomely in crisp white like a loaf of fresh bread. As she talked her voice appealed to him as the keening expression of the land that had bred her, having in it the feathered dryness of its willows and cottonwoods, the flatness of its tile-blue sky, the strength of its clean, hard rock tragically pervious to the wear of time; bearing him on like a song or the turbid red flow of the country itself. To the south a line of mountains peaked beneath a bank of cloud—"*The*

La Sals!" Jenny cried, grasping his shoulder and pointing like a child. Abruptly the highway plunged into a red crevasse of buttery rock smoothly sliced as if by a knife, and she cried again: "The Colorado!" They followed the river as it ran, clear and low now in early September, beneath a roof of sky cut exactly to fit it, and catapulted without warning from the lung-red rock into the green valley above the clean and pretty town, leaving the river to flee away like a serpent, gliding down into wildernesses of cracking, crumbling, pulverised rock—the land, he thought, where everything runs perennially to destruction and they call it beauty.

"Oh!" Jenny exclaimed, drawing her bare feet from under her bottom and sitting very straight and solemn on the seat. "I guess I'm home," she said.

Directing him through town, she sat very still in her bird-dog position, encouraging him to admire the wide, swept-looking streets fronted by the corniced red-brick buildings, the willows dusty-gold and pendant before the rows of white bungalows kept safe within the circling wall of purple cliff.

"Do you like it?" she urged; and, because he couldn't bear to speak, he reached to press her knee with a sweating hand.

2

HE TRIED DIVING deeper into sleep like a sounding whale, but the tinny, insistent bell pursued and he woke the rest of the way with a start and sat up on the sprung sofa, scratching his tonsure of silver hair and muttering, "Gosh dang it." The bell rang once more and he shouted, "Coming!" in a thick voice, and began scrambling in his stocking feet between the indefinite shapes of trunks, packing boxes, and broken furniture that stood piled in the heavy blue light of the attic. At the head of the stairs he stumbled against a child's rocking horse, its paint cracked and faded and with part of one rocker broken off, and yelled *"Coming!"* again in a furious voice, as if it were a curse. *Why the gosh dang* he protested as he started down the stairs *don't she answer the gosh dang doorbell?*—a tallish, thickset man with a sunburned face and pale, short-sighted eyes made bloodshot from the nap he had taken, as he had every Saturday afternoon for twenty years, from whom sleep hung like the loose nylon shirt he wore unbuttoned over the white under one. Reaching the second floor he padded down the hall and pivoted heavily about the newel post, his breath coming in harsh and irritable gasps. By the time he got there whoever it was would have gone—Nellie must be working behind the house somewhere. They rarely entertained visitors and the mail had been delivered hours before: he promised himself if it were a salesman he would give him a piece of his mind and get rid of him quick before he could talk to Nellie. The bell sounded one final time as he descended to the entry; he jerked the door open and stood, blowing hard and squinting into the still-bright day at two people, a man and a woman.

The man was tall, broad-shouldered, and dark, with the brutal good looks of a TV cop and wearing a battered black hat; the woman was very young, with long mahogany-colored hair and a pale, scared-looking face that memory hinted he would recognize in another second. Then he did recognize it and, half-shutting the door against them, wheeled round in the hall and began to bawl, "Mother—Nellie—get in here quick—the front door—!"

She came hurrying from the chicken-yard, wearing jeans and an old paint-spattered shirt of his and carrying a garden trowel, her features bleared by moistened face powder and the groping expression on her small uncertain face. She scuttled through the kitchen and into the hall, her sneakers making a soft, rapid patter on the worn carpet, holding the trowel before her as though it were a knife and crying, "What is it, Sven—what's the matter?" in a tense, nervous voice. For answer he threw the door wide again, stepping back dramatically like a sideshow barker displaying an exhibit, as, letting go the trowel, she gave a little scream.

"They brought her home!" he declaimed, letting his thick arms fall helplessly at his sides. "What has she done *this* time, officer?"

3

"MY NAME IS Chuck Richardson," he told them. "May we come in, Mr. Petersen?" And then the four of them stood staring at one another through the open door, while he felt the sharp pressure of her nails in his palm. From behind him came the rattle of children's toys along the sidewalk and the long, diminishing rip of a rebuilt engine. At last Mrs. Petersen bent to pick up the trowel, which lay near Jenny's feet. Straightening up, she said, without looking at the girl, "You better shut the door now, Sven. The neighbors may be watching."

He shut it, and they stood silent again until Mrs. Petersen suggested, "Why don't we go into the kitchen and sit?"

It was a bright, sunny room, with windows along two sides and an antique coal stove facing a modern range and refrigerator across an oilcloth-covered table with a centerpiece of tiger lilies in a green glass vase. Beside the coal stove was a straight-backed rocking chair and a maple-wood rack for magazines. Jenny and Richardson took places opposite each other at the table and Mr. Petersen seated himself in the rocker, leaning forward with his hands between his knees and reaching occasionally to scratch perplexedly at his back hair. Laying the trowel on the sideboard, Mrs. Petersen drew her wedding ring back and forth over the knuckle of her thin, dirt-stained finger.

"What can I get for you, Mr. Richardson? I'm trying to think—we don't keep tea or coffee of course, but there's milk and orange juice and I think maybe fruit punch—"

"Just plain water would be fine, Mrs. Petersen." On the wall behind her was a framed sampler into which the words THE FAMILY IS FOREVER had been stitched and he saw that the rack contained, besides what appeared to be church publications, a ball of wool with knitting needles stuck in it and several pieces of opened mail, among which he recognized two envelopes bound with a rubber band.

"How about you, Jenny?" Mrs. Petersen asked. "My, you've gotten fatter."

Jenny blushed angrily. "Nothing, thanks."

Mr. Petersen made a grumbling noise in his throat. Then he took a handkerchief from the back pocket of his pants and spat carefully into it. "Maybe they'd like a piece of that cake Darlene gave us, Mother."

Richardson raised his hand in polite declination, and Jenny said crossly, "I only weigh a hundred and thirty-five, Mother."

"It's awfully good cake," Mrs. Petersen explained. "Darlene Thomas baked it for our Relief Society luncheon last week and they had so much food left over they made me take it home. Of course *I* don't need it, and Mr. Petersen isn't allowed sweets because of his diabetes, and I said to Darlene, 'Why don't you send it home with someone that's got children. . . .'" She went on talking and drawing the ring over her knuckle, staring above their heads the whole time, while her husband brought out his handkerchief again and began folding and refolding it as if in embarrassment. When Mrs. Petersen stopped talking, he said, "You folks been having a nice summer up in Wyoming?"

"Hot, and very dry. It's been lovely but we're going to need all the moisture we can get this winter."

"You do much fishing up there?"

"Some."

"Trout?"

"Yeah."

"What kind of equipment?"

"Flies mostly."

Mr. Petersen gave a disapproving grunt. "I troll for bass ever' fall in Lake Powell."

"I'm told they have good fishing there. I've never tried it myself."

Mr. Petersen wiped his mouth on his handkerchief, which he inspected carefully before tucking it into his shirt pocket. "So you've had a real busy summer," he tried.

"Busy enough." He glanced quickly at Jenny, who was watching intently the forefinger of one hand stroke the middle finger of the other. "How do you think your daughter looks?"

Mr. Petersen started as if he had been shot. "Good, oh—good," he exclaimed. "Don't she look good, Mother?"

"Oh yes, she looks real good."

"You bet she does—she looks good."

Richardson told them, "We were trying to figure on the way down here how long it's been since you've seen each other."

"How *long?*" Mr. Petersen repeated, his pale eyes appearing to unfocus themselves. "Oh, well," he said. "Let's see, Mother—how long *has* it been, now?"

Her mouth stretched in a puckered blear across what must once have been, he thought, a pretty face, though the skin was loose on the bones now, flaccid with age and self-pity. "How long?" she echoed helplessly, and he noticed that she tottered slightly on her feet. "Why, I guess it would be before she went to work for the—ah—"

" It's been *exactly* three years and two and a half months," Jenny interrupted.

"Well, now, you see, that's what I was about to say—it would have to be a little more than three years, Mr. Richardson."

A long pause followed, which he broke finally by asking, "Did you receive the two letters I wrote you?"

The Petersens exchanged looks and he heard Jenny draw a sharp, astonished breath. Without looking at her he added, "I mailed the second one over a week ago." He could tell she was looking at him now, but in puzzlement probably, without hint yet of doubt or suspicion.

"We got em," Mr. Petersen said. His plump cheeks sagged and his upper lip made a beak for the wide mouth that had dropped abruptly at the corners, giving him the stubborn appearance of a snapping turtle.

"I was hoping maybe to have heard from you about that."

Sven Petersen looked once again at his wife. Her face was a frozen mask but she gave him a tight, almost imperceptible nod.

"We kind of figured there wasn't anything to say."

Under the table Jenny kicked his foot: she was staring at him with an expression of urgent inquiry. Frowning, he shook his head discretely at her. "Is that in fact the case?"

"You call yourself a lawyer. How do you figure it?"

"I figure you for decent parents who love their daughter and want to do all they can to help her, but also for pretty shaky correspondents."

Petersen's stare was definitely malevolent now.

"How about *you*—call *you*rself a decent man?"

"Not very, until I met your daughter."

Sven Petersen stood and, lifting the lid of the coal stove, spat in it. Then he dabbed with the handkerchief at the corners of his mouth. "We keep up with what's going on—read the papers, watch TV. I think you're some kind of pimp, if you want my honest opinion."

Richardson laughed. "I haven't sold Jenny into white slavery yet. I'm trying to defend her against the possibility that she could spend the rest of her life in prison for a crime for which she has no responsibility. In order to do that I need your help, and I haven't hesitated to ask for it."

"Call that defend," Mrs. Petersen said.

Again he received a kick; her reddened eyes seemed to implore him.

"What I want to know," Mrs. Petersen said in a harsh voice, "is what kind of a man would take deliberate advantage of a helpless girl half his age—"

"A pimp," her husband put in, "a seducer—"

"—that had gone wrong even though she had a moral, God-fearing upbringing and was being punished for it, needing to ask Heavenly Father for forgiveness instead of being led into greater sin—"

Jenny was on her feet now, flying across the kitchen: they heard her running footfalls followed by the slam of the front door. After that was silence, disturbed only by Petersen's nervous coughing and his wife's harsh breathing, which ran on and on like a racehorse after it has crossed the finish line.

"You've ruined my daughter," the old man said. (But he can't be that old, he reminded himself: maybe forty-five or fifty.) "Ruined her and ruined us, so's we can't hardly hold our heads up anymore."

"Yes," his wife went on. "Church-going people that, through no fault of their own, raised a daughter that as far as Heavenly Father is concerned might just as well be dead, and even then there's those that believe—If you only knew how terrible it has been—those awful TV reports, the newspapers—her father's not well, it almost *killed* him—"

"I understand," Richardson said. He started to rise from the table and discovered that his legs would barely support him.

"Get out now," Petersen said. "Before I call the sheriff."

He felt their eyes like shotgun barrels on his back as he went out through the hall and down the narrow concrete walk to the truck where Jenny lay, crumpled but dry-eyed, across the seat. He went around to the driver's side, found the door locked, and had to tap several times on the window before, raising herself on one hand, she lifted the button to let him in.

"I *told* you," she said. "They don't like surprises."

4

Tapering toward its stony point, the mesa drew the world to convergence about them while, swollen and heavy with final heat, the sun balanced precipitously on the horizon beside the triangular shape of a distant mountain peak.

"*Hurry*, Chuck," Jenny urged him impatiently, "or we're going to miss it!"

She sat forward on the seat, gripping the edge with her hands. "We have the most beautiful sunsets in the world—I wanted to take you in by the switchback, only there isn't time. It's just an old cattle-trail, Chuck—it goes right up the side of a huge cliff like this!" She turned to face him, making zigzag motions in front of his nose with a graceful, flickering hand. "That's how we always used to go in, so nobody would see us." She sat back looking pleased with herself, and he reached over to rub between her shoulder blades.

"What would it matter if they *did* see you?"

She shrugged, her face glowing with sunset, and wrinkled her nose. "It wouldn't, I guess. It's just—why let anyone know anything if you don't have to?"

She had demurred at his suggestion that they rent a motel room for the night and he had been impatient with her until finally she had said, "I know what we're going to do—I've been thinking about it all day!" Then she had directed him to the City Market, where they had bought supplies—bacon, beans, bread, eggs, coffee, matches, and beer; the Army-Navy store, where they added two blankets and an iron-ware coffeepot; and the state liquor store, for a bottle of red wine. "Now *hurry!*" she had insisted, drawing her feet onto the seat and leaning her weight against his shoulder: "I don't want you to miss the sunset!" and they had driven out of town past the motels and restaurants, the gas stations, and the float-trip headquarters with their waiting fleets of buses, jeeps, and rubber rafts.

Abruptly the sun lurched from the horizon, plunging the world below them into blue shadow like an ocean bed from which the waters had cataclysmically been drained and drawing the blush from her face, which shone faintly now with a pale sheen. Mile upon mile of grassland stroked past them, and the occasional skeleton of a corral built against a tumulus of sandstone. "They used to run cattle here before the government took it," she said, and he felt he could almost hear memory pounding like blood in her temples. The sun had left a pink thumbprint on the green sky and now a silver moon lifted above the eastern range, giving a shine to the land as if it were created of silver from which the moonlight were polishing the tarnish. Dropping her feet to the floor, she moved away from him and sat still and silent, her profile edged in light, oblivious of him as of the jolting of the truck on the hard road.

"*Turn here!*" she cried suddenly.

Her voice was sharp as a pistol shot in his ear and he turned obediently onto the divergent trail, twin shadows running in parallel lines across a silver meadow, giving way at last to the hunched, druidic forms of pinyon and juniper whose roots lay exposed on a pitched floor of dried needles, berries, and shards of weather-polished wood. He thought of his childhood summers in Maine—of following wooded spits until they broke off in the ocean and you were left at the uttermost margin of the earth. Abruptly the road vanished as if it had been a trick of the moon, leaving him with a terrifying vision of cliffs descending carelessly into the abyss. "For Christ's sake, Jenny—!"

But she was already out of the truck, an antic, eager shape in the headlights. "We'll have to pack in the rest of the way," she cried; "—just the food and the blankets. We don't even need a flashlight, with this moon!" Then he heard her scrabbling, raccoon-like, in the bed. "*Hurry*, Chuck! It's so beautiful and I'm so *hungry*—aren't you?"

Like a leisurely, indulgent husband he followed the waffled prints left by her silly striped shoes in the red powder which was soft and fine as moondust, picking his way among the junipers whose hard waxen berries exuded a perfume around the little trees that were alive only at the heart, supernal life preserved in a splintered wrap of cuticle; while ahead of him her footfalls went, chuffing faintly in the powder and whispering across bare rock. Then he lost her, and continued for several minutes to plunge ahead until a tree at his elbow split suddenly in two and she jarred with rough playfulness against his shoulder, ordering in a fierce, exultant whisper, "*Set it right here!*"

"See!" she cried. "It's *perfect*—let me show you. Look!"; and, seizing him by the wrists, drew him behind her ambush, where a hood of rock rose to a height of three feet, forming a cavity nearly as deep and fronted by an apron of sandstone. "It's a natural oven!" she went on in the same exultant whisper. "There's even a kind of seat where I can sit to cook our supper." Letting go his hand, she hitched herself lightly onto the hood and posed there like a singer atop a piano, looking pert. "You're not supposed to gather wood, but I don't see *why*, there's nobody here to miss it. And you can't see the fire inside the oven."

He made a pile of the wood under the rock and lit it, and Jenny knelt in the sand and thrust a can of beans among the fragrant coals, the green flames shooting up like blades of new grass. In the ruddy light her face was an opened flower and he caught the sweet aroma of perspiring young female flesh. Brushing her hair from her shoulders he laid his hand on her bosom, but she gave him a shove that knocked him back on his heels in the dust. "Go on now," she said, "and bring the wine."

When he returned with the bottle she was still working on her knees at the fire, her hands quick and sure, heaping the coals into glowing pyramids with a stick, retrieving finally the blackened can. "Now," she said, "we want coffee for later"; and when the water boiled she cracked an egg and added the albumen to the pot.

"This is for you," she told him, handing him the loaded plate. But when he squatted with it she said sharply, "Not here!" and he rose and followed her out of the circle of fire-light and into the forest of bristle-cone and juniper. "Don't slip now and drop your supper," she warned over her shoulder, and he realized then that she was no longer using the harsh whisper but speaking instead at full voice above a sound—far, static, dense as cotton—that seemed to describe motion without having motion in it. He watched her figure going on ahead of him, soft-footed through the trees, while the mysterious sound grew not louder but more *present*, as if it were being drawn slowly out of time, like sea-sound from a conch. Then, abruptly, he collided with her and she said—whispering again—"*Careful*, Chuck—now sit *down*," and he sat, holding his supper in his lap and watching the sound shimmer in the vast and intricate mold in which it seemed eternally frozen.

They ate in silence, passing the wine between them and staring at the sheer, unobtrusive ledge where the moonlight poured smoothly over and fell motionlessly a thousand feet to the first bolgia of clean rock from whence came a remote wind shushing the dust and sagebrush; and at the river, another thousand feet down again, shining in silver segments where it angled against the sky. At long intervals they heard the sound, like breaking china, of loosened rock clattering in the canyon's depth.

When they had finished eating Richardson lit a cigar and Jenny came and sat with her back against his. Stretching his legs luxuriously, he felt his boot heels suspended piquantly in space.

"Where do we go from here?" she asked after a while.

"Go?"

"You know what I mean."

"Like I said—either we keep moving, or we go back. Thurlow's going to try to hang Munger on me somehow, like he'll try to hang the Collinses on you. We might still make it into Mexico if we're lucky."

"I don't want to live in Mexico," she told him in a decided voice.

"As a matter of fact, neither do I. A couple of years ago I tried to hire on with the Border Patrol so I could shoot the bastards as they came across the Rio Grande."

"Well then, you'd better come up with something else."

"*I'd* better?"

She did not answer, but a minute later leaned away from him and he heard her doing something in the dirt, as if she were scratching with a stick. "Chuck."

"What?"

"What did you write in those letters?"

He had known of course that she would ask; the two sheets of cheap stationery had been a pervious wall between them all evening. Taking up a bit of rock, he flung it over the cliff and waited to hear its faint, minuscule impact before answering.

"Do you love me?" he asked.

"Um."

"Then don't ask me to tell you that. Not ever, Jenny."

"Okay," she said simply.

She rested her back once more against his and together

they listened to the sound of moonlight in its mold of gelid rock. "Chuck."

"What."

"Promise you won't be mad?"

"No."

"Why not? I haven't said it yet."

"Then maybe I won't be mad after all."

"Quit being smart, all right?"

"All right."

"Now I'm going to tell you."

"Tell me then, for Christ's sake. You're starting to make me nervous."

She drew a long breath and said, "You're going to be a father."

He scrambled to his feet then and stood swaying a little with two thousand vertical feet at his back. "Good Lord. You're *not*, Jenny!"

Hugging her knees under her chin she looked up at him and nodded gravely. "Is it that terrible?"

Richardson removed his hat to give the question its due consideration. He brushed the hair back carefully from his ears and patted it down at the back of his skull, and with the toe of his boot made a hole in the powder like a tiny grave and covered it over again. "I guess it's not the end of the world," he conceded.

They lay together in the cold sand while he thought about the briefness of time and the incredible burden it was imposing upon him, beginning a new life when he had already used up half of the old one; and presently he heard a different kind of sound. It began deep in the sky, midway between dome and horizon, and swelled quickly to a driving organ note before assuming actual shape: a streak of silver hurtling forward at terrific speed and drawing itself up more slowly behind; sending down a portentous rumble that bored into the night like an augur. Half across him Jenny lay, heavy with sleep, drooling a little onto his shirt, and he stared over her at the smear of vapor stretching itself like a tape above the vast wilderness of rock in absurd, futile attempt to take the measure of all and of Man triumphant against it. After all, he thought, feeling a sudden access of something like peace: You can't stop them from trying.

5

TOWARD MIDNIGHT A figure that for several hours had lain without moving under a juniper tree sat abruptly and, after looking around itself as if to discover its whereabouts, got stiffly to its feet. For a while it stood, gazing across the moon-chalked canyon to the river, shading its eyes with its hand as if against the brightest sun. Then it bent and, after a struggle, raised a second figure from the ground, which it threw over its shoulder sack-wise and made off with into the trees. The wide hatbrim cast a mask of shadow across the eyes, so that in the light of the moon only the lower part of the face was visible, grinning.